Mysterious
Track

Mysterious Track

Lech Lebek

authorHOUSE®

AuthorHouse™
1663 Liberty Drive
Bloomington, IN 47403
www.authorhouse.com
Phone: 1-800-839-8640

First published by AuthorHouse   05/11/2011

ISBN: 978-1-4567-8114-9 (sc)
ISBN: 978-1-4567-8307-5 (ebk)

This book is dedicated to **Joan Haywood.**

"You are the one who tells nonsense. Your lives have nothing to do with any religion. Actually I am not too sure how to say that but first of all you seem to be not mature enough to have any religion and it seems to me that you created all religions to prevent your dirty lives, to cover your dirty matters and to use them for your own advantage . . ."

Chapter 1

Lisa got up shortly before the sunrise. She was strolling slowly through the house, looking at the flowers then she entered the bathroom. Somewhere in the house, the telephone rang, soon after she started to prepare the bath so she went to take the call. After she picked up the phone there was no voice on the other side.

'I came too late', she thought and went back to the bathroom.

Lisa stood in front of the bath, looking into the water in such way as she could see something inside then slowly she took off her clothes. There was a big mirror on the wall so she could see her whole body. She started to brush her long, blond hair, looking at her reflection in the mirror with some happy enjoyment. Once, her sight went into her blue and a little greenish eyes. She moved her face closer to the mirror and looked deeply inside them as she never seen her own eyes before.

She stood for a while then she went to the other side of the bathroom and from many different cosmetics, she has chosen one bottle and poured the liquid into the water. As soon as her hand has been deepen into the water, she felt very sweet taste in her mouth. She put the bottle back on the shelf and stepped into the bath, and set down. The sweet taste became very irritating and she thought about a drink but then she felt that she could not stand up. Surprisingly the sweet taste became quite nice, could say, like a very good chocolate.

Lisa was lying in the bath and felt very comfortable. Somewhere from the house, she could hear soft and relaxing music, mixed up with a sound of the birds, singing happily behind the windows. She tried to say something to herself but suddenly it became impossible, as she could not move her lips, which turned into a smiling shape. She took the water into her hands and wetted her hair. As soon as she took her hands off the head to take some more water, she held into them most of the wet hair, which went off her scalp. Lisa tried to say something again but only her lips looked more smiling then before. She looked surprisingly at her hair with silence and her strange smile.

She has forgotten about the sweet taste. Slowly she deepened her hands in the water, holding most of her hair. Suddenly she sight at her legs and then at her hair. The water around Lisa's hands with the hair turned into a whitish colour as they started to melt and turned into a liquid. Soon it became difficult to believe that not long ago, she had had beautiful blond hair and now they could not be even seeing into the water.

With a smiling face, she looked at her legs and someone could be very surprise to see her lying peacefully in the bath, and watching as her muscles started to vanish. Her face became badly damage as well. On one side of her forehead, there was a deep wound but there was no blood coming out of it. The same happened to her face on which she had big wounds. All the wounds moved inside and create deep hollows.

Now the water became again clean as all the hair already vanished. Shortly there were no muscles of her legs and after some time all parts of Lisa's body, which were under water started to vanish. Soon she had no legs, no corps and no hands. It could be beyond a human's imagination and difficult to believe but that was left from her body by now, were only tin strings, just floating strings. One ticker in the place where she had her corps and then in the place where should be her legs, she had two strings. The same happened to the hands, which have turned into strings as well. All together looked like a children's drawing, who very often drawing strings in stand of a proper body, legs or hands. The main string was still connecting to the head, floating in the water.

It was obvious that Lisa is death but it seemed that she still looks at floating strings, and smiling. After some time her eyes started to be more and whiter, until they became completely white with some blue and green shades. Her lips were white as well but still with the same strange smile.

With the time, Lisa has badly damaged head with all the strings floated on the water. Her head looked like a white and partially destroyed monument.

There was no open window in the bathroom, which means that there should not be any wind inside and it could be beyond any common sense how it was possible that Lisa's head and all the strings floated in the water without any wind. Someone could be only sure that she was death but what anybody can be sure to see an incident like this one. Whoever will look at her must ask a question, what moves everything. If it is not a dream, why it is still floating?

Perhaps there is an answer in the future, who knows.

Chapter 2

John was not in good mood this morning; even another beautiful day of the summer just began. He was sitting in the office with his legs resting on the desk, next to his coffee cap. He did not open his eyes when the phone rang. With lazy move, he picked up and listened for a while. On another side of the line was his partner, detective Oscar who has spoken with excitement in his voice.

'Inspector, you have to be here right now. It looks that a woman vanished.'

'Do not you think that she might be gone shopping?' John asked ironically.

'Inspector, her head is in the bath.'

'Oscar, I'm sure that she has forgotten to take it with her,' John answered still joking.

'This is very serious matter inspector and you have to come here as soon as you can.'

'Look, I'm not in a mood for stupid jokes, especially in the morning and I don't care about woman which goes shopping without her fucking head. This time of a year I should be gone fishing. By the way, I thing that you should be in the office by now, am I right or I am still dreaming.'

'Inspector, I was on my way to work, when I received a call, that a woman has been murdered so I am here.'

'I'm still not too sure if you are not in a pub but if it is so then you might find yourself in fucking shit situation.'

'Inspector, I do not know what is wrong with you this morning. After many years we have been working together, very strange ideas are coming to your mind. Why?'

'Ok, ok Oscar, give me the address and I will be there as soon as I can.'

John finished his sentence and at the next moment to the office came his boss, opening widely the door. 'What are you doing here?' He asked loudly. 'Did you come here to have a rest or to work?' His voice was full of anger.

'Need you to fuck off from this office now and remember, do not come before the case is finished.'

* . . . . . * . . . . . *

John did not take long to come to the place given him by Oscar. He passed a big gate and entered Lisa's property, slowly driving towards a big, white painted house. Around the house, there was a beautiful garden. Next to the entrance of the house there were parked few motorcars. John stopped behind them and at the same time, a police officer came to him.

'Good morning inspector,' said young policeman and he continued, 'I am very glad to have a pleasure, to show you the way, inspector.'

John looked at him for a while then he said, 'good morning young man and I think that I might find the way on my own.'

'Oh yes, inspector, I am sure you can but it will be much quicker because the house is very big and the bathroom is on the first floor. I mean the bathroom in which the house cleaner found the body of the death woman.'

'I was told that there is a head only,' answered John.

'Oh yes inspector, just a head. To be honest inspector, I have never seen anything like that in my whole life.'

'What are you fucking talk about? Have you ever shaved yet? You didn't pass a quarter of the life,' John was very unfriendly this morning.

'Inspector, if I said anything wrong, I am very sorry but if I have to be honest, I wish to have three quarter left.'

'I wish you too.'

'Inspector, it is behind that door where the policeman stays.'

'Thank you very much,' John answered and a moment later, he entered the bathroom, where a few people already worked. His sight went to the bath with a woman's head. He stood like in shock for a while.

'Good morning inspector,'

'Fuck,' John said and after a while, he added. 'What is it?'

'I told you inspector,' Oscar answered looking at Lisa's head and they stood silently for some time then Oscar asked.

'Do you see?'

'What would like to say Oscar is fucking blind or what?'

'Inspector,' Oscar answered, 'when I entered the bathroom everything was floating and never has stopped but there is no wind inside; I really don't know how it is possible.'

'Perhaps somebody stirred the water or what so ever.'

'I was here for about one hour before they came and everything was floating, funny.'

'All I can say is that it's looking quite exciting but for sure somebody has poured very strong acid into the water.

If I look at the bath it seems to me that the head is in the place as it supposes to be after somebody set in the water.'

'I'm quite sure that you are right inspector but how it could be possible that a human's body turned into some strings?'

'Why are you asking me? You are very good detective so perhaps you can give me an explanation because I think about a strong acid.'

'The man from labour said that the water is clean.'

'I can see that the water is clean and don't any labour to tell me this shit. By the way, why there is no blood in the water?'

'Yes inspector, from the very first moment I have thought about the blood. I don't know what to think.'

'Oscar, do you really think that clean water can make such think with a human's body?'

'The man has tested the water but a full report can't be ready on the same day.'

'What about the photographer, is he finish with his job?'

'Oh yes inspector, he left shortly before you came in and now as you can see only fingerprints have to be taken.'

'It could be possible that I am not yet fully awake so perhaps I am not too sure what I see. I think that it could be very good to see that again. Oscar, I hope you have to call the photographer back but ask him to take a video camera so we will have a possibility to see this strange shit again, later on.'

'Shall I call him, inspector?'

'I think that I was clear, Oscar and tell him to be here as soon as possible.'

'I could be right inspector, because it is difficult believe that it is possible. It looks like a dream, a head together with strings floating on the water and no blood. There are deep hollows in the face and the head which looks like its empty.'

'Who found the body; I shall tell rather the head.'

'The house cleaner, she comes here every morning and she called the police.'

'We need to talk to her but I still can not believe that it is clean water.'

'It is really very interesting and difficult to believe but there in another room I have seen a fish tank so I thought that we can to pour a little water from the bath and see what will happen.'

'Oscar, what fucking ideas are in your mind, it seems that you will to kill a fish but from another hand it might be interesting to see how a fish is changing into a string.'

'Well, perhaps not because it could be possible that somebody has poured a chemical which already steamed, in other wards the water is clean.'

'The best if they will take the whole bath to the labour.'

'Inspector, I don't think that it might be possible.'

'Why not, we can pull down the wall and take the bath down the staircase.'

'If we can get permission of course and I don't think that it is possible and that the boss will never let us to do.'

'I know Oscar so better lets see the house cleaner,' John answered and they went to the same room, where Lisa for the last time in her life has picked up the telephone.'

'Good morning,' said John and continued, 'I am inspector John and this is my partner inspector Oscar. I hope that you wouldn't mind to ask you a few questions.'

John looked at a young girl, sitting in the big chair. From her eyes was falling tears.

'Inspector,' said young police woman, 'I will be outside, if you need me.

'Thank you very much,' he answered kindly and looked at her as she was leaving the room then he asked the girl.

'Tel me please, what's your name?'

'I am Shivana,' she answered with crying voice.

'How long are you working here?'

'It will be already a year, sir.'

'Do you work here every day?'

'No sir, I am off on weekends.'

'At what time did you come here this morning?'

'I came just before eight o'clock, sir.'

'Could you tell us, how did you found the body?'

'I just went to the bathroom, sir and saw that Miss Lisa's head is in the water, she was so kind for me, sir.

'Do you remember what time was when you went to the bathroom?'

'I do not know but it was just I came to work, sir.'

'Tell me please,' asked Oscar, 'are you going to the bathroom every morning before you start your work or you have to start from the bathroom?'

'No sir, but today I felt that I have to go into the bathroom, sir.'

'Who stays in the house with Miss Lisa?' John asked.

'Miss Lisa stays alone, sir.'

'Do you know any friends of Miss Lisa?'

'No sir, I do not know anybody,' the girl answered with some irritation.

'Do you know where Miss Lisa works?'

'No sir, I do not know and I have never asked. Most of the time she spent at home and I do not know if Miss Lisa works at all,' she started to cry before she finished her answer. Both police officers realised that they would not learn too much at the moment, as except the name of the death woman, the house cleaner did not say too much.

'I think,' said John, 'that I haven't got any more questions at this moment. What about you Oscar?'

'No, I have no questions,' he answered then he thought, 'well, if I could know how it happened, it could be cool.

John sight at him as he was trying to say that he knows Oscar is thinking about then slowly he turned his sight to the police woman and asked, 'do you mind to take Shivana to her place?'

'Not at all inspectors, I'll do it with a great pleasure.'

'Miss Shivana, I think that it could be better for now if you'll go home but if you will remind anything that you will think that it might be important, make a phone call, please, here is my card.' John said to her and added, 'the police officer will take you home and will take care if you'll need anything.' Then he said to the police officer, 'perhaps you will notice what could be important so, please make a call at any time.'

'Of course inspector, it will be my great pleasure to help with the investigation.'

'Thank you very much.'

Two young women left the room and nearly at the same time came in the photographer together with two another police officers and their boss, Captain Paul, who said to John. 'Listen, I haven't got too much time but after I have learned that you are going to make a movie, I came as well, perhaps I can take a part, if you will allow me, of course.' He said that with a voice filled with irony.

'Sir, I am not making any movie but very strange thins are happening here and I thought that it could be very good to see it again or to show it to somebody who is more capable in a matter as that one.'

'Captain, it isn't a common case,' said Oscar.

'What's happening here?' asked Captain Paul.

'Actually, you have to see it for yourself, sir,' Answered John and they went to the bathroom, and John stopped surprisingly next to the bath, next to him stood Oscar. The two man busy with fingerprints noticed that something is not right so they stopped their job and looked at the bath as well. No one of them could understand how it was possible that all the strings and the head where now in standstill. There was no movement in the bath.

'Perhaps there was really a wind coming from outside,' said Oscar.

'What wind are you talking about, Oscar?' Captain Paul asked and added, 'are you ok today?'

John sighted at Captain with a smile and said, 'now you can see on your own, sir that we are facing big problem here.'

'Don't play fool with me, John,' Captain answered sharply.

'Sir, not long ago everything here in the bath was floating and now it is standstill.'

'Why it makes you so surprise. If you like to see it floating then stir the water but then you don't take any photos because everything will be in big mess.'

'Sir, something there isn't right and please don't take us incorrectly. The reason that I've been asking for a video camera is that everything here was floating and it isn't any joke.'

'John, I was here not long ago and I promise you that I didn't see anything floating,' said Benjamin the photographer.

'I came here before you,' replied Oscar, 'and everything floated in the bath.'

'In your dreams perhaps because I took photos here and I never noticed anything,' the photographer answered angrily.

'Ok, ok, enough because there is no time to quarrel.' Captain stopped their conversation. 'There is no time to be waste, what we need is to solve the matter.' Captain Paul finished and sighted at John.

'Yes sir, you're right because I have a job to do, not to drive up and down only because of somebody's imagination. What shall I do now? What I have to do with the video camera?' Benjamin was slightly irritated.

'I don't know,' answered Captain and added, 'personally I don't see any use of it.

'Sir, I am very surprise and I don't know what to say but it could be very good to use the camera.'

'Captain, it is a part of my job to look for any evidence of the case and I've been checking the house but when I was here everything was floating. They saw it as well. Never mind that but for the very first time I did not found even who is this woman and all we know is her name. There is nothing in the house, just nothing that we might be able to push the investigation forward. If the house cleaner said incorrect name, we have to accept it for now as well,' said Oscar.

'Ok gentlemen,' said Captain, 'I have to go and better I'll do it as quick as possible before you'll come up with some more fantasy. By the way, I do not see any reason so you have to be as much excited, the matter should not be too complicated. It looks to me a very common case and all what you have to do is to find out who did this shit. Wish you good luck.'

'Did you hear it?' Asked Benjamin after Captain Paul left the room.

'Yes Benjamin, I did and it seems that no one case is complicated for all of you. Everything is simple but why cannot you try to solve at list one of that simple cases.' John was not too friendly.

'Listen, I am a photographer and I have to do my job, and you are the one who has always complains. Now, what can I do for you this time?'

'Look Benjamin, at the moment I don't know but if you are here, perhaps you can use the camera.'

'An excellent idea but if you wouldn't mind then I rather leave the camera and will be gone to work. I hope that you know how to operate it.'

'Well, it looks similar as mine but tell me a few words and then you can go,' John answered softly.

'It's very simple, just press here then look here and you will know everything you need,' Benjamin answered and he asked. 'John, can I go?'

At the same time from the bathroom came one of the men busy with fingerprints and said to John. 'Inspector, come and see this fucking bath.'

John entered the bathroom and couldn't believe his eyes as everything floated again as it was before, so he stood for a while and then he left to call Benjamin.

'Benjamin, take your camera and come to the bathroom, now you'll see on your own how everything floats in the water.' John said that with some excitement but happiness as well and he went back to the bathroom. I took a few minutes and Benjamin came to the bathroom as well. As soon as he entered, there was no movement in the water.

'What now?' He asked.

'What the hell is going on?' John looked at the water then at Benjamin.

'Something is going on here which is difficult to understand,' Oscar was surprised as well. He stood for a while then he said, 'I think Inspector that it will be much better if I will check the house once again, is possible that I have been walking too quickly and I have missed something.'

'John, you know how to operate the camera so perhaps I will assist you only.' Benjamin proposed looking at the bath.

'Ok Benjamin, give me the camera and I'll go out the door. You will open and I will enter with the camera ready to shoot.'

'All right,' answered Benjamin and a moment later he was alone in the bathroom. 'Oh no,' he said to himself looking at the water. There in the bath everything started to float.

He could not believe himself so he stood standstill in front of the bath. Soon from behind the door came John's voice filled with irritation.

'What's wrong with you? Can't you open the door?'

John entered the bathroom and sighted Benjamin, standing without any movement. Slowly he turned to John and said, 'John, I am sorry, I am really sorry, you were right, it moves, everything moves.'

'What moves?'

'Everything, the head, the strings, everything, John I am very sorry.'

John sighted at the bath and asked, 'what moves? I don't see anything moving.'

Benjamin turned towards the bath where again everything was in standstill. 'This is beyond my imagination. Few moments ago, it was floating on the water. Why it has stooped?'

'Please, do not ask me because I do not understand.'
John answered slowly. 'Anyway, take your camera and
capture the bathroom, the entrance and what ever you like.
He gave the camera to Benjamin, who worked with it for
some time. He came very close to the bath in hope that it
will be possible that the water will move again somehow but
without any luck. After he finished his job, John said.

'Benjamin, I thank you very much, I don't know how it
might help but at least you could see on your own that I
didn't call you here without a reason.

'John, I told you that I am very sorry and I am. I think
that if you will tell to anybody about a matter like this,
nobody will believe you.'

'You right Benjamin, no one can believe but something
is that I am not to sure about. The time, you worked with
the camera I thought that the lips of the woman did smile
more then before. I just have such impression. Anyway
Benjamin, thank you for your help and let me know as soon
as you will get the photos.'

'I will make them as soon as I can,' answered Benjamin
and left the house. John stood in the bathroom for a while
then went to see Oscar.

'How are you doing,' he asked. 'Did you find
anything?'

'Not really Inspector.'

John together with Oscar still was busy searching
the house when the telephone rang. After very short
conversation, he said. 'Something happened by Shevana's
place, I don't know exactly but the owner of the house
called police because she couldn't open a door so we have to
go there, Oscar.'

'What could be wrong, she left together with the
policewoman.'

'Nowadays people rather call police in stand a locksmith.'

'It's strange.'

'Lets' go and see what's going on.'

They left the house and drove trough very beautiful garden surrounding Lisa's house.

PUT SOME GARDEN, PERHAPS PARK

'Inspector,' said Oscar, 'I do understand that there has to be something in the water but it could be possible that the chemical has dissolved because if not then the head will be gone as well and nobody will ever know that the woman was killed.'

'You right,' answered John and continued, 'it looks that the chemicals were active for short time only.'

They arrived to the address given them on the phone and John parked his vehicle behind another police one. Nearly same time a police officer came to the motorcar and said.

'Good morning Inspector, you have to go to the first floor. My partner is waiting for you over there, sir.'

'Thanks.'

As soon as they reached the first floor, an old woman greeted them and invited them inside her flat. 'I am Mrs Brown,' she introduced herself and made a way for John and Oscar.

There by the door stood the same young police officer, whom John already met by Lisa's house.

'I didn't expect to meet you so soon,' John said to him, while entering the flat.

'Me too Inspector, we have been driving near by when came a call so we are here,' he answered.

Inside the flat, they met the same police officer, who took Shivana to her place. 'Could you tell me what's going on, please,' John became quite gentle.

'We came right after the call and according to Mrs. Brown, Shivana should be inside her flat and even the key is inside but it seems that there is nobody. We thought that there will be a need brake the door so I thought that the best will be to call you, Inspector.'

'I hope that you don't mind if I will talk to the owner of the house,' John answered and added. 'Anyway, I thank you for your help.'

After the police officer left the flat he said to the old woman, 'I am Inspector John and this is my partner, Inspector Oscar. Did you call police?'

'Yes sir,' she answered, 'for more than a year this young girl stays here and I never had any problem and suddenly, this morning, she came with police.'

'I think that anybody can come home with police and I don't see anything wrong with it, Mrs. Brown,' said Oscar.

'Sir, the floor is wet and it seems that the water is going out of the bathroom. I knocked on the door but there is no answer and it seems that there is no one in the flat.'

'Do you have a spare key?'

'No sir, the only key for the flat has got Shivana. Many times I was about to cut one but never did it.'

'Oscar, could you open the door?' John asked him with a smile.

'I can try but I am not too sure. By the way, three cops coming here and they do not know if anybody needs a help but no one can open or break the door. Only what they did was a phone call so what they are paid for,' answered Oscar. 'Show me the door Mrs. Brown,' he added and they went out the door.

The door was open within few minutes. John did not allow enter the flat except him and Oscar. They went inside and soon have learned that there was nobody in the flat. The floor was wet all over but the taps in the bathroom where closed.

'This is unbelievable, Inspector,' said Oscar.

'Oscar, somehow the floor is wet because the water went out of the bathroom but it seems to me that she took shower and left.'

'Then how it could be possible that the door was locked from inside. Inspector,' Oscar's voice sounded excited, 'come have a look at that strings on the floor.'

'Shit, it really looks the same. Don't try to tell me that she vanished as the other woman.'

'It seems like but there in the house there was a bath and here is a shower only so how it could be possible that,' Oscar suspended his voice and started to examine the strings on the floor in the bathroom.

'Oscar, I can see that the strings look very similar as there in the bath but it might be very serious matter. It isn't too difficult to pour some chemical into the bath but here must be a geyser.'

'Inspector, if this is the true that this girl has turned into strings then we might face big problem'

'Oscar, call people from the labour and tell them that they must come here immediately. And call the boss, because I'm not too sure about this case.'

The time Oscar was busy with phone call, John has walked around the flat then he came back to the bathroom. Oscar came to him and said, 'Inspector, I think, well, I am quite sure that the strings are the same and . . .'

'You don't need to finish, Oscar, if the strings are a part of Shivana's body then the water might be poisoned in the whole city and this is not a joke. I do not know what we shall do about it.

It did not take too long and soon there was in the flat Captain Paul with the people from the labour and Benjamin. John asked everybody wait outside and invited inside his boss only.

'John, what's going on, why did you call all the people?'

'Sir, we have very serious suspicion that the water in the town could be poisoned.'

'John, don't you think that you have too many crazy ideas today? Do you know what are you talking about?'

'Sir, there is a bath in the house and we can expect that there was a chemical in the water but here is a shower only.'

'What do you mean? Is anybody death here?'

'Sir we called the people from the labour as we think that the house cleaner from the other house has turned into strings like the other woman.'

'Did you found a head as well?'

'No, there is no head. We think that there in the bath any chemical could dissolve before it reached the head but here the water was coming from the top, right on the head so it is understandable that it vanished as the first.'

'Wait a minute, perhaps the strings look similar but it can't be true, no it can't be true. The other thing is that it is not as simple as you think. No, it is impossible. How can you close the water in the whole town, it cannot be possible. No, John you strictly have some terrible day.'

'I'm worried that there is no other option,' answered John and at the same time, his phone rang. He took the call and after he finished, said, 'it was Benjamin, I don't know what's wrong today but definitely it isn't a good day. Benjamin said that the film went blank and he ahs no photos. Except that he said that he checked the video camera and there is nothing as well.'

'What do you mean nothing?' Captain Paul asked.

'I don't know, that what he said,' answered John.

'Why can't he go back and take the photos again, can't he think a little?'

'He went there then he said that he went inside the house. After he entered the bathroom, he sighted a police officer's uniform on the floor. Except that, Benjamin said that there in the bath are more strings then before. He said that is waiting for us urgently.'

'What the hell is going on? Not a half a day and so much trouble,' said Captain and added, 'I want to go and see the place again.'

'I do believe that we have to go there as soon as possible. Oscar, you have to carry on here.'

'Actually, what I have to do first, I mean what do you think is the situation with the water.'

'Well, the labour people have to give us an answer as soon as possible so we will have a proper view in the matter.'

'Oscar, if there is any suspicion that the water is poisoned then I have no idea what we'll do with the matter.' Captain said that with nearly crying voice then added, 'one is very important, the matter is highly confidential. Lets' go John.'

After they left Oscar stood in the flat and started to think about his family. 'We took the shower quite early but I think that I should phone home and warn, well, we need water. Shit, better they must check the strings right now.'

He opened the door and invited the two men inside. 'Look,' he said, 'here in the bathroom are some strings which seems to be like that in the other house in the bath.'

They entered the bathroom and Oscar pointed the string on the floor.

'Inspector, here are only pieces of strings and to say exactly if they belong to human's body, we have to take them to the labour or perhaps to the house over there and compare if they the same. It seems that if the strings are the same then the water on the town contains some chemical.'

'Don't talk nonsense,' Oscar answered. 'I took a shower this morning and what, nothing wrong with me? We do not know if anybody ahs been kill here.'

'Ok Inspector, we've got some string so we can go but to be honest it looks strange because here is a shower only and I can't understand how a human's body can change into strings.'

'Listen,' said Oscar, 'do you think that a wild strawberry can turn red if they become ashamed?'

'Is it a joke?'

'No it isn't a joke, one friend of mine told me about it long ago in army.'

'Are you serious?'

'Of course that I am serious but not about strawberry only about my friend because he really said something like that,' Oscar answered and they laughed but not for long. Their faces became serious as they realised that the matter, which they are dealing with, is far from any joke.

'Ok Inspector, we are leaving.'

'Remember that I'm waiting for the result as well.'

After they left, he began to search the flat and surprisingly again he could not find any photos or any other things telling something about the girl. 'I can't understand it,' he thought, 'another woman that I don't know anything about her.'

Suddenly he reminded his family and he saw himself entering his house and the bathroom where he found strings in stand those who he loves. 'Shit,' he thought, as the strange vision will not leave him. 'Perhaps I should phone my wife,' he thought. It was difficult for him to stop himself from a phone call, as he understood that now many people could be death in town. 'No, I have to believe,' he nearly said that loudly.

Chapter 3

'I like this place,' said Captain Paul after they entered Lisa's property. 'Everything here is very unique. Dark wood and glass set up in forests and parklands with waterfalls then rolling lawns. Can say that some harmony exist here.'

'I wonder what is the price of this property,' said John.

'I'm sure it has to be a lot but John, how it is possible that you don't know anything about the woman?'

'Sir, I'm sorry but it is a true, we don't know anything, except her name which told us the house cleaner. Captain, look there,' John changed the subject as he spotted Benjamin standing in front of the house. They stopped behind his car and Captain asked.

'Benjamin, why are you standing in front of the door?'

'I'm waiting for you people,' he answered.

'Did you take the photos?'

'I can't go there, I can't.'

'What a fuck are you talking?' Captain was not friendly at all.

'Ok, we can go there together but do not ask me to go there alone. I've got my family and except that I have to tell you that I am quite sure that the film as ok and there is nothing wrong with my video camera.'

'So?' Captain looked at Benjamin and actually did not know what to say.

'You don't understand that there is very strong power in the house,' Benjamin was very worried.

'Let us go inside and all what we need from you is to take photos. If you think that you need a leave, we can talk about it but now let's go inside,' Captain finished and moved towards the door. They entered the house and soon after they came to the bathroom, Benjamin said.

'Captain, you can go in but I can't. I can't go inside.'

'Stop your shit and come to take photos,' Captain was angry.

'Ok, you go first then you can call me but I'm not too sure if I should.'

'All right, let's go John.'

'Shit,' John nearly shouted as they entered the bathroom. 'I can't believe it.'

'John, I wasn't serious when you told me about floating strings but what I see now is even worse.'

Two men stood in front of the bath and looked at something, which they could not understand. Except damaged Lisa's head and the strings, which was left from her body in the water they saw more strings. The extra string looked exactly as Lisa's but lying on opposite side and everything was floating in the water. It was obvious that the strings belong to a human been.

'Now you know sir, why I've been asking for a video camera,' said John.

'Yes, yes John,' he answered and went to the door. 'Benjamin, come here to take the photos.'

Benjamin a little worried entered the bathroom and quickly started to take the photos. Suddenly John said to Captain, pointing the water, 'Sir, look here.'

'What is it?'

'I don't know but it isn't right, exactly the same story as before,' said John and went to search the uniform, which was on the floor still talking. 'I wonder if somebody forced the man go into the water or he entered on his own. Perhaps he tried to check how the water would work on his body. Fuck, this is not right.'

'What's now?'

'This seems to be the same man, I have spoken early this morning,' John answered holding ID in his hand.

'I remember him but perhaps the strings don't belong to the same person.'

'To be honest, I don't feel too well, I wasn't too kind with him,' John said sadly.

'If I have to be honest, I am glad that is you are busy with this investigation not me, John,' Captain try to joke.

'I told you that here is very strong power,' Benjamin was very serious.

'Benjamin, take the photos once again and work a little with the video camera. By the way, did you put a new film into the camera?'

'Captain, I am working for you more than twenty years and now you are asking me if I've got a new film and very soon you will ask me if I know which side of the camera shall be pointed to the front. I think that you better bring somebody else to do the job.'

'Don't be cross Benjamin it was just a naïve joke,'

Without one word more, he started to take photos. Shortly Benjamin finished the first film and inserted another one. After the second film was finished, he asked Captain, if he can go back.

'I can't stay in this place any longer,' he explained.

'Benjamin,' Captain did not know what exactly he suppose to say, 'you should know that as policemen, we have to face any risk connected with our duty.'

'Captain, I am not a policeman but a photographer. Do you know, when I came here everything was floating then suddenly it stopped. Nothing, not even a small move on the water and this is not a joke, here is strong power.'

'When we came, it floated as well.'

'You see, I told you and I tell you more, the best if you go away as well.'

'Benjamin, did you see anything else?'

'No, I did not see anything and I don't need anything to do with it. Perhaps I heard some voices but I am not sure what it was. I am finish and let me go.'

'Ok Benjamin, we'll talk in the office.'

Benjamin left the bathroom but did not go out as at the same time come people from the labour so he asked, 'what are you two doing here? Don't you have better place to spend your time?'

Captain heard them and quickly asked about their results, 'what can you tell us?'

'What we can tell you?'

'Don't make story too long, please. We have to know if there is any possibility that the strings belong to human's body.'

'We have to compare them. No one can give any answer just to look at strings. It can be anything.'

'Then do it,' said John and added 'try to be quick David.'

He put n gloves and took a plastic bag in which there were strings from Shivana's flat. As soon as he sighted the bath, he said, 'I think that here are more strings then before. Well, it looks like somebody took a bath.'

'Oh yes but look here,' John pointed police officer's uniform.

'Shit, we have checked the water and I do believe that there was nothing in. How it is possible?'

'Do you think that the strings belong to human's body, David?'

'Captain, it looks alike but I can't be sure. Do you think that I can drop one of this from the bag into the water so we might see more exactly?'

'David, do whatever you think you need to do but be quick,' Captain was nervous as the matter started to be more and more complicated.

Soon David dropped one of the strings into the water and all the men could witness unbelievable phenomena. The water was standstill but all strings started slowly to move. Then everything was floating together with the head. Suddenly something took place that no one of them could imagine, the small piece of string started to move towards Lisa has wounded head. It was breath-taking incident and everybody looked at it silently.

'We have to call Benjamin back,' said John, braking silence and quickly went out the door. 'Benjamin, come quickly with your video camera.'

'Why, what for?' he looked at John surprisingly.

'Man, don't ask only come quickly,' somebody repeated as everybody went outside the bathroom. After they came back, they could not be more surprise because into the bath there was no movement.

'What the hell is going on in this place?' Captain asked with excitement.

'You should be with us,' said John to Benjamin. 'We could get everything captured and it's over. I don't understand what's wrong with you but seems to me that you are not serious.'

'I told you that we can't stay in this house. Don't you see that they are not death?' Benjamin looked very worried.

'Do you need a doctor?' asked Captain.

'I have a family and I must leave this place. It looks like all of you are not serious, blind and very stupid.'

'Benjamin, if you need a leave, we'll talk but now I getting piss of with this shit of yours' so take your things and fuck of to work. The photos you took must be finish immediately. Now you better go before I'll do something very bad,' Captain raised his voice. 'I have to go and you have to be in touch with me, John,' he added.'

'Sir, what about me,' asked Benjamin.

'You've go your car,'

'Sir,' John came into the conversation, 'he seems to be in shock so better you take him with and we'll take his vehicle to the station.'

'Ok John, I'll take him with and just let me know if you'll need any help.'

'I don't know at this stage what I need. The situation with the water is quite serious and I think you have to make some preparation so there will be no panic in the city.'

Captain looked into the window and kept quite for a while then he said with very soft voice, 'it might be big shit but since now on before we don't know too much about the situation, nobody will be here alone. Fuck knows what has happened to Benjamin. I need results, John.'

Captain left together with Benjamin and John started thinking loudly about the photos and blank film. He knew Benjamin since he started work and never before happened something like that.

'John,' David came to him closer, 'you see it might be possible that there is a radiation coming from the bath or from the strings, difficult to predict but I don't see any other explanation.'

'We will see the next film and I hope it will be ok because it could be possible that he had some old staff from the shop. It is quite common nowadays but if really we are dealing with radiation, as you said then we have big shit. Seems to me that I have to call Oscar,' he said and took his telephone.

'Oscar,' he started, 'I have to tell you that it is very important that it is necessary for you to leave Havana's flat as soon as possible but before that, you have to wait until somebody will come over there. Except that you have to make sure that, nobody will enter the flat. This is very important.'

'Inspector, what's happening?'

'Perhaps nothing but is possible that a lot. Another thing is that it could be good to take the owner of the house to the office.'

'Can you say something more, Inspector.'

'I'll see you in the office, Oscar. I will be there soon after somebody will come here because according to Captain nobody is allowed to be here alone.'

Shortly after the two police officers came and John instructed them that at all times they have to be together and no one is allow going into the house then he left for the office together with the people from the labour. He did not even look at the nice garden, which he liked so much before. The only, what was on his mind was that the water in the city contains some very danger chemicals.

John knew that the situation is very difficult but it was even more difficult for him to understand that the water in town is not close yet. 'Why we have to wait,' he thought, 'many times there was a water shortage in town, we can reopen soon after it will be clear that there is no danger for the people.'

Chapter 4

John arrived to the police station and as soon as the officer on duty has spotted him, he told him that Captain need to see him very urgently. He walked slowly towards Captain's office as after he came it surprised him a lot to see Oscar sitting on the chair.

'I can't believe Oscar that you are so quick.'

'He is quick, have a sit John,' said Captain.

'Thanks', seems to me that it is very official meeting,' John joked.

'You are right John it is official and very serious meeting.'

'What is it now about?'

'John, I have to tell you that no one policeman has been sent to Lisa's house and no one to the house where stays or use to stay Shivana, I think this is the proper name of the young house cleaner.'

'I didn't get you, Captain.'

'Look, no one call has been received here in the station and no one have been made.'

'Sir, I had a call from Oscar and he most probably had a call from here then the cops which we have met in the flat get a call from here as well.'

'Yes John Oscar call you and he called to bring technical staff to the house but the question is that somebody call him and for sure no one from here.'

'Now I'm getting completely confused.' John looked at Captain and then at Oscar's face then he asked.

'Oscar, how did you know that Lisa is death?'

'I received a call from officer on duty, as I thought.'

'Actually I don't know how it might be possible I think that there must be a record.'

'There is no record, we checked.'

'Then somebody call wait a minute, how anybody can call Oscar on his mobile. Seems to me that somewhere is a big mess or someone is playing fool with us.'

'You right John somebody is playing fool and is playing big time and we have to suspect that the patrol which was there in the flat has nothing to do with police.'

'Sir, the man is death and I found his ID.'

'John, I took the ID before I left the house and gave to check so we will find his family and I have to tell you that for sure the person those not exist in our records. He has nothing to do with police. Most probably he is not the one whose strings are there in the bath.'

'Shit, I wouldn't think for a moment even that I have spoken to some stranger, perhaps a criminal even,' John was partly surprised and partly angry.

'We informed all the patrols to look for them but I don't think that it will bring any positive result.'

'They are using police's vehicle.'

'It doesn't matter. The thing is that they know more about us than we know our self. Except that, we are dealing with very good professionals. Firstly in the morning they called to Oscar then the ex policewoman took the girl to her place and again another person has been killed.'

'Sir, the old lady made telephone call to us'

'Perhaps she did but no call has been received here but by those people.'

31

'How they can do it?'

'Our technicians are working already in the matter and I let you know as soon as I will know anything about it so do not say that I am not helping you people. Well, I have nearly forgotten, Benjamin is in hospital.'

'What's wrong with him?'

'You have seen there in the house that he isn't ok but it become terrible, he is in very bad mental condition and he has some strange things on his body. Very bad looking blisters and the doctor said that it might be a radiation.'

'Sir, what about us, we have been in both places.'

'John, I went to this places as well so do you think that I am not interested what's going on. I will let you know but now you have to carry on with the investigation. In addition, remember that I have to know everything about the matter. If there will be a need for an action, I have to know it.'

'We will do whatever we can, sir.'

'One more thing, I am busy organizing specialists to check for any radiation in both places. Take the matter very seriously because we do not what we are dealing with and as a fact the case went somehow to our bosses, and they are waiting for a report. How it could be possible that they know about everything, I do not know, but they know. Ok, you can go but remember that something has to be done and quick.'

* . . . . . * . . . . . *

Far in the passage was sitting Mrs. Brown, who came to the station together with Oscar. They stopped next to her and Oscar said. 'Sorry Mrs. Brown that you have to wait for such long time but we had to attend very urgent meeting.

We are quite busy at this time of a year, please, come inside,' he invited her to the office.

'Have a sit, please,' said John and asked. 'Would you like a cup of coffee or tea perhaps?'

'A cup of coffee will be nice, sir.'

John made three cups of coffee and put them on the desk. Soon after the hearing has began but there was not too much, they could learn from the old lady, who from time to time asked if Shivana is ok and where she might be gone.

'At the moment we don't know where she is but I hope that we will find her very soon,' said to her John and continued. 'Mrs. Brown, you told us that for sure nobody left the flat but I'm still wondering how could be you so sure about that.'

'Sir, I saw hr coming home with police and thereafter I've been out the door. Perhaps you have seen the small garden next to the entrance. This is the only entrance to the house.'

'I seem to be very difficult situation because somehow she left the house and is missing.' John tried to get as much as possible information abut the case.

'I do not know sir, I never have had any problems with my memory and I cannot understand what is happening with me now, sir.'

'How did you find out that something isn't right the in her flat,' John asked.

'Actually, I don't know. It is strange but somehow I looked there, I am sorry, I do things as if that and I have no idea why I did it today but something pushed me to check in the flat. I saw the key in the door but though the key, I could see the water on the floor.'

'What happened later?'

'I was very worried so I made a call to the police, sir.'

'Do you remember the voice of a policeman, you have been spoken?'

'I do not remember but if could hear it I will recognise it. It was a man with very nice deep voice, very gentle like on radio.'

'Tell us please, did you know Shivana well?'

'Not really, sir.'

'She stays by you quite long so you might know a little about her.'

'Yes sir, she stays long but to be honest, I don't know her at all. About a year ago, I put an advert to the paper and she came first. She paid deposit at the same time as she came for the first time and she came to stay on the next day. I do not talk to her too much. She is very nice person but somehow she is mostly alone.'

'Did you see any friends coming to her?'

'No sir, for all the time I didn't see anybody.'

'Did she go out over the weekends?'

'No sir, it surprised me a lot because she is young and pretty but all weekends she's spending alone in her flat.'

'Tell us please, did you notice anything unusual about that girl except that you have told us already.'

'I am not sure but I think she is a little different and somehow she is separated from the world.'

'Ok Mrs. Brown but now tell us something else, do you remember the police that came with Shivana in the morning?'

'Not really sir but I think that it was the same woman who came later.'

'Have you spoken with her?'

'Yes sir, I have spoken with her but it was shortly before you came to the house.'

'She is still very young but do you think that she will be a good police officer?'

'Oh yes sir, she is very kind and very intelligent.'

'I hope that you remember what was the conversation was about.'

'Sir, I do not know what is happening to my memory today but I do not remember anything. 'We have spoken quite while but I really don't know what it was about.'

'Mrs. Brown, the young policewoman was in your place at the time when I was looking around Shivana's flat, did she tell you anything before she left.'

'Sir, I sorry that I do not remember but I am quite sure that she told me something, one what I remember is that she was very kind.'

'I think that it will be all for now Mrs Brown and if there will be anything that you will inform us then please contact us at any time.'

'Sir,' she said slowly looking into the window, 'I think there in the room, you see the door was pen for a while and I think that there was a picture on the wall which I didn't see thereafter.'

'Do you remember what picture was alike?'

'I can't tell you exactly because I never had have the possibility to see it properly but it looks as some stars or stones. I'm sorry but I can't be sure what was on the picture.'

'When did you see the picture for the last time?' The hearing started to be more and more interested.

'I can't be sure but I think that it the same time when the police came to me, you see, the door isn't close at all times. Oh yes, it was the time because I have been checking if somebody is out the door.'

'I see.'

'And you know, I think that she had some stones there in the room.'

'Do you remember what stones she has have, Mrs. Brown?'

'I don't know sir, but I have never seen stones like that in my life.'

'Mrs. Brown, you told us that you don't go inside the flat,' John asked her with smile.

'No sir, I don't but it must at the time when you two went inside the flat, I think so,' she answered turning nervously on the chair.

'Do you remember anything else Mrs. Brown?'

'Sir, this woman from the police and Shivana . . .' she did not finish her sentence.

'What about them?' John asked.

'I think that they look very similar.'

'What do you think about them, Mrs. Brown?'

'I don't know but they talk very similar and they have same very special personality.'

'Do you think so?'

'Yes sir, there is something about them but I do not know how to explain that.'

'Perhaps you are right and if there will be anything more, you'll have to tell us, please call at any time,' John noticed that the old woman is looking for attention and started to feel comfortable in their company. He walked her to the door and thereafter he poured himself another cup of coffee.

'Oscar,' John said and set down by his desk, 'there is something important with this case.'

'What is it Inspector?'

'It seems to me that somehow the killer or the killers providing us with information. We're receiving phone calls without any record about them and seem to me that we know about the matter only as much as they will let to know, strange.'

'You are quite right, Inspector.'

To the office came Captain Paul and started his speech from the door. 'I don' think that you will move the case a millimetre sitting and drinking coffee. I am waiting for a progress.'

'Sir, we have finished a hearing with Ms. Brown, the owner of the house where stayed the young girl.'

'It doesn't matter, I have spoken with the people from the house and they told me that there is some radiation. You have to go there and find out more about the matter, perhaps all of us will go to hospital to join Benjamin.'

'Sir, perhaps it isn't as bad as you think.'

'John,' Captain raised his voice, 'you mustn't tell me anything because there is already bigger shit then you think. I've got no idea how everybody knows about the matter.'

'Sir, the same I was telling to Oscar right now, these people inform everybody, they want. Firstly, they are killing people then they call cops. The thing is that they don't use a normal way of communication.'

'Soon you will tell me that we have to sit and they will come here to introduce themselves.'

'Perhaps they won't come here but they must make a mistake because the way they work is quite complicated.'

'Oscar, are you telling me that they are working and, ok let say that this is work but for me is just a shit crime.' Captain was about to say something but he left the office talking to himself something.

'Oscar, I'm going to Lisa's house and it could be good if you'll make some order with all the information, we have up to now. By the way, there is something not right with the old lady, seems to me that she knows something but her memory isn't too good.'

John left and slowly drove through the town. His thoughts went to different directions and he wandered if there is anything more trouble with the matter he was busy with. In front of the house, the two police officers halted his motorcar.

'Good afternoon sir, may I see you ID, please?'

After he shows him his batch, the police officer gave him a book and asked to write his name into it.

'I hope that you are true policemen,' John joked writing his name and the time into the book.

'Yes sir, we are.'

After the formalities, he drove again through the beautiful garden thinking who looks after it. He parked behind other vehicles and the two police officers greeted him. It impressed him that the house has such good security. In the bathroom, he met a few people.

'Good afternoon,' he greeted them and added, 'I am Inspector John and I am busy with the case.'

'Good afternoon Inspector, we heard about you already. I am Bob and together with my people we trying to find out what's going on in this place.'

'Do you have any results?'

'Not really, Inspector but we know for sure that here exists some type of radiation.'

'What radiation?'

'That's the problem; I have never experienced something like now. We know that the radiation comes from the bath but funny, it doesn't exist at all time.'

'What do you mean? A radiation is radiation and if here is any it supposes to be at all times.'

'Inspector, we don't know what radiation we are dealing with and from our information you couldn't get any photos as the films have been damaged.'

'That's right.'

'What we know by now is that it affects a film but you'll be very surprised that the radiation occurs when we've been trying to take photos. Our films went blank as well.'

'You must be joking.'

'Incidentally not, Inspector, we made a couple experiments but it is too early to say anything.'

'Do you think that a radiation can destroy a human's body except a camera's film,' asked John.

'Quite difficult question,' Bob answered shortly.

'One of our people is in hospital,' said John.

'I know about it, Inspector.'

'Do you think that it has connection with the radiation which is here?'

'It is highly possible because I don't see any other reason for that type of illness.'

'Is it possible that we might land in a hospital as well?'

'I don't think so because we are prevented with the screen.'

'Well, there was no screen before and we spent a lot of time here in the bathroom.'

'Inspector, we are still busy and we are in contact with the doctors in the hospital. I will inform you if there will be any danger to your health but now I can't say anything.'

'In other words you are saying that I have to leave you alone so you will have some progress in your work, well let me go and I hope not to finish in a hospital, bye Bob. Before I go, I would like to ask you about another matter.'

'What is it?'

'There is another place where we have found some number of strings and we are quite sure that they remind a human's body and I need to know if in that place is any radiation or not.'

'Well Inspector, we know about the place and I do believe that there are already my colleges so there is no need to worry about.'

John left the bathroom and started to walk slowly from room to room. He came to the lounge and set down on the same chair, on which set Shivana. After a while his sight to the wall in front of him and suddenly he spotted a space that most probably was a picture in this place not long ago. John stood up, came closer to the wall, and became quite sure that there was a picture. He reminded Mrs. Brown, who told them about a picture as well. His phone started to ring which stopped his thoughts.

'Inspector,' it was Oscar on the other side, 'we've got very interested matter.'

'I think that we've got shit matter, anyway, is it the only reason that you're calling?'

'No Inspector, I have to tell you that I have sorted all the files, we've got and now I have to go to hospital.'

'What do you mean, are you sick?'

'Oh no, I am well but I have a feeling that I have to see Benjamin.'

'If you'll be long enough over there, we might meet, Oscar.'

'I don't get you, Inspector.'

'I'm not well, I feel dizzy and it's strange because I was ok not long ago and now I don't know if I'll be able to drive a car.'

'Shall I come to see you, Inspector?'

'Thanks', I'll be all right, Oscar but tell me, do you remember if in the same room where we have spoken with Shivana was a picture, just on the wall opposite the coffee table.'

'I haven't noticed anything, Inspector but it could be possible because Mrs. Brown was telling about some picture as well.'

'I don't know what's wrong with me but now I have a felling that I saw stones somewhere here as well.'

'Missing pictures, stones and on top if that Mrs. Brown was telling about a language that she couldn't understand.'

'All this things are exciting but I'm getting more and more dizzy.'

Chapter 5

Oscar arrived to the hospital and after he entered the building, he looked around surprisingly as he did not expect as big space inside it. From outside the building seemed to be very small.

'How they are building nowadays houses that it looks so small from outside and is very big inside?' Oscar asked himself as he walked through the passage to the room where he was told is Benjamin.

'Hi Benjamin,' he greeted him from the door. 'I couldn't find you in his big building, it's really huge.'

Benjamin did not answered lying on his back and looking into the ceiling.

'You don't look sick at all and I don't know why they put here. Look, I brought you some fruits and cookies.'

There was a silence in the room as Benjamin didn't moved his head even only his lips moved slightly as he like to say something or praying. Oscar stood next to the bed and did not know what to say. Suddenly Benjamin turned his sight to Oscar; he looked for a while and said.

'You shouldn't be here, Inspector.'

'What are you talking about?'

'I know what I am talking about and I'm telling to you that it will be better for you to go away.'

'Benjamin, you've got here the cookies,' Oscar put the plastic bag on the side table. He looked at Benjamin for a while and thinking that the man does not looks to be ill at all. Perhaps he has some lumps on his body, the face did not look too well with the lumps but Benjamin stopped his thoughts, saying.

'I don't need anything, I'm fine.'

'May I ask you something?'

'I know what you will ask me but I don't have any answer because I don't know anything and much better if you'll go. They are not death and I am telling you Inspector that they are everywhere. They can go wherever they want to.'

'What did you see over there, Benjamin?'

'I didn't see anything, I told you already.'

'Benjamin, I know that you saw something and you have spoken to someone.'

'Oscar, I told you, I didn't see and I didn't speak to anybody. I am tired by now and I need some sleep.'

'Why can't you help us?'

'Listen, they are very strong and if you will avoid problems then leave me alone. They can go inside your body and talk to you from inside, and you have to listen.'

'Benjamin, you are telling a big crap to me but it doesn't mean that I will believe that you are very sick, I won't. You know something and you are hiding it but it doesn't matter, we will find out sooner or later but we will.'

Benjamin turned his head and pointed his sight again into the ceiling. Oscar stood next to his bed for a while then finally realized that Benjamin will not say a word more. 'Benjamin,' he said to him, 'I hope to see you soon at work and at the mean time just think about all the people in the city who might go to hospital like you, it's up to you, bye.'

Oscar set in his motorcar holding the keys in his hand rested on the window and in such way that he does not know what to do, start the motor or go back to Benjamin. It went through his mind that there are many people who might be in the same situation as Benjamin. He started the motor as soon as he had a vision of his wife. Her clear picture woke him up and soon he drove away from the hospital.

* . . . . . * . . . . . *

Oscar entered the office and surprisingly looked at John. The office was with big glass windows so everybody can see from outside, who is inside but he did not noticed that his partner is in already.

'Hi Inspector, did not expect to see you so soon.'

'What did you expect, did you thought that I will be in hospital by now, or what?'

'No, I thought that you're still in Lisa's house.'

'You must be joking, by the way, the day is nearly finished and we haven't got any progress in the case.'

'Inspector, it isn't any surprise, you can't tell that we are solving all the matters on very first day. We started the investigation only in the morning.'

'Perhaps you are right but tell me how is Benjamin.'

'To be honest, I don't know. His head is covered with lumps, some of them are swollen badly and the same is on his face. This is not all because he talks without any sense. I think that he saw something but seems that he is worried to talk about.'

'Let's have a hope that he will be ok very soon. Besides, we have very difficult case.'

'You right, firstly, a head in the bath then strings which most probably belong to people.'

'I think that they do belong to people but the most serious problem is that we don't know if the town might be in danger or it was only a killing because of the pictures and the stones.'

'Are you sure that Shivana is death, Inspector?'

'Could you give me another explanation, Oscar? By the way, did you notice if there in the house, in the lounge just opposite a coffee table is missing picture?'

'No, I didn't but to be honest, I didn't look there so perhaps there is missing picture, perhaps not, I think we have to check it.'

'You right, I have had some imagination. Is that what would you like to say?'

'No, not at all,' Oscar answered and changed the subject. 'I still cannot believe that so many people are death in such short time.'

'Wake up,' John said and stood up to pour him more coffee. After he set down, he said to Oscar that the strange strings could not be anything else but destroyed human's body.

'It isn't all Oscar because there in the house is some radiation which occurs from time to time so we might be going to hospital to join Benjamin.'

'Inspector, please do not say that because it sounds very bad, actually, I do not understand, or there is a radiation or not.'

'Bob, the man who works over there said that it is at the time when they tried to take photos.'

'This is a real joke, isn't it?'

'No Oscar it isn't any joke, those people are still there in the house trying to solve the matter. It is difficult to believe but Bob told me that they made a few experiments and the radiation is registered at the time when they tried to take photos.'

'It must have some connection with Benjamin.'

'You told me that he doesn't will speak.'

'That's right, except some crap.'

'Wait a second, are you telling that I'm talking nonsense?'

'Inspector, you don't listen to me at all, why? He talks like someone who is totally mad but it must be connected to the radiation, which you are talking about.'

'Why do you think, actually it must have some connection. I wander why he doesn't speak.'

'You see Inspector; he is telling that they are not death. Perhaps it is some shit because is telling that they have big power and go inside human's body then they talk and he has to obey their orders. By the way, how are you felling, Inspector?'

'What the hell are you talking about? Do I talk crap as well?'

'No no but you have told me that you are not well so I just asked.'

'Better we go back to the matter, Oscar. Oh, I nearly forgotten, I have found a slip from the bank and funny thing is that Lisa's money has been paid in India. I have contact with police over there in Delhi but they did not answer yet. I hope that we will be able to find out much more about that woman. The next thing is her expensive motorcar. It looks as she didn't drive too much, if she did at all.'

'At least we have something. I have sorted all the information, we have and there must be some connection between those two women. The name Shivana sounds like Hindu but I wouldn't say that she is from India.'

'You right, the first part of her name are the same as Hindu god and we really can find her relatives over there but I don't think that she is from India, she doesn't looks as an Indian's with her blue eyes at all.'

'Inspector, Mrs. Brown has told us about a language that she couldn't understand, do you think that she was talking about a conversation between Shivana and ex-policewoman.'

'It looks alike but I'm not too sure, we have to talk to this woman again and very soon. We have to do it as the first thing in the morning because the story with the pictures and the stones are not clear at all.'

'I see one very positive part in this matter.'

'You see a positive side in a killing, Oscar, there must be something not right with your brain as well.'

'Everything is all right Inspector, the positive thing is that there is no need to panic because if killers used a radiation, means that there is no danger for the city except just a few death people and then if there are stolen goods then we are going somewhere.'

"We are going nowhere Oscar, the time I have spent here, it came to mine knowledge that defence force is involve into the case and it could be much better if they will take over the matter so I might go for leave.'

'I think that they are the right people to solve the matter with radiation, Inspector.'

'If I have to be honest, I don't like to give up but if there will be a need then I don't have anything against that, Oscar.'

'The day is nearly over and it is difficult to believe that so many things happened in a short time.'

They have spoken for some time without any enthusiasm. Their voices sounded very hopeless and mostly a silence filled the office. It was already time to leave the office and John proposed to stop to have a drink on the way home and soon to the office came Captain Paul, who heard his last sentence and said.

'Oh yes, this is an excellent idea but before you will be gone I have to tell you that the case, you are busy with is very serious.'

'I thought that all our cases are very serious,' John answered smiling.

'It isn't any joke John,' Captain answered angrily. 'I need from you a full report about the case because I have to give it to different people, defence force as well. They knew about the case before I have spoken with them about the radiation. I do believe that at this time all your strings are in their labour.'

'Sir, we are still in good shape, why you see us as death people.'

'John, you are trying to joke but you don't even know that we are playing with fire. This is very danger crowd of criminals using highly advanced technology. Technology, which worries me and everybody because it is highly possible that we might face an aggression.'

'Sir, perhaps they are not from this earth?' Oscar forwarded a question, which made Captain even angrier.

'Do not talk shit Oscar, all I need is the result and report. If you like, they can be from hell but it does not mean that you will seat here and dream.'

'Sir, nothing we can do with the information which is available at this stage.' John came with help his college. 'We are waiting for a report from India and it will put another light on the matter. On top of that, we know that those people stole pictures from both places and some stones. Mrs. Brown told us about a language that she could not understand which means that the ex-policewoman and

Shivana knew each other before so why are you telling Sir that we have nothing in the case.'

'I am not saying anything except that those people know about us more then we know. How they can stole a picture from the flat if as you said the old lady is watching the house at all times.'

'We don't know but it wasn't real police for sure and we agreed in this matter, Sir.'

'Sir, the next thing is Benjamin, he was taken to hospital and he is in very serious condition.'

'Well, as far as I know, we all might finish together with him but what I have noticed is that he knows something and doesn't like to talk about.'

'We have to wait for him to come back and then we'll see if he can give us any information in the matter.'

'Sir, after we will receive a report from India we will have much more clear situation as well,' said John. He suspended his voice for a while then he added, 'apparently, we know as much as they let us to know only.'

'It seems to me,' said Captain slowly, 'everything very strange and personally if I look at a person driving very expensive motorcar, leaving in luxury house then there always is something wrong behind that matter. For me the person is potential criminal as there are not too many people who can get reach in a right way. Anyway, is getting late so I won't stop you and perhaps shortly I'll join you for a drink as well.'

'Sir, you welcome,' John said while Captain was leaving the office.

Shortly after him, John and Oscar left the office as well so no one of them could hear the telephone, which rang for quite long time. They set by the bar and soon Captain Paul joined them. In general, they did not spoke about the

49

case but it was clear that the matter is on their minds. It was clear that they are tired after difficult day. John was the first who decided to go home.

'I don't feel too well,' he said.

'It's strange but I don't feel too good as well,' said Oscar and added, 'it might sound funny but since we have entered the pub, I've got a felling that somebody is watching me at all times. I have never experienced a thing as such.'

'Oscar, it is an obsession,' laughed Captain Paul.

'No sir, it isn't any obsession and except that I still see the sight of that ex-policewoman. It's funny but I do remember that I have noticed that something isn't right with her.'

'What I do remember is that she was good looking girl. I would say very attractive,' joked Captain, 'do you think that she could be somewhere around here.'

'I don't know why you are looking at me, sir,' said John and added, 'Oscar is hoping to see that girl not me, and by the way, I hope that you'll be in the office in the morning.'

'Why I shouldn't be, Inspector?'

'Well, you might look for another missing woman,' Captain Paul was in good mood.

'Well, I am gone and wish you luck Oscar, you might be lucky to meet the girl with blue and little greenish eyes.' John laughed and then he left the pub.

Captain Paul and Oscar did not stay too long and soon they left as well.

Chapter 6

John came to his house and strolled from side to side. In the kitchen, he stood in front of the fridge then he opened the door. He did not feel hungry so after a while he closed the fridge. He poured himself a glass of whiskey and set down in front of TV, changing channels without any interest. All the time to his mind was coming the case, which he started, investigate in the morning. His sight was on TV set but all what he could see was the situations which he experienced during the day. John finished the whiskey and poured another glass then he set with it until he fell asleep.

It was about a middle of the night when the phone's ring woke him up. He was very tired and with slow move, he picked up the telephone.

'John speaking,' he said that and after he heard Oscar voice, he said, 'don't you have anything better to do in the middle of the night? Oscar, what's wrong with you?'

'Inspector, I'm really sorry to wake you up but I'm calling from Mrs. Brown house, she is death, Inspector.'

'What? Fuck this shit life; I'll be there just now.'

John left his house as quick as he could, practically immediately as he slept on the couch dressed as he came from work. He drove through the town thinking what possibly happened to old woman. He arrived to the place and looked very surprisingly as except Oscar's motorcar there where parked many more vehicles in front of the flat. What surprised him the most was that Captain's Paul car stood there as well? Inside he learned that there were people whom he never seen before. John came to Oscar and asked.

'What's happening here?'

'She is death, Inspector and the doctor said that he never saw something in his life. He isn't young,' Oscar added.

'You don't have any respect . . .' John did not finished as came to them Captain Paul together with another man and said.

'John, this is Captain Robertson,' then he continued his introduction. 'You know already Oscar and now this is Inspector John, who is responsible for the investigation.'

The introduction was not too long and shortly after Captain Paul informed John and Oscar that they will work together with Captain Robertson, which did not made John too happy.

'Are you trying to tell me that I am dismissed, sir?' John asked.

'No John, you have to carry on with the investigation and Captain Robertson will assist you guys,' Paul answered with smile.

'You see Inspector,' Captain Robertson came into the conversation, 'the matter seems to be very serious and there is a serious suspicion that we are facing a group of terrorists or, as some of our officials saying, an aggression against our state. Very well organized group does things that we can't understand.'

'I don't think that it could be as bad, Captain,' John answered.

'Perhaps but it is not a place for this type of conversation, Inspector. What I can say is that the matter is highly confidential. Perhaps you know already that after the first killing everybody was well informed in the case but nobody knows what's going on and how.'

'Captain Robertson,' said John, 'there in the house is some radiation, I hope that you have some information what is it about.'

'Inspector, our people are still busy with the matter but now we do not know too much, I would say we don t know anything. What we know is that the radiation might be the main case of killing.'

'Captain, I hope that you wouldn't mind if I'll ask you how did you knew about death of Mrs. Brown.'

'It is quite interesting because we are receiving some phone calls and we don't know how. The case is well known to us since very beginning.'

'It means that somebody is playing with us at all times and in this case there isn't any suspicion of some aggression as you have told me. No one will attack a country and inform about the matter their citizens. What with a matter like that has an old woman?'

'Inspector, you might be very surprised if I'll tell you that Mrs. Brown has same swollen places as your photographer Benjamin.'

'Do you know about Benjamin as well?'

'I told you Inspector that we know about the matter as long as you know and our job is to ensure safety of our citizens.'

'Excuse me please, may I ask a question, please,' said Oscar, who stood quietly for all the time.

'Go ahead, Inspector,'

'Have you been in the same bar with us last night, Captain?'

'Well, I was not there personally but yes, some of our people where in the same bar.'

'What can you say now? Did I gat an obsession? I strictly knew that somebody is watching us.' Oscar said that very proudly.

'I'm sorry Oscar but I didn't mean anything wrong,' said Captain Paul.

'Very shortly after you guys left the office,' said Captain Robertson, there was a phone call. We tried to trace but it was impossible. They making phone calls but they don't use any mobile phone or land line.'

'It is impossible,' said John.

'Perhaps not but it is a fact,' answered Captain Robertson.

'Captain,' said John, 'you have told us about a radiation but now what about our health. We are exposed for a radiation as well.'

'Apparently here isn't any radiation and this is a second question but don't worry because just in case we are protected with a screen. Our technicians are busy with it here as well.' Captain Robertson answered.

'Captain, as far as I do remember from school a radiation can occur or not but that what I heard from your people it is from time to time only. I can't understand that the radiation is gone and suddenly is coming back again.'

'Well Inspector, I can't give you any answer in this matter as our technicians still working on it. Those people showed us that they could produce and stop the radiation at any time. The most interesting thing is that how they can do it if they are not present in the place where the radiation occurs.'

'The cold war is over and all the things are beyond my understanding,' said John.

'Captain,' said John's boss, 'you are telling that we are not in a danger zone but I see that your people are wearing protective uniforms. Why?'

'Well, they didn't take them off but I can ensure you that we are completely safe and nothing will harm us. Don't think that I will be standing together with you without any protection and endanger myself for some unknown illness.'

'I've got another question Captain,' said John, how could you explain that the radiation is coming from the bath and most likely the strings are emitting it so how could you explain that phenomena.'

'Well, I told you already that I don't know and I can repeat only that our people are busy with the matter. We are equipped with very advanced technology and I hope for some answers very soon.'

As they have spoken, one of the men came to them and said that their job is finish and they have to take the body to the labour and as soon as John heard that, he said.

'Sorry, sorry,' his voice sounded very exciting, 'how could you tell us that the place is safe if he told us only now? The other thing is that I have been wake up to come here just to learn that there is no radiation and the woman is death. Could I see the body at least?'

'Nobody said that you can not see the body. You are busy with the investigation and you do whatever you think is necessary for you,' answered Captain Robertson.

'Thank you Captain,' John answered and went close to the body of Mrs. Brown. He stood in silence and looked very carefully. The old woman was sitting with her head resting on the back of the sofa.

'She doesn't seem to be death at all,' he said and added. 'I can see that she isn't breathing and it is the only sign that she isn't alive.'

'Look more closely, Inspector,' said Captain Robertson and added. 'Here on the head and in many places of her body are some lumps. Swollen places like this can be after a nuclear explosion. Your photographer has similar symptoms.'

'We have been planning to have a chat with her in the morning. I wonder what the hell she did that they had to kill her,' John asked.

'Inspector,' said Oscar, 'she knew too much. Firstly, we know that she was too interested what is going on with her tenants. Then, she told us about the picture and stones, and some language as well. Who knows what she knew more about the all mater.'

'It makes sense. By the way, I feel very tired and if you don't have anything against, I would like to go home to get some rest.'

'Inspector John, as far as I remember, you've been complaining last afternoon as well,' Captain Robertson asked.

'I see that you are watching us very closely, Captain.' John was upset. 'Do you still need my presence here?'

'No, Inspector, not at all. You can go if you do not feel well. Besides, I'll be going as well so we will finish our conversation in the morning.' Captain Robertson answered.

'Then I'm gone, see you in the morning.'

Soon after John left the flat, Captain Robertson went to the other side of the room, where stood, looking into the window one of his agents and said to him.

'Listen Glen, take Jeffrey and follow Inspector John, perhaps it isn't necessary but I will to know a little more about him. By the way, he was very close with this shit radiation and didn't look too good.'

'Ok Captain,' he answered and left the flat. Glen set in the car and said to Jeffrey, who already slept.

'Start up the engine and follow him.'

'Follow who?'

'Follow Inspector John and hurry up before we lose him. Can you see the light?'

'Ok, Ok,' he answered and started the motor. Shortly after they drove behind John in a distance that he could not suspect that anybody is watching him. Both motorcars moved slowly through nearly empty town. Suddenly John turned into direction of the freeway. Jeffrey did the same but quickly John's rear lights where far in front.

'Why he is so in hurry?' Jeffrey asked.

'Fuck knows, don't ask me, and just follow this idiot. I think that our boss smells something about this guy.'

'Glen, I've got full speed.'

'Fuck, he is too fast; I cannot see his lights any more.'

'Shit, he is gone. What a fucking car is he driving?'

Jeffrey slowed down as he spotted right behind them traffic cops.

At the same time, John went very strange experiences. After he left Mrs. Brown house, he drove slowly towards his house and suddenly he saw in front of him a light. Firstly, he thought that it is another motorcar then he realized that it is not any vehicle but just a light. John fell something like a magnetic field. The light was in front of him in the same distance. He did not know why but just follow the light. As the light turned into direction of the freeway, he has followed it. John did not look at the speedometer, which somehow was not working any longer. After he reaches the freeway, his speed became very high.

John saw that the blue light stopped for a while then turned to the left from the freeway. He took the same turn and after about twenty-five miles on his right side, he saw very strong lights on high poles. He could not recognize the place and did not know where is going to. Actually, he did not control his vehicle at all. He went to many places while going fishing but never went on this road. After another five miles the light has turned to the right again and John followed it as well.

'Why I'm going here?' he asked himself but could not find any answer. He started to feel more and more tired. His head become very heavy. On his right hand side, he still saw very high poles with strong lights. Suddenly gravel road went over a small bridge then turned to the right. Shortly before he took the turn, far in front of him, he could see high Rocky Mount.

He still drove behind the light but now on one side, there was open field and on another side, he saw a fence but not as high as there where he saw high posts with the strong lights. John started to look at the landscape with some interest. He thought that behind the fence has to be a farm as he saw a few lights but what surprised him the most was a blue colour of grass. Far on the left side, there was a very high construction, which seemed to be much too high for any farm's building.

John passed a gate with a small light and a board. He could not see what was on it but he thought that there was a picture on it. He saw a straight road and further some small buildings. He still drove along the fence and become sure that the colour of the grass is surely blue. John fell that is driving around a very big farm and once he thought that he might be lost and face difficulties to find the way back but the blue light was still in front of him. He drove quite long distance; he came back to the same bridge, which he has crossed before. He did not know how but soon he found himself on the freeway. Soon after, he arrived to his house.

* . . . . . * . . . . . *

Just after Glen and Jeffrey lost John, traffic cops halt them for high speed and it was not too good experience for them especially when they found themselves standing with their hand rested on the roof of the vehicle. Traffic cops took their firearms but soon the situation has been clear up. The only unclear was John's motorcar.

'Man, you can't tell me that you didn't see any other vehicle except us.'

'Listen, you drove faster then any other vehicle during many years on this road and you where here the only people we spotted and it is on our record.'

'I could not go faster but if I could, I will but you must seen the other vehicle, the light was clear.'

'Don't tell us that we are blind or we slept. We didn't see any other idiots who want to make suicide.'

'I'm sure you must see something.'

'Listen, the first off ramp is in town and the other is quite far from here so how do you think could we miss any vehicle.'

The conversation did not go anywhere and as soon as traffics left them, Glen made a call to Captain Robertson to tell him that they lost inspector John. Captain went furious and his speech mostly contained swearing then any other words.

'I am fucking sure that you lost him still in town. The freeway is straight and does not talk to me shit.'

'Captain, he drove twice speed then we could, perhaps even faster. It was like a plane before taking off.'

'You must be joking. What a fucking reason he might have to run away. I don't know what you did but I'm sending somebody to his house to make sure that everything is in order.'

Jeffrey started the motor and they drove slowly towards the town. Just before the off ramp, there was a fuel station. He stopped the car in front of the shop and Jeffrey went to buy coffee and a snakes. After he came back, they set in silence for some time. After they finished their coffee, Jeffrey lit a cigarette and said.

'Glen, do you think that he stopped here without lights and we went further leaving him behind'

'I don't think so but in this fucking case anything is possible.'

They set a little more than forty minutes speculating about any possibility of loosing John and suddenly Jeffrey spotted in the rear mirror a light coming with very high speed.

'Look there Glen, I think that he is coming back.'

'Shit, start the motor but quickly,' Glen answered and at the same time John's motorcar passed the station. Jeffrey left the station and tried to keep as close as possible to John's vehicle. It was not too difficult because Inspector slow down his speed just after the station.

At the time that Jeffrey started the motor, Glen made a call to Captain Robertson. 'Captain,' his voice was filled with excitement, 'he is back. He is really back.'

'Where did you see him?'

'Captain, you told me that you will send someone to his place and he will be home now, now and this is the reason that I have to call you.'

'Ok, try to follow him to his place and then fuck off.'

Chapter 7

John did not expect to meet Captain Robertson very soon, practically, he even forgotten about him. It was a big surprise for him to see Captain behind his desk.

'Good morning Captain,' he greeted him.

'Good morning Inspector, sorry to take your place but somehow it was most comfortable seat here. By the way, I am here for quite long time and I have to tell you that you have very good coffee. Inspector, I came here because I have to see you very urgently.'

'What is the reason?' John said and added; 'I hope that you don't mind that I will have a mug of coffee as well,' then he poured him nearly black liquid and set down opposite Captain Robertson.

'I'm listening,' he said.

'I need to know where you have been diving through the night.'

'Captain, I don't know.'

'How I have to understand that you don't know, Inspector?'

'Captain, I know most of the places around the town but I have never ever gone on this road.'

'I am worried that you have to tell exactly where have you been, even it is very personal.'

'Captain, once again, I don't know the place. You can believe me or not but I went somewhere and I have no idea where, and I do not know how I came back.'

'Inspector, I hope that you remember where you have been gone.'

'Well, I do remember but not clear. Captain, what is going on here? You are on everybody's back. Why don't you trust anybody? Perhaps you know much better where I've been gone to.'

'Inspector, don't be cross, you know very well that we have to know everything about the case. This is the only reason that I am here but now tell me please, where did you go. The killers know about us everything and we know zero and please, tell to me about your adventure. Even it is very personal, nobody will know anything except two of us.'

'Captain, to be honest, I don't like this conversation at all but anyway, firstly, I started the engine and drove towards my place but then like a dream, in front of me there I saw a blue light. It was like a dream. Firstly, I thought that it is a motorcar in front of me but it was not. There was a blue light and actually I couldn't see anything else but just have had a feeling that I have to follow the light.'

'Don't tell me Inspector that you didn't see anything on the way.'

'Captain, firstly I think that except the light, I didn't see anything only thereafter. I think that I remember since the moment when I started to drive on the freeway.'

'Do you remember the speed, which you've been driving?'

'Not really, actually I didn't look at the clock but to be honest I think that I lost control over my vehicle.'

'Did you see any other vehicle except you?'

'No Captain, I didn't. Except that funny light, I had to follow, I did not see anything else. Only sometime later, after I left the freeway, I saw on my left a very high fence with strong lights on high poles. There was a gate with two big stones on both sides and a board but I do not know what was written on it. A little deeper in the field there was a building and a big but I mean big satellite dish. Except that there where small dishes as well and a plenty ropes. It seemed to be a military base but I'm not too sure because I never saw any base around here.'

'Do you remember what was on the other side of the road?'

'I think that there was a small motel in some distance from the road but I have never seen it before so I'm not too sure about it.'

'Ok Inspector, carry on, please.'

'After some time the fence become smaller and there was no lights. I do remember that I crossed a bridge and shortly after I turned to the left but before far in front I saw high Rocky Mount.'

'It is quite interesting, Inspector.'

'The road become very badly and I didn't know where I'm going to, and what for. I think that there was a farm but I cannot be sure about it. Captain, the most funny thing was that the grass on this side and far behind fence, which was mostly broken there was a green grass.'

'Are you sure about it, Inspector?'

'Captain, whatever happened to me last night; I will never forget the colour of the grass.'

John finished story about his journey and Captain Robertson kept quite for a while then he asked, 'Inspector, tell me please, have you been in this place before?'

'No Captain, I have never ever been over there.'

'Could you tell me please about your drive since you have reached the high fence?'

'Sure,' he answered and started the story again. Now Captain listened more carefully and from time to time asked questions. Some of the question he repeated, which made a little nervous Inspector John. Nevertheless, Captain was giving more and more questions asking for different details and finally he said.

'Inspector John, if I have to be really honest, I'll tell you that you are trying to make me full. Strictly, it is impossible that you've been gone to the place, which you've been telling me about.'

'What do you mean, Captain?'

'The biggest problem is that I know the place and I know that you never went there last night but you must know about this place before.'

'Captain, I told you the true story and this time seems to me that you are trying to full me.'

'According to your story you drove along one of our base and it is. I'm telling you once again strictly impossible because it is a few thousand miles from here.'

'Captain, you are talking shit to me,' John gets very cross. 'If we have to this conversation the way we do up to now then I rather will keep quite.'

'I think that it is not me who talks shit but you, Inspector so it could be really better to tell me where did you go last night.'

'I told you and I have nothing to add to my story. I have no reason to keep a secret where I am going to and you are trying to tell me some nonsense. Where is the point?'

'The point is that you are trying to tell me that you went to the coast and back within not even fifty minutes.'

'Captain, there wasn't more than a quarter of tank if the fuel and that is impossible for me to go to the coast. I must be gone somewhere around the town and I am sure that you are making some big mistake and mixing two different places.'

'No Inspector, by the way, after you come back, we checked your vehicle and it really didn't looked that you made such long distance. For that reason we have to check your vehicle once again and I hope you wouldn't mind to give me your keys, Inspector.'

'Of course I do mind because you are threatening me not better then some criminal but well, you will take the vehicle anyway so here is the keys.' John gave keys for his motorcar to Captain, who left the office to make a few phone calls.

The first call he made to the base GP-2 and as soon as he heard a voice in the receiver he said, 'Robertson speaking, listen, you have to check for me as soon as possible if there around the base you have notice any turbulence. I mean after a midnight. I need a full report and I need it on my desk immediately.'

The next call he made to his office and asked for all the information about Inspector John then he gave the keys from John's vehicle to one of his people and asked to take it for a test and come back to the office. After he set down, he said.

'Inspector John, you have gone to our place but before, I would like to give you some more questions.'

'No problem Captain,' John answered.

'I do not know where have you been but tell me please, id it possible that after you start to drive you lost conscious.'

'I cannot answer this question but what I can tell you are that I have no idea why I did not go straight to my place.'

'You drove with small amount of fuel, so it means that you are very good driver,' Captain laughed.

'At least you like my economical driving,' John answered.

'Oh yes, there are some very clever chaps who can use three times more fuel then they really need but let's go back to the matter. If I am not mistaken, you came here from the coast and it means that you have stay not far from the place about which you are talking. How it is was possible that you never saw it before.'

'I do not know, Captain.'

'Tell me please, do you remember a condition of the road after you passed the motel especially around the bridge.'

'Not exactly but I think that the road was very muddy. Yes, definitely, the road was muddy but I did not notice any dirt on the car in the morning. Well, perhaps I did not look, I do not know.'

'Inspector, I have to take you with me and there you have to see a doctor.'

'Captain, I do not feel to see a doctor.'

'Perhaps you not but you have to and quite urgently, I do believe that you don't like to see a doctor and perhaps everything is true about the story, you are talking about but I have to find out much more about the whole matter which is very unclear.'

'Perhaps I did not go anywhere and dreamed only, how could I know.'

'How could you explain that you did not see the base before?'

'Captain, if you need me to go with you and see a doctor, is all right but I do not understand anything.'

'You did not dream Inspector, our people lost you just after you have reached the freeway and that is what I know for sure.'

'You strictly spy on me, Captain,' John was angry. He stood up and went to pour more coffee. 'I do believe that

I am a free man and I have a right to go wherever I like to go.'

'Yes, you are right but we have had to follow you so now we are having shit. One you have to know that you drove with a speed that normal vehicle can not achieve.'

'What speed?'

'Nobody knows and what I know and I believe is that you are telling me big crap.'

'I told you the true and now I can tell you that you told me crap that I drove a few thousand miles, Captain.'

'Inspector, to make the conversation shorter, I have enough evidences to look you up so, you better thinks before you say a crap. We have to know where have you been and we will. By the way, there is no time to be waste so finish your coffee and let us to go, Inspector.'

* . . . . . * . . . . . *

Oscar met Captain Robertson and John briefly just before they left the building. He entered empty office and set down. He looked around then poured himself coffee and set down again. He looked at John's desk and at a plastic bag on it. 'Why I did not see it before?' He asked himself. Oscar stood up and picked up the bag. Inside he found stones what surprised him a lot, as they have spoken about it but no one of them saw it.

'It has to be brought here by Inspector john and he must forget to send it to the labour.' Oscar continued his meditation and suddenly the telephone rang. It was from switch—board. The police officer on duty has informed Oscar about a death body in Lisa's neighbour house . . . .

Shortly after he finished the conversation, he made a call to switch board to confirm the information, which made the man on the other side of the line a little angry.

'I am sorry to call you back but I need to make sure where the calls are coming from.'

'I thought that you know my voice.'

'Once more, I need to know, what I need to know.'

Oscar drove his car thinking about the case. Since he left the yard of the police station all what come to his mind was Lisa's head in her bath. Mostly the smile on the death woman's face stood in front of him. He tried to answer why Lisa had such fancy smile. He could not understand that she had a smile on the face while her body vanished and it would not be possible that she did not see it. Next to Lisa's house, there was armed police officer and just by the next house stood another one. Oscar slows down.

Before he entered the property, he had to write down his name into registered book. After that, he drove slowly toward the entrance. Suddenly he thought about coming weekend and the promise, he gave his family that they will go sailing. Oscar owns a small sailboat and every time he could, he went sailing together with his family. For short time, he set in the car then he shrugs his arms and walked to the house. Surprisingly, he met there Inspector John and Captain Robertson.

'I thought that you went to see a doctor,' Oscar asked with smile.

'We will Inspector,' answered Captain Robertson before John could open his mouth then he added. 'You see Inspector, soon after we left your place, came up this matter so we are here.'

'Oscar,' said John, 'you have to see who is in the bathroom.'

'Again in the bathroom,' Oscar was surprised and added. 'I am quite sure that it has to be the same killer or killers.'

They entered the bathroom together and Oscar could not believe his eyes. In the bath there was the same man, who's ID was found in Lisa's house.

'I thought that he is death,' he said.

'We thought the same but now is another question,' said Captain Robertson. 'There was somebody there in the bath but now we do not know who that was.'

Oscar stepped forward but he could not come too close to the bath, as there was a screen to prevent them from any radiation, which was detecting in other houses. He looked at badly damaged body. It was obvious that the man died the same way as other victims. His body has been mostly vanished and in the water were strings in stand of legs. The same happened to his corps. The parts of the body, which did not, vanished there were deep hollows. The head was without hair and with many hollows. As before, there was no blood in the water.

'How they can do it?' Oscar asked and after a while, he added. 'It looks that is nothing inside the hollows. Why there is no blood in the water?'

'Inspector, we know as much as you know,' answered Captain Robertson.

'Captain, do you think that these people can take photos?' Oscar asked.

'That I do not know but they have to try and I am sure that they achieved some progress in this matter. Now, I think, we are winning. You should see what they do in their labour, quite exciting.'

'Well, I will be glad to see it, Captain,' he answered.

'One you have to remember, the time is very short and we are facing quite high urgency. This is the reason that they have to work day and night. I do hope that our scientists are very close to solved problem, we are dealing with.'

'Sorry Captain,' a man who worked with big camera came to them. 'There is something, I would like to show you Captain.'

'What is it Clive?' Captain asked, walking closer to the camera. 'I cannot believe it,' he nearly shouted and called John and Oscar. 'Listen guys, come and see it.'

'We started with infrared rays but it did not work so we made some modification and finally we have a picture as you can see, Captain.'

Everybody looked at the monitor and at the victim's body in the bath. They saw some phenomena, which they could not understand. There in the water was body of the victim, which has turned into the strings then as they looked at the monitor; they saw a man without any wounds. Somebody might say that the man is just resting in the water. The only sign that he is death was that he did not breathe.

They have spoken for a while about the matter and many different possibilities but even long explanation about some rays; they could not understand how it might be possible to see two different pictures. Most probably even those who worked over there did not know how they have achieved that unusual situation.

'The most interesting is that the man his funny smile on his face. It looks like he is happy that his muscles are getting vanish,' said Oscar.

'Captain,' John came closer to the monitor, 'this is the same but exactly the same colour as I saw there on the field.'

'Excuse me,' said Clive, 'did you see a light like that before?'

'Yes, I saw it last night. I was driving and I have seen grass which was exactly the same colour,' John answered proudly.

'A grass,' repeated Clive and asked. 'Where did you see grass with a blue colour?'

'I was driving somewhere but actually I don't know the place.'

'I sound strange.'

'He drove around the farm, which is next to our base GP-2,' said Captain Robertson.

'When was that?'

'Last night.'

'Captain, do I look like as idiot?' Clive asked a little upset.

'No, you don't but if I tell you that he did that distance in forty minutes you will say that I am an idiot.'

'You people talk some crap so better leave this place and go to do something better than that.' Clive said that and opened the door for them so there was no other option just to leave the bathroom.

Just before they left Captain asked, 'Clive, do you think that you can get any photos from here?'

'Well, I hope so but we need a special emission. We are getting here some shit, infrared mixed with gamma and fuck knows what else. I can tell you that we have registered some other type of radiation, which is from time to time only but what it could help you to know all the information, I do not know. Practically nothing here is steady. My people are very busy and I hope for good and quick results. It is beyond my imagination, a normal man on the monitor and wrack in the bath. I cannot understand what the man on the screen has hair and in the water is bold. The other story is that there is no blood in the water, not at all.'

'Anyway, it is very fascinating,'

They already left the bathroom and walked slowly through the house. Captain informed Oscar that he has to carry on with the investigation because he and John have to go to Captain's office. Oscar was not too happy about that and asked only.

'Captain, I was told that the body was found by the house cleaner but I did not see anybody here. Where is she gone?'

'She was taken to hospital because of shock,' answered Captain and added. 'Sorry Inspector but we have to go and if there will be a need, you can contact me, here is my card.'

Oscar stood in the front door and looked s Captain and John where leaving the property. He thought about the strings and become sure that they look similar, and then he thought that all what would come to his mind, he should write so they will get as much information as possible.

He thought about very high technology used by criminals and suddenly it came to his mind that perhaps they are not normal people. He knew that there in Captain's labour are working best scientists who are using best equipment in the world and soon it will be possible to get more answers in the matter. For a moment he thought about DNA test as it come to his knowledge that there is some problem with this matter.

Suddenly he reminded about a blue grass that John was talking about in the bathroom. Actually he could not understand what was the story abut and why he spoke about a grass in such colour. 'Perhaps there was some light that turned a natural colour into another one,' he thought.

Oscar turned to go back to the house and suddenly he heard brakes behind him. It was Captain Robertson together with Inspector John.

'We decided to see the house before we'll go to my office,' said Captain after they left the motorcar.

They went back into the house and started to walk from room to room. Oscar opened the first door on the left and entered the main bathroom as he thought. There was a double bed in the middle and it looks like somebody slept into it last night or not long ago. He looked at the clothes, which most probably belong to someone who slept here. Opposite the entrance to the room, there was a small pantry with a few cupboards. Right next to the pantry there was an entrance to the bathroom. The bathroom was much bigger then the one where was the body of the victim. In one corner, there was a big bath and in other was a shower.

Oscar stopped in front of the cupboard with lots of cosmetics. He looked at them for a while then he shrug and asked himself why the man did not took a bath here, only went to another side of the house. He came back to the bathroom and started to search cupboards. They have been build right up to the ceiling and contained plenty of clothes. Except that in one of the cupboards there was a big safe. Oscar looked at it for a while and then he went to the bed. He picked up a par of jeans and searched for keys but doesn't find anything. There was a dressing table. Oscar opened drawer after a drawer. He didn't find any keys but in one of them there was a photo album. He started to look at the photos and couldn't believe his eyes. Most of them have been taken by the sea and on luxury yacht. He looked at them and didn't know if it is true or a dream as there was on most of the photos Lisa together with the victim found in the bathroom.

'At least we have something', he thought looking at the photos.

Oscar was busy paging the album when to the bedroom came Captain with John.

'This is interesting,' he said and gave the album to Captain and added. 'There in the cupboard is a safe as well.'

'Did you try to open it?' Captain asked.

'No ways, not this type of lock.'

'No problem, our people will open without any damage.'

At the time when Captain looked at the photos, John went into the bathroom so he couldn't see that most of them have been taken in the town where he used to live most of his life. Captain knew the place but didn't say anything as there was a need to find out about John's journey.

'I do not understand why the man went to another bathroom if it is obvious that he slept here in this bedroom,' said John after he came back.

'It is possible that here was some fighting but we have to have a hope and wait for doctor's opinion, if they will be able to give any.'

They left the main bedroom and finally entered the kitchen. All agreed that the house must be worth a fortune. The kitchen was very clean. Two fridges were full but there was no sign that anybody used the place for quite long time.

'It looks very clean but well, a house cleaner was here so it is understandable.'

'Yes Oscar, you are correct but there are questions that we still don't know anything,' Captain answered then they left the kitchen and entered big lounge. John put his hand on one of the chairs covered with pure leather. He liked the set up of the house a lot.

'Only this furniture must be a couple thousand,' said John and added. 'Let's see the other part of the house.'

Suddenly he sighted at the wall behind the sofa and spotted a clear mark after a picture, which must be taken not long ago. 'It is very strange,' he said, 'except the pictures nothing else is gone from all the places.'

Suddenly Captain Robertson decided to leave the house and he asked Oscar to continue his work then they have walk of the house but through the garage. There was standing same Mercedes SL cabriolet as in Lisa's house.

'It seems that the vehicle was used not long ago,' said John.

'Our people have to check the car,' replied Captain and added. 'Perhaps you will be lucky to find more interesting matters so I wish you luck and now we have to leave.'

Captain and John left and Oscar was left alone in the garage. He checked roughly then he went to search other parts of the house. A smaller then the main lounge there was a smaller one but with leather furniture as well. He passed the coffee table and went to the next room. There were a few chairs and in the middle a three quarter pool table. A board on the wall showed that some people used the place intensively.

Oscar left the pool room and went upstairs. There was one room which was turned into an office. He stopped next to the desk and switched on the computer. Next to the PC there was Lisa's photo which has proved that the two of them had close relationship. In the drawers he found plenty of disks. In one of the drawers there was another photo album. Oscar turned pages and looked at the photos very carefully especially at one of them which shows similar construction like that one which Inspector John was talking about.

In the office there were many signs from the sea and all the maters connected with sailing took a lot of Oscar's attention.

Chapter 8

'Have a sit Inspector,' said Captain Robertson after he entered his office together with John. 'Would you like a mug of coffee?'

'Oh yes Captain, I think that I like coffee very much,' John answered.

'Inspector, you have to enjoy the coffee and I need to solve some serious matter so before I'll be back, you can check a news paper. I you'll need more coffee, help yourself, please.'

Captain Robertson left the office and entered another one. He picked up a telephone and dialled GP-2 number. He didn't see any report from the base and with very serious voice asked for the reason of the delay.

'There wasn't anything special, Captain so I didn't think that you need it,' answered officer on duty.

'Listen, it is not up to you to decide what is special and what isn't. I need the report and I need it now.'

'Captain, it was night like any other and it was the reason that you didn't receive any report but I will send it right now. By the way, there was some disturbance after a midnight but actually nothing serious. It happens every now and then.'

'We'll come back to discipline and now I need the report, and tell me if you seen any UFO.'

'Captain, too many of them lately so we cannot look at them separately,' answered officer on the other side of the line.

'In other words you cannot even tell me if there was something unusual or not. It is very important, ok send the report because I see that we cannot understand each other at all.'

'Ok Captain.'

The conversation was over and Captain came back to his office. Soon after to the office came very tall man and greeted them from the door. It was George who knew about already about the case of Inspector John but this time he said to Captain about the report.

'Captain, it came now, now,' he gave the report to Captain.

'Inspector John, George will take you to the doctor,' said Captain to him and then to George. 'You have to come back as soon as you can so we'll continue our job.'

After they left the office Captain Robertson tested his cold by now coffee and before he took the report, which brought George, the telephone rang. It was Oscar on the line. He made the call soon after he saw the photo with the funny construction.

'Captain, I am quite sure that this is the same construction, which Inspector John was talking about,' he said.

'Perhaps it is the same construction but not for sure, Inspector,' he answered.

'Captain, the matter is more and more interested because on the photo is the same man who was killed in the bath.'

'Is it?' asked Captain.

'It isn't all because somehow on the same photo he is together with Lisa. I cannot understand what they have to do with the farm.'

'So am I but we have to finish because I have somebody in the office, who came right now,' Robertson finished the conversation and greeted the man who came into the office. 'Have a sit Robert,' he said and the man set down in front of him.

'Robert, I am glad to see you,' Captain continued.

'Doesn't sound too good this invitation, sir,' answered smiling Robert.

'Well, do not be sceptic.'

'Captain, I went through the reports which come from the GP-2 base and it isn't too good. Something wasn't well over there last night.'

'I think so, Robert.'

'George brought me a copy but I never have had time to check it.'

'I was told that you are waiting for it so I came with my copy, Captain.'

'Did you analyze it?'

'Not yet but I can see that there was something wrong with electricity last night.'

'Tell me Robert, do you think that there were more flights during last couple days or not?'

'Definitely Captain, even if I look at this report, I can see that there were some very close flights but many of them don't exist on the records.'

'How could you explain that because if we record them then they have to be on the records?'

'It is quite complicated matter but it is like that. The last record which you have in front of you can prove it.'

'Do you think so?'

'I don't think, I know.'

'Why are you getting cross so quick?'

'Look Captain, you are asking me the same questions every day and I keep a special record.'

'Robert, if I could know what to do with the matter, I wouldn't ask you, I think that it is simple.'

'Well it looks like but is not. The best example is Inspector John, you have told me on the telephone. The matter is getting more complicated by now because how he could in short time drive around the base and the farm nobody can explain at the moment. Could you, Captain?'

'It took him not even fifty minutes if that what is telling is true because personally I don't believe in this shit. It is possible that for some reason he don't like to talk.'

'Captain, it really looks funny but we are busy with UFO and suddenly some cop, who is busy with a case of killing, is involved into our matter. I heard about some radiation but you are looking for some strange connections.'

'I don't know what I am looking for but this crowd of criminals is using very highly advanced technology. Except that there are some problems with DNA test and at the same time the whole country is well informed about the matter. Do not be surprised that I am looking for some connections because we are dealing with terrorists or even worse, invasion.'

'Perhaps it isn't a common killing but I wouldn't look at the case as bad, Captain,' answered Robert and at the same time there was a knock on the door.

The office entered Glen and Jeffrey, and before they greeted them, Captain said, 'good to see you, perhaps now I will know a little more about your fucking work last night.'

'Captain, everything what happened last night you know very well and there is nothing to say,' answered Glen.

'Perhaps but I need to know exactly about the matter.'

'Captain, it was still in town,' said Glen and continued. 'Jeffrey has followed this man and as soon as he reached freeway, start to drive such speed that there is no vehicle which could follow him. It was a speed that he could fly perhaps.'

'Did you see any light in front of him?'

'No Captain but if there was a light very close to his car then we couldn't see it.'

'I didn't ask him how far the light was but he said that there was a light in front of him and it worked as a magnetic field.'

'Well, is possible that he saw something but it must be too close so it was invisible for us. Captain, we drove quite close but when he speed up then it was a moment and he was gone like that,' Jeffrey clicked his fingers.

'How a motorcar can vanish?' Robert asked.

'How I should know? It was empty road and soon after traffic cops would like to arrest us. Likely there was no fight.'

'What fight? What are you talking about?' Captain becomes a little cross.

'How could you feel if someone will tell you that there was no vehicle on the freeway but the man drove in front of us?'

'Inspector John told me that he drove around the farm which is next to the base GP-2.'

'Nonsense but from other hand he might be gone around the world.'

'Captain, he went to another dimension,' said Robert.

'Robert, do you still believe into the story with another dimension?' Glen asked ironically.

'Then, you have to give me another explanation,' Robert answered.

81

'Well, if you will prove it then we can talk about another dimension but now I have no idea how he vanished and boss knows that we are not able to do our job.'

'I have never said that and what is important you shall know, safety of our country,' said Captain.

'Where is the cop?' Jeffrey asked.

'He is gone for a test but what is important, he told something about a light in front of his car then about another story a blue grass on the farm. The same colour was on the monitor where a man has been killed.'

'Captain, if we have to look at the matter seriously then there is some possibility that he saw another colour. Did you ask him about the colour of the grass on our base?'

'No, I did not but I think I have to because it is interesting. At the moment our people are checking his vehicle and the matter with the colour I am giving to you Robert.'

'I don't understand you, Captain. What I have to do with that matter?'

'Put it into your dimension,' laughed Glen.

'Robert,' said Captain, 'I think that you should understand because you are working on the matter so don't be too surprised. To be more precisely, you have to go to the farm and find out all about the grass and perhaps you will be lucky to find why he drove over there.'

'You must be joking, Captain.'

'No, I am not and to tell you more there is a photo of a man who has been killed and he is on it together with another dead person on the farm.'

'If I didn't know you Captain, I would ask you to send somebody else but to be honest it isn't good time for me to go anywhere.'

'You are very familiar with the information and perhaps you will find over there some time to find more about your dimension,' joked Captain.

'I see Captain that you are still joking about this matter but from other side you are sending me to the farm and practically you don't know what for I have to go there.'

'Robert, we are working on the UFO case for quite long time but never looked at the farm and most probably it was a mistake. If by now we know that the victims somehow are connected with the farm, we have to check it. There is another matter, one of victims said something about stones so it might be possible that there are some minerals and you have to check it as well. Mrs. Brown, who was killed in her house said abut stolen stones and a picture with stars but about the mater we will talk later.'

'Quite interested matter, I would say.'

'Well, I hope for quick results, Robert.'

'Captain,' said Glen, 'it seems to me that we have to do police work.'

The conversation has stopped as to the office came young woman and greeted them from the door. It was another intelligent agent, Alice.

'Good morning Alice,' Captain greeted her and other people as well.

'What are you doing here, Alice?' asked Robert.

'I think that I came to tell you good morning,' she answered shortly and came closer to Captain's desk then she said. 'Captain, we've been checking the house and I took the telegram. It came not long ago.' She gave it to Captain. He opened and nearly shouted.

'What? This is too much. This is really too much.' Firstly he put it on the desk then after a while he picked up and started to read. Now everybody learned that John's father has passed away just after midnight. There was a silence in the office and then Captain ordered twenty minutes brake. 'We will meet here in my office after the brake because this matter is giving another light on our case. I am totally confused and I have no explanation.' He stood up and everybody left the office.

The brake was over and again everybody set in Captain Robertson's office. They needed the brake so everybody could straighten a little their thoughts. During the brake, on the way to the canteen, Captain asked to find out everything about the farm. Everything about people who are living there and about the production and on his way back he received already the information, he asked for.

'As you can see the matter become quite complicated but I hope my operation plan is, I think very simple,' Captain opened the meeting and continued. 'If you will have any suggestions, you are welcome to tell about them. After Alice brought the information about Inspector John's father, we need to put our attention into this matter and this is very serious.'

'Excuse me Captain, I might be sorry that someone has passed away but I do not know why it become as much important,' said Alice.

'Well Alice, you do not know yet but the time when you went to his house, he took a ride around our base GP—2. This is making the matter so complicated.'

'I was told that he went somewhere for fifty minutes.'

'It was not even fifty minutes but during that time he went over there and came back.'

'It is fantastic but without jokes, where he went?'

'Alice, this is true and this is the matter that we are sitting here especially after that telegram, which tells about his father dead.'

'Captain,' Robert started but Captain stopped him.

'If you like to forward another theory then I thank you because we have no time for some nonsense. Inspector is on a test and other people are checking all possible information, they can get about him. What counts here is facts only and nothing else. I am not too sure as I have no proving but he is somehow involved into our case. The fact is that his father has passed away at the same time, when he went for his journey. Personally I do not believe in telepathy but in this particular case, I have to consider facts.'

'Well, Captain, now you are very close to my theory,' Robert said that seriously.

'I am not too sure but it seems to me that even Inspector John is not involved onto the matter personally, somebody is very interested with him and we cannot ignore this situation. Firstly, he has to attend the funeral of his father and since now on there is a need that we have to know all about him.'

'Sorry Captain,' said Alice and asked. 'Why are you steering at me?'

'Well, somebody has to take care about him and you are the best for this matter, Alice'

'Me? You must be joking, Captain,' she answered with some anger in her voice.

'Alice, firstly, because this is my order and secondly because he is single and you will go there as his girlfriend or fiancé or what ever you name it,' answered Captain.

'Do you think that he will accept that?'

'Does he have another option? I do not think so and this is the best solution to ensure his family that he is on leave and you are with him. This situation will give you the possibility to stay there as long as there will be a need.'

Alice did not say a word but it was obvious how much she dislike the idea to Inspector John's family. There was a quite in the office for a while but then she said.

'Captain, I do understand that I have to obey your orders but to be honest, it isn't correct to make a comedy from other people tragedy.'

'Alice,' replied Captain, 'you have a job to do and I do not like to hear any more comments. You have to be ready for the trip at any time and there is no need for you to stay here any longer so you are dismissed and wait for my telephone call, thank you. By the way, one you have to remember, we have to consider an invasion as well. There will be more to talk about but after John will be back from his tests and I will know more about his case.'

'Captain, how long do you expect me on the mission with this cop?'

'This is difficult question and I told you already that it will be as long as the situation will need it, and now go.'

'Ok, bye.'

'Alice, remember that Inspector is still young and good looking, said Robert while she was already by the door.

'Hey listen, I am here to do my job and if you feel that to go with him might make you happy, just talk to Captain because I will stay here with a great pleasure.' Alice left the office nearly slamming the door.

'Now you Robert,' Captain said to him after Alice left the office. 'As I have told you earlier, there is a need for you to go to the farm. It is not far from the place where John's family stays. We know that most of UFO flights are around our base GP–2 but now there is something more.'

'Sorry Captain, ma I ask a question, please?'

'Go ahead, Robert.'

'I have a feeling that we have to do cop's work.'

'I do not understand what is wrong with you people. Please, no more stupid questions because we are working on UFO and suddenly very serious incidents took place. Once again, most of UFO flights are around the base but it is possible that we are not looking into the matter as we suppose. The country is very big but UFO is over the base mostly. It might be possible that somebody is looking not at the base but at the farm. You might be right that John saw blue grass because of the speed but we don't know anything for sure. He told me that he saw a blue light in front of his vehicle and this is interested as well.'

'Sorry Captain, I am quite busy at the moment and how do you think, I have to carry on with my work if you are sending me on the farm?'

'Robert, I said that already and once again, we might face terrorist's attack or an invasion as well and please, stop giving me stupid questions.'

'Ok but somebody has to do the job.'

'Do not worry, we will find some solution. In very short time you will have more possibilities to look into many matters over there in the base so be ready for your plane.'

'What about us, Captain?' Glen asked.

'At the moment Jeffrey is going to work on Lisa's case and you will look into the matter of her house cleaner, Shivana. Any information, you will need, you have to contact Inspector Oscar, who is busy with all the cases. By the way, I am going to work together with him or let me put that more clear he will work under my supervision. There will be a need to deploy some more people but I have to think about the matter later. What I know for sure, there is a need for some clever system so we can have quick progress. It is very important to solve the problem as quick as possible. Through me and Oscar you will any important information. Before you go, once again; that job is very dangerous and you have to learn about the case as much as you can in very short time. Just now I will make a call to Oscar and arrange a meeting for you and do not say that you working for police because it isn't like that. I do not think that Oscar's boss, Captain Paul will like the situation but I have no other option as to interfere into his work but now you can go and prepare yourself for the trip.'

At the time when John came back from his test, Oscar was in Captain's office as well. It was very important for Captain Robertson to organize a meeting with him as quick as possible.

'I am a little surprise that you are here Oscar,' said John.

'You shouldn't Inspector because since you went for test, many things took place and the matter become quite complicated,' said Captain.

'Not for me because at this moment I do not know if I really drove or I have a dream only, Captain,' said John.

'Inspector John, firstly I would like to show you a photo but before that take a sit,' said Captain and pushed a photo towards John.

'This is the building which I saw last night,' said John.

'Well, it is not all what I have to show you. Something else,' Captain didn't know how to tell him about his father. The situation was complicated especially that he will send Alice to attend the funeral. Captain sight at the window for a whole then slowly moved his sight to John. He picked up the telegram and gave it to John. 'It came not long ago,' he said.

John looked at the telegram in silence for quite long time, going through the text over and over then he put it on the desk. 'You spy on me, Captain,' he said.

'I just do my work and I do as good as possible.'

There was a short conversation between them and after John learned about Captain's plan to send Alice together with him to attend the funeral, he became nearly furious. He stood up and walked through the office a few times then he set down again and said.

'I am very sorry for my father and I can understand that he has passed away but I do not and I do not want to understand how you can send someone to spy on me, and make a comedy in my home. Do you know what are you doing, Captain?'

'You are mistaken Inspector,' answered Captain and continued. 'You are going to the funeral and see your family. Now you have to understand that I have to not answer to my bosses but make sure that my country is not in danger. There is way that anything will stop me to do so, not even your father's death. You know the place on the photo and most probably you didn't see it before last night but I am not too sure about it, Inspector. At the moment I know that your life might be in danger.'

'This is really amazing; a woman will look after my safety.'

'I do believe that she will,' Captain said smiling.

'I think that it could be too difficult to change your decision but I hope that you have already arrangement with my boss about my leave.'

'No Inspector, he does not know about this matter and you have to deal with it yourself. All I can say is that before you'll we will have meeting so everything will be organized and you will avoid problems.'

'Problems, I think Captain that you don't know what you are talking about.'

Chapter 9

It wasn't good time for John and Alice. Since the plane took off they didn't talk at all. She understood him very well and didn't try even a conversation. Luckily for them the flight didn't take too long. Soon they drove from airport towards his parents' house. They kept quite for some time and Alice was the first who broke silence.

'Look John, I have learned about the trip yesterday morning and do not think even that I like to be here together with you. I do understand your situation very well and I am very sorry.'

'Thanks' a lot,' John answered shortly.

'You have to know that it is an order and we have to work out that my presence here will be not too difficult for both of us.'

'I do not go to attend a picnic. My father has passed away and I do not feel to go there together with you, and talk to them shit. Why can't you stay in a hotel?'

'Sorry but it is impossible and you know that, and as I said I do not like to pretend to be your girlfriend at all but I have to make sure that you will be safe at all times. Except that I have to find out as much as possible about the case, we are working on.'

'Oh yes, and that you will do right in my home. It is very interesting and do not say that you are not going to spy on me.'

'I am not going to spy on you but you have to understand that the journey of yours over the other night isn't a common.'

'Why cannot you say that it was a vision? Perhaps you shall put me straight into a mental hospital. What actually my father has to do with the matter?'

'Until now nobody know how work telepathy but it might be possible that your father will put your attention on some very important matters. You already know that we are working on a case with UFO and you drove around the base where most of our job is done. Something very important might be behind your journey.'

'You can say straight that I am a suspect.'

'You are not a suspect and it is pointless to carry on with this conversation the way you do so it seems to me that we have to cooperate rather.'

'Look lieutenant, I am going to attend the funeral not to play a comedy.'

'If I am not mistaken you know my name and we have discussed the matter in the office, and if you like then make a call to Captain Robertson so he might call me back from this mission but if there will be more problems then you might not go to be on the funeral but be escorted back, and believe me that I am ready to do it.'

'Please, do not think that I am fool. I was told that my leave will be as long as you will decide, so what is my situation.'

There was a fuel station on the way and Alice asked John to stop so they can have a snack and something to drink. She didn't feel hungry but their situation wasn't pleasant at all so she will change the atmosphere a little. John stopped the car and switched off the motor.

'I hope that you will enjoy your snack,' said John.

'I thought that we will go together.'

'Thank you but I rather stay here, lieutenant.'

Alice shrugged her arms and left the car. It was about midday and the sun shined nicely. John took deep breath of the fresh air, the air which contained smell of the ocean. He likes the place a lot as he grew up here. On another side of town there was his home where he grew up. He remembered the time, he spent with his father but he was for short time alone because Alice came much quicker as he thought. She was very stunning lady and well presenting dressed in a grey leather skirt and white top with short sleeves. Alice set down in the car and said.

'John, I brought a beer for you and pizza will be soon, soon.'

'Thanks' but I have never told you that I like to have a beer or pizza.'

'Well, I know that you like a beer but if not then I can change it and if you do not like pizza then I will eat myself, no problem.'

'I see that you know about me everything.'

'Not everything but a lot, John one you have to understand, I have a job to do so there is no need for you to be cross. The truth is that if not me then it will be somebody else but for sure you cannot be here alone.'

'I know, I know,' John answered and they kept quite for a while then Alice said.

'I think that you are interested with this mysterious trip of yours as well. Don't you?'

'Right now I am not too sure about anything. Did I go or I did not but had a dream only, difficult to understand. What I know for sure, my father is gone and I am suspended. Perhaps it will be up to you if I will still be a policeman or not.'

'Don't you think that you have to work with me?'

'I thought that you know that I am on my way to attend funeral.'

'You see John, I have never been in a situation like that one and I hope that you will not make it more difficult as it is already, and this is more then work together.'

From the restaurant came the waiter with a big pizza and after he gave them it he asked if there is anything else they need. John ordered one more beer.

'Anything for you, madam,' asked the waiter.

'Thank you, I am fine.'

The waiter left them and John said, 'you are going with me but how I have to tell my family that you are my girlfriend or worse even fiancé if the know that I am single.'

'Well, you have to tell them that you have decided to have one as to be alone was to boring, simple but remember that I don't like to be any one of them.'

'It's cool because you are not my type.'

'That's ok and I like it that at least one matter is solved.'

They stopped the conversation as the waiter walks back with beer and after he left, Alice asked. 'John, you might be cross but the pizza is really good, would you like have a piece?'

'Thank you,' he answered and took the plate. He remember the place and very tasty pizza, he used to eat long ago. After he finished, he said. 'I don't remember when for the last time I was here but I have to say that they have very good pizza, thank you.' Thereafter John lit a cigarette and set more comfortable in his chair.

'I see that it was very good idea to stop here,' said Alice and set quietly while John looked around. The place has changed a lot since the last time he was here. They set for some time then John started the motor and has pulled away. After they passed the town he stopped in front of his home. The gate started to open before he ring the bell.

'Why nobody is looking who is by the gate?'

'Who could be, they expect me at any time,' John answered smiling and added. 'There is my mom. Now is time to start a comedy.'

Alice didn't answer as she was in very uncomfortable situation, perhaps the worse in her life. She watched as John left the car and gave hug his mother.

'Mom, as I have told you on the phone this is the surprise, let me to introduce you my sweet Alice. She wouldn't me to go alone in such difficult time. Alice, this is my mom.'

Mrs. Carol was in her early sixties. Her brown hair were a little grey on both sides but her slim figure made that she looks much younger then she really was. She came close to Alice and hugged her then she said to her. 'Alice, oh my dear, I am so glad that john isn't alone any longer. I new that he will meet someone, oh my dear, I am so happy to see you but come inside, please.'

'I am sorry Mrs. Carol, I am really very sorry what happened to you and I wish that our meeting could take place in another time.'

'My dear, you have to know that my husband was very ill and it was time for him to leave us. Come, come inside, you look beautiful my dear. Would like to have a bath?'

'Oh no, Mrs. Carol, the flight wasn't too long and I am fine, I thank you very much.'

Alice answered as they entered the house.

'Paul should be here any time. Paul is John's younger brother,' said Mrs. Carol and she asked. 'I hope my dear that you are not working with John for police. This is very danger, my dear.'

'No Mrs. Carol, I am an architect,' answered Alice.

'That's good my dear, I cannot understand why John works for police, my dear.'

'Mom, I am on leave and how many times I have told you that my job is as any other and it is very important for other people so please, leave my work on side.'

'John, don't you understand that I am worried about you my dear.'

'Mom, leave my job and I hope that you would not mind if I will make a coffee.'

'Do not be funny John, it is still your home my dear and I keep best blends of coffee just in case, you will be here. I think that Paul is by the gate.'

'I know that this town is safe but you just press the button before even look through the window or listen to someone on intercom.'

'John my dear, I know that Paul is by the gate and I heard when his car stopped next to the gate.' Mrs. Carol left the house and now they heard a car stopped in front of the door. John and Alice went outside as well.

'Hallo John,' Paul greeted him from his motorcar. Soon he came closer and said. 'I think that something is not right with my sight or you are not alone,' he laughed. After the introduction he said to John. 'I see that soon one more policeman will be in our family.'

'I am sorry Paul but she is an architect and by the way, she is not a member of our family,' John answered.

'Difficult to believe but it isn't my business.'

'Hi, I am Betty and here are our kids, Allen and Rose,' Paul's wife introduced herself to Alice. Mrs. Carol hugged her two grand children happily. 'I am so glad to see you,' she looked very excited.

Alice made quick friendship with Betty and soon they became very busy with their conversation. They looked like two women who met again after very long time. John, who rather seldom visited his family, now was busy with Paul.

'Long time didn't see you, you must be very busy and spending your free time somewhere else.'

'Well, I didn't take a leave for few years by now and if not the story with our dad, I wouldn't be off from work at all. You see Paul it isn't easy to be off in my profession. Even at this time of a year we are quite busy.'

'John lets go outside,' said Paul and they left the house and set down on the veranda.

'Where did you find such nice girl, John?' asked Paul.

'Why are you asking that, I have never asked where you looked for Betty,' asked John and took a sip of beer which Paul brought with.

'Well, I told you but tell me something, do you think that we can go fishing sometime together?'

'Wait, what do you mean together, me or Alice?'

'Don't be silly, of course with you,' Paul answered then added. 'I did not know that you might be joules.'

'am not but you are talking about her in way that I thought that you like to go fishing with her, by the way, I do not know for how long I will stay here. It might be a week but I am not too sure because they can call me back at any time. Paul, you are talking about fishing but I feel shit that I have never come to see our dad. If I could know that things will go this way, I will make sure to be here long ago.'

'John, you cannot change anything.'

'You right I suppose,' John answered and lit a cigarette.

'If you will smoke as you do, you cannot even dream about good health. How much are you smoking a day?'

'Do you know that in China people smoke since they very young and they live very long?' John defended himself.

'Our father smoked as well and you see what happened.'

'Perhaps you are right but he was already seventy six.'

'He went sailing a lot but you are living in a big city. Actually, do you still have oxygen over there?'

'No, we have to buy it at the time when we do our grocery. Tell me Paul, when dad went sailing last time?'

'It was a few months ago and at that time he was still in good condition but John, there is something that he was talking very often.'

'What is it?'

'He had a wish that you will look after his yacht.'

'Paul, I have no time and he knew about it as well. Except that I don't stay here.'

'You cannot say that because he had spoken about that for many times and you cannot change his will which means that you cannot say no.'

'I do not stay here, Paul.'

'Perhaps he thought that if you will get married one day then you might to come back here and now . . .' Paul suspended his vice for a while and John asked him.

'What do you mean, now?'

'I strictly mean that by now you are together with Alice.'

'Paul, once again, I do not stay here and I have my job. Another thing is that I have no plans to marry Alice. Except that there is something which is much better, I think. If you will look after the yacht together with your kids, they will be very happy, I think.'

'No, no uncle, we have our yacht,' said Allen who came to them and heard their conversation then he asked quickly. 'Uncle John, when are you going to make wedding?'

'What wedding?' John asked.

'Uncles wedding of course with Aunty Alice.' I like her very much and if I was you, I will make the wedding tomorrow.'

'Allen, your grand father died and it isn't good time to think about matters as such.'

John did not like that conversation especially because he knew that children are much better psychologist then adults but likely Mrs. Carol came to them and said.

'Come inside, please, I prepared lunch and you have eat.'

'Mom, I am sorry but we have to go. We came to say hallo to John,' answered Paul.

'But you cannot come for a minute and go.'

'We will come back still today or tomorrow after work but now I am really sorry mom. By the way you might be sure that we will come to say hallo to my new sister-in low.' Paul laughed.

'Did you have many of them in the past?' Alice laughed as she came outside as well and heard last words of Paul.

'You see, the problem is that I never had one so now I am very surprised. Do you know, even Allen said that John has to make your wedding tomorrow.'

'Paul, why cannot you find another subject to talk about? Our father is dead.'

'I know but the life has to go on and it isn't any reason to stop you to get married. At least Alice can help you to look after the yacht.'

'John, you have never said that you have a yacht,' said Alice surprisingly.

'Because I haven't got any yacht,' John answered.

'John has no yacht, he has to look after our father's one as it was his wish.' Paul explained.

'I wish to help but I have never ever have contact with sailing in my life,' said Alice.

'Don't worry Aunty Alice, I will teach you everything,' Allen came quickly into the subject. 'Actually it isn't too difficult.'

'What are you talking people about? I have my job and Alice has her, and we are not married yet, and it's possible that she will never like to marry me.'

'John,' said Alice coming to him closer, 'I won't be against if from time to time you will go sailing and perhaps some time I might join you as well.'

'Aunty,' Allen likes to put her attention on him, 'I have never see uncle sailing but I went many times with dad and grandpa.'

'I think that for us is time,' said Paul and added. 'Actually we should be gone already because we have to take Camellia to the airport.'

'Who is Camellia?' John asked.

'She is a student from France and she worked here during her holiday.'

'She is very sweet,' said Betty.

'Oh yes you right because she is very sweet, perhaps too sweet because on the very first day after she came here, she fell in love with our neighbour's son.'

'Paul,' said Betty, 'I don't see anything wrong with that, they went to town today and shortly before we came here she brought big bunch of flowers. Isn't it sweet?'

'I have to say that I love her very much and I hope that she will be back next year,' said Mrs. Carol.

* . . . . . * . . . . . *

'John,' Mrs. Carol said after Paul and his family left, 'I don't know where you will be sleeping. Your room is ready as usually but there is a single bed only and I think that it might be too small.'

'Mom,' John sighted at her and said, 'we are not sleeping together. Alice can sleep in my room and I will go to dad's office.'

There was consternation for a while and Alice said, 'I don't see anything wrong if we will sleep together in your bedroom and I hope that your mom wouldn't mind as well.'

'Not at all my dear,' she answered and added. 'I will go and make sure that there is clean enough.'

'I do not like talk about that any more and I go to make coffee,' he said.

'Please, do not make for me,' said his mom and left them.

John set up the coffee machine and came back to the lounge. He switched on TV and said to Alice that she might be interested to watch it and he will be in his dad's office. Alice answered that it will be much better if they can be together so after he poured coffee, they went to the office. John didn't like that she will be with him and as soon as they were alone, he said.

'Don't think that I am stupid but at least let be myself in my own home.'

'John, just be a little friendly and do not look at me like an enemy. It is not that I need to be here with you but it is very difficult for me to be with your mom. I really try my best but, oh by the way, I don't mind to sleep in one bedroom . . . .'

'But I do mind,' John answered unfriendly.

'John, to sleep in one bedroom does not mean that we have to sleep in one bed.'

'I think that at night I can stay without supervision.'

Alice ignored what he said and changed subject, 'I can see John that your father liked the sea very much. The office looks like a ship. All the photos on the walls are very beautiful.'

'I think that you know very well that my father was an artist photographer and a sailor.'

'I am thinking if it could be possible that your father had anything to do with that trip of yours. What do you think?'

'I don't think anything and if you will know some more about my father, you have to check his log-books. They all here and except that there are all the maps, it might keep you busy for some time. It will give you his picture because he went sailing a lot and if you are alone on the sea then you need to do something so he wrote a lot. All his races are very well recorded.'

Alice looked at the photos on the walls then she took one of the log-books and somehow the book has opened on the place where a photo, which shows a spaceship, was. She took it out and asked.

'John, did you see this photo?'

John looked at here like at some magician and asked, 'where you get it from?'

'You are smoking too much and I will stink like an ashtray. The photo was here in the book.'

'I think that you put it in.'

'Don't talk nonsense. Do you think that it is a true UFO?'

'If on the photo is UFO then he took the photo of UFO and I can't see any reason to make some shit I mean photomontage.'

'I never said that it might be photomontage. Would you like more coffee?'

'If you don't mind, yes please,' John answered.

Alice left the office and in the kitchen she met Mrs. Carol. 'Alice, my dear just tell me if you need anything.'

'I came to get more coffee for John. I try to assist him as much as possible as I believe that h shouldn't be alone in difficult time as that.'

'My dear, thank you very much and it is very kind of you. I am very glad that you are with him and support him,' answered Mrs. Carol.

'I think that your husband liked sailing a lot because everywhere I see pictures from the sea.'

'Oh yes my dear, he was gone sailing before I met him.'

'Did you go sailing together with your husband, Mrs. Carol?'

'Only occasionally my dear because I don't feel too well on the sea,' she answered.

'Tell me please, did your husband suffered a lot before he died.'

'Not really but who knows. He spent last days in the hospital but until the last moment he was very conscious and it surprised me a lot, my dear.'

Mrs. Carol suspended her voice for a while then she added, 'yes my dear, he was surprisingly conscious. He knew that is leaving this world but somehow he made us take it very peacefully. I do not know how to explain that but somehow I did not feel that I am losing him for ever. I fell that he will be back just after a while.'

'I am very sorry Mrs. Carol.'

'My dear, by now after I know that John isn't alone I don't feel so lonely and I have to tell you once again that you are with him, my dear.'

'I think that he is waiting for his coffee so excuse me please.'

'Of course my dear, I won't keep you any longer.'

John looked at the door after he heard that she is back. 'Did you go to Brazil to get the coffee?' He asked.

'Well, I hope that you will like it but tell me, what do you thin about the photo?'

'I have nothing to think about and I have to remind you that I came here to attend the funeral of my father.'

'But I have to remind you that I have a job to do and you should help me as much as you can.'

'What the hell it has to do with me or my father?'

'Perhaps a lot because I have to tell you if you don t know yet that we are busy with UFO.'

'Look, I feel that you are here to spy on me and I am interested how the photo went into my father's log-book. Except everything how do you see my help?'

'John, you are very good detective and the only difference between us is that we are working, I would say for two different departments. Except that the job is practically the same so be so kind and answer my question.'

'I gave you my answer already.'

'Once again tell me if you see any connection between that trip of yours and dead of your father.'

'I don't know.'

'John, do you believe in telepathy?'

'What about you?' John answered with question.

'I do not know,' she answered.

'Why are you asking such question if you told me that you are a cop as me?'

'Well, I have to collect as many information as possible.'

'If you start from telepathy then I wish you luck but one think I have to tell you, do not question my mother.'

'What do you mean?

'Exactly what I said, do not question her, please?'

'I don't, we have a little chat and for your information, I feel shit to be here. Anyway, what do you think about the photo?'

'What can I think about it; just a space ship falling into the sea, he answered.

'Why are you telling that the space ship is falling into the sea not out from the sea?'

'You must be joking. Just imagine how much luck must have somebody to be on the deck to wait for UFO coming from the sea. As far as I think they don't fly as underground trains according to the plan, if they fly anyway.'

'Perhaps you are right but we cannot be sure because your father might be busy with other photos at the same time.'

'Well, the photo must be taken in the middle of the sea and what do you think he might be busy with. Who might be interested to take a photo of a calm sea?'

'Perhaps you are really right but we cannot be sure.'

'What do you mean, we? Talk rather about you and please exclude me from this case.'

'John,' she wouldn't like to give up, 'I have very strong feeling that your father knew something about UFO and somehow liked to put your attention in some matters. It is my explanation of the trip you went for on the other night.'

'Perhaps but it's getting boring. I think it might be much better if you go to watch TV. It will be nice to be alone for a while.'

'Perhaps you are right at least I can have a nice conversation with your mother.'

'I think that I told you to leave my mother alone,' John said with anger.

'Perhaps a drink will be good for you. I think that I can get one as well,' Alice said ignoring him.

'Ok but this time I will go so what would you like?'

'Scotch with soda will be nice,' she answered and he left the office. In the lounge he found his mom. 'I came to make drinks for us; I hope that you wouldn't mind.'

'You are asking me about everything every now and then and I don't like it too much as it is still your home my dear. Do you know what? I am very happy that you are no longer alone. Alice has very good heart and I can see that she loves you very much. I hope that you two will be very happy together.'

'Mom, please do not say too much.'

'I can see and do not tell me anything because I have my eyes and my heart as well. I know what I am talking about.'

'Please mom, it isn't good time.'

'Better in that very bad time then never my dear, we worried with dad that you will stay single for the rest of your life my dear.'

'Mom, I don't stay here and how do you know with who I stay over there? Perhaps I was never alone.'

'John, you didn't go out with anybody before, did you? You never brought anybody home and now I know that if you wouldn't be together with Alice, you will never bring her here with you. Would you?'

'Mom, I would like to make drinks, could I?'

'Then make it and go because she is waiting for you, my dear.' Mrs. Carol said smiling.

John stood for a while with widely open eyes then after he made two drinks and went back to father's office. He put the drinks on the desk and set down. Alice fell that something isn't right and she asked him.

'What's wrong?'

'What's wrong?' he repeated her question and continued. 'It isn't right my mother really believes that we are together. This is wrong if you will to know.'

'I know that,' she answered.

'What have you told her?'

'Actually nothing but I am very sorry for the whole situation. Not my but Captain Robertson is guilty in this mess.'

'I will help you and here is your drink.'

'I am glad to hear it, John and I am happy that you changed your mind.'

'It has nothing to do with my mind. You'll get your information we will leave as soon as possible. That is on my mind.'

'At least something,' said Alice smiling.

'Do not smile but tell me what I have to do.'

'John, the whole matter is very strange, the photo it took from the log-book and now I realized that I should check where possibly it was taken. I mean during which race.'

'Well, the photo might be in the log-book incidentally but if not then perhaps we can try to find out where it was when you opened the log-book.'

John took the log-book and tried to open in the manner that it will be open in the same place where the photo was. Every time the book opened in another place. Finally he asked Alice if the photo was somewhere in the middle and after she told him that it was more or less in the middle, he checked where the race took place.

'John, did you go sailing with your father a lot?'

'Well, it was long ago but I can see where he went and where the photo could be taken if it was taken during that race which is here in this log-book. It is possible that the photo was here just incidentally.'

'Do you think it might be possible for you to recognize the place from the photo?'

'Don't be funny. The sea is the same all over the world. From a photo you cannot say which sea or which ocean is on it. This is impossible but if I look at the log-book, I think that I know where he went.'

'Do you,' Alice asked with interest.

'I told you that the photo might be here incidentally but if not then it was taken during one of the two races but I think that there isn't too many options.'

John took a map from the shelf and put it on the desk. 'This is the map which might show the race,' he said and added. 'Your boss told me that the base, which most probably I was driving around, is close to my town so it must be somewhere here.'

'Sounds interesting,' she answered.

'I think that we should talk to my brother.'

'It is not applicable. We are not pathfinders and this is serious matter. Our government is spending lots of money on it and we cannot ignore it, and the case is highly confidential.'

'Look, he is a sailor and knows a lot about father's races.'

'No, don't even think about that.'

'Ok, whatever you say, you are the boss.'

'It isn't about who is the boss. John, I see here are many of undeveloped films and I think that we have to send them to be processed as soon as possible.'

'Are you hoping to find more UFO?'

'I don't know but we have to do it quickly because anything is possible. John, if your father took a photo of UFO why do you think he did not published it?'

'How I can know it? I have no idea.'

'I wonder why the photo wasn't published. You see, we are working on the case with UFO for quite long time and everything is important. Anything what can have even small connection with the matter.'

'Do not tell that I am connected with UFO as well.'

'Why not, firstly the trip of yours isn't clear and now the photo. Well, there is another thing, which is that your father has passed away at the time when you went for drive.'

John shrugged his arms and took a sip from his glass. He didn't know what actually think about the whole matter.

'I did ask you about telepathy because if there is one then it is possible that your father tried to tell you something or as I have told you already to put your attention on some very important as he thought matters.' It isn't any joke and we cannot ignore it.'

'Listen, there are dead people and don't tell me that it has any connection with UFO.'

'Perhaps not but we don't know it because the killing seems to be highly professional and must be supported with plenty money.'

'Perhaps you are right but one what is on my mind is to attend the funeral and go away from here.'

'There is something I would like to ask you but don't be cross.'

'What is it?'

'If your father knew something about UFO and I think he knew then there is strong possibility that he didn't died naturally.'

'Oh no now you went far too far, and don't try to dig into this matter.'

'Well, we have to go to the hospital right in the morning and I need to see him. There is nothing wrong to go there, I think. It is obvious that people go to see their relatives before a funeral is taking place. There only thing is that I have to be with you, John.'

'This is another prove that we are not working together which means that we are not partners but it doesn't matter, we can go there and it might be better then sit here and play the comedy.'

Their conversation didn't went too well and after some time Alice decided to go to the bedroom so she asked once again if John will join her but he didn't liked the idea to sleep in one room so she left him alone. As soon as she entered the room, she made a call to Captain Robertson and he sounded rather friendly to hear from her.

'I am glad to hear you, Alice.'

'I am ok except some problems with John but I hope everything will be alright. There is something very important, I have to tell you.'

'What is it?'

109

'Captain, in John's father log-book I found a photo of UFO going into the sea.'

'Well, I can understand that you found a photo but how do you know that it goes into the sea not out, Alice.'

'Perhaps is going into another direction but it does not matter. A photo in the log-book and except that there are undeveloped films. It could be useful to see what is on them.'

'You quite right but wait until somebody will contact you, it might be even tomorrow and at the moment you have to base on the material which is available,' said Captain Robertson.

'In the morning I would like to go to the hospital where still John's father is,' she said.

'Ok Alice, wish you luck,' Captain finished d the conversation and at the same time John knocked on the door. He entered the room and said to her ironically, 'sorry partner to disturb your privacy but there was no need to finish the call.'

'John, I have to report to Captain Robertson how the situation is and again, if you think that he will call me back then ask him. Why not? There are undeveloped films and you know very well that we need to see what is on them. My boss he the right to know is everything is ok.'

'How anything could be ok if my father is dead.'

'Do not turn my words, please and remember that nobody can change the past.'

John didn't say a word. He shrugged his arms and left the room. Alice didn't feel too well and however she tried to look at the matter, she couldn't see another option except to wait for the morning with a hope for better day.

Chapter 10

Robert was a very highly marked intelligence agent, who for quite long time worked in the office. The news that he has to go to the farm, did not make him happy at all especially that after his life has been a little stabilized, without any extra hours, he really felt ashamed to say to his wife that he has to leave the family for couple days. Practically he didn't know even for how long he has to go over there.

The farm where he was going to was in the neighbourhood of the GP—2 base and only now he learned a little about it. On the farm there were leaving people who were mostly homeless and in many cases maladjusted, without any possibilities to live on their own.

Firstly Robert flew to the base and spent their first few hours on checking how the information is collected before it is send to the head office. It was very interested even he was here for many times before. UFO flights have been registered but incidentally no one could be photographed or as it was planned taken down. Now with all the unknown crime it became very serious matter. Thereafter he was taken with a helicopter over the farm and studied a little about it. Robert looked at the farm with some irony as he could not understand what could happen in such place. Mean time he had to go through most shocking time in his life.

Robert did took too seriously when to the base came an artist to characterize him so everybody could say that he for sure is homeless or let's say it straight a hobo. After he was prepared and ready to go on his special trip, he was taken to the south part of town, where was the head office of the farm. From there he walked to the gate and rang the bell. After a while a small window has open on side of the gate and a young girl asked.

'Are you Pete?' she asked. He was announced before in the morning.

'Yes, I am Pete,' Robert answered and a moment later the gate opened and the girl said to him. 'Come in junkie,' she invited him sarcastically.

Robert entered the yard with some unpleasant feeling as the girl wasn't too kind with him and except that there was something that he fell that he should not to be here.

He looked at the girl and thought, 'well, it isn't her fault, it was me who has chosen this job. This is my fault only.'

He understood that the situation need from him to be dressed with very old, dirty and torn clothes. At this moment he really presented himself how's life did not treat him too well or can say one, who become lost somewhere into the labyrinth of the his journey. Now he walked behind the girl to the other side of the house and as soon as they entered the back yard the girl said to him.

'You have to wait here,' then she pointed old and hardly used chair. 'If you will need a toilet, you must walk over there around the corner,' she added.

'Thank you,' Robert answered and asked. 'Where will I sleep?'

'I told you that you have to wait here and after Theresa will come back from town, she will attend you. I must go,' she said and left him.

Robert for the very first time in his life was in a mission station. He looked around and couldn't believe his eyes. He knew that there are people in the world who are living in very bad conditions but that what he saw right now, was beyond his imagination. Along the wall of the house on his left side there were two old and half broken tables, and a few broken chairs. In front of him there were two double banks covered with torn and dirty blankets. The yard wasn't too big but a crowd of small and dirty children have enough space to run around and carry each other in broken plastic crates or playing with heavily injured dolls, making high or even too high noise.

Robert's sight went to a child, which was lying just in front of two double bunks right on the ground. A girl who was about seven or eight years old and couldn't walk, and talk. She moved her hands and legs without any controlled coordination. The girl looked at him for a while then she turned her face down to the ground and licked dirty pavement and sand. Next to the small girl stood very tiny skeleton-like man, who watched Robert for some time then he came to him and said.

'I am Mike,' he introduced himself.

'Hi, I am Pete,' Robert answered and shook his small hand worried not to break it incidentally.

'Have you got a cigarette?' mike asked.

Robert gave him a cigarette and lit it. Mike took very deep pull and said. 'You shouldn't give away any cigarettes. Later on you will be short of smoke and everybody got his own tobacco twice a week'

'Then tell me where your fucking tobacco is?' Robert asked the way that it was obvious he is one of those whom the life gave trouble.

'You see Pete, I have tuberculosis and for me isn't enough.'

113

'If you want to kick the bucket, I will give you some more cigarettes but if you have TB then why are you smoking? You should not smoke at all.'

'They are stealing from everybody,' Mike didn't answered the question, 'they can steal anything but you will not stay here.'

'How do you fuck know where I am going to crèche?'

'Here are people, who are working in town and you will go to the farm.'

'Don't talk sit I am not a fucking farmer,'

'There is no need to panic, there on the farm is much better and you will like there a lot. Would you like a coffee?'

'Sure I will I didn't drink anything since last fucking morning.'

Robert found himself in completely different world and as soon as Mike brought him a mug of coffee, he tasted it slowly then he drank it very quickly because the taste was very bad. He wasn't prepared to experience such things and couldn't think about the farm where the situation might be even worse. He met some more people and soon he learned that as long as he has cigarettes everybody is very friendly.

'Hi, I am Norman,' another man came to him and soon as he introduced himself, he asked for a cigarette. It was too much for Robert and he asked him.

'Before I will give you a cigarette, tell me whose girl over there on the ground is?'

'This is my daughter,' he answered.

'Then I would like to tell you that you are fucking ass. You are worried about a smoke but at the same time your daughter is lying on the ground and licking the same sand on which dogs have pissed. If you and your fucking wife cannot give you child a blanket then I cannot give you fucking a cigarette.'

'We all have to suffer because Jesus suffered for us as well.'

'What a fucking shit are you talking about? If you fucked up your life is your problem but do not say that this is the reason that your daughter has to suffer.'

'We all must suffer, He suffered for us and we have to.'

'Why cannot you see that he tried to tell you how to live? Will he let his daughter liye on dirty ground? You have no right even to mention his name.'

Robert didn't like his language but there was no other option if he will go to be on the farm. He looked by now how the man has spoken with his wife and after a while the girl was on a piece of a dirty blanket. The girl looked at Robert with smile and he fell a little better. Norman came back to him and Robert gave him a cigarette and said.

'I am broke and have no place to crèche but I see that as long I have smoke, everybody will like me here but it doesn't matter, perhaps one day you can give me a cigarette. I have to tell you that you must after your girl. Remember that she isn't like other kids.'

'Of course, you are very good man. Thank you very much.'

'You are welcome.'

'Are you going to the farm?'

'I don't know where I am going to.'

'I think that you will go to the farm but the truck will be late, we are waiting since yesterday.'

'What do you mean since yesterday?'

'We should be gone last night because we stay on the farm but the truck never came.'

'Where did you sleep?'

'Here in the house, women and children inside and men in the yard.'

'But I see two double banks only.'

'No problem, they bring mattresses and blankets.'

'What about rain?'

'Don't you see a roof up there over the pavement? Anyway you shouldn't worry because you will go to the farm and you will like over there, I am telling you.'

'Do you think that I will?'

'Sure and this is a good place, and nobody will ask you anything. Many people stay there and they like it. Do you see that fat woman over there? She has six children and some of them stay here as they go to school and over the weekend they go to the farm.'

Robert learned from Norman about most of the people in this place and about many matters which surprised him a lot. For sure he came here too early and slowly he became angry for his job and his life. Suddenly he became one of those people who for many reasons cannot look after themselves. He fell sorry for those people but there was nothing he could do about it.

It was late at night, about ten o'clock when Aunt Theresa came to Robert and asked to help by the track. He went to see her soon after she arrived home but at that time she didn't had time for him. Now she had spoken nearly shouting.

'You must help to load the track as well and there on the farm they will take care of you.'

'Yes mom,' he answered and went to the front of the house where other people were already busy loading food on the track. After that the people started to go on the track and before Robert went on it the same girl who brought him to the yard came to search his bag.

'Listen junkie man, I have to check your things because you might have some drugs or alcohol. You cannot take things like that to the farm.'

Robert did not say anything as he understood that he doesn't look too well and after she finished, he went on the track. Surprisingly he didn't see Norman on the track and after he asked someone, the answer was that there is no space so those people must wait for another day.

'It is strange,' he thought while there was a lot of space, 'well, this Theresa must be very good woman Robert continued his thoughts but after a short travelling, the track stopped soon everybody left the track. Robert was approached by a man who told him that he is a leader in this place and he will show him where will sleep. They walk through the tents standing between trees. The leader told him a little about the farm then they stopped in front of one of the tents and Robert learned that this is the place where stays single men, and he will stay here as well.

'In the morning I will write you to my register,' said the leader and left.

The farm was situated quite far from any civilization which makes the place very quite and peaceful. Only the wind blows between trees and actually Robert might enjoy the time if not a stinking blanket given to him by the leader. He faced problem to manage that the smell doesn't go into his nose and finally he covered his head with the jacket and fell asleep.

In the morning he received a cup of coffee and went back to his tent. It was six o'clock. At seven there was a breakfast, and after that everybody attended church. Thereafter the leader called Robert and put his name into the register book. What surprised him the most was that nobody asked him to show his ID and practically anybody could come and in that place stay.

On the first day on the farm Robert was sent to work together with other people and help them to bring gravel from one side of the farm next to the kitchen. Now he could look more closely at the high construction, which he already knew from the photos and he knew that Inspector John drove around the farm with the same construction as well.

'Why this construction is so high? He asked a man who worked together with him.

'You see, the man who sponsored the building a year ago did not like it so it is not finished.'

'I don't get you; it cannot be that the building was done without a plan.'

'Aunty Theresa decided that it has t be high because if somebody will play volleyball then it has to be big.'

'Does anybody play volleyball here?'

'Most of the people on the farm cannot properly walk even and they cannot for sure play but some time Theresa's husband with her sons and other people coming to play.'

Another place which Robert was interested with was a workshop. There was a man worked by a motorcar in front of it and he has learned that vehicles are coming from different people as a donation and after they are fixed then they are for sell.

'I don't understand,' said Robert to his new friend, 'this vehicle looks quite good and we came here with old track which we had to push to start the motor.'

'You will stay longer here then you will know much more about this place. The track that you came here last night is not even on the road but it cannot be fixed as it will never bring some profit.'

Robert spent a day on the farm but his search didn't give any results. He was cross to be here and look at the people whom he couldn't help. One matter came to his mind, many of the people he met were mentally ill. Perhaps not too seriously but ill enough to be unable to look after themselves and another matter was that they have been threaten very badly. He took some photos when the leader beat an old man. It wasn't nice. It happened that the leader spotted him and said.

'You see Robert, this fucking people cannot work because they have no power but when they go to eat then they are looking to get extra plate.'

He kept quite as he knew that after any intervention they might send him away from the farm so the mission will be over and then he will face lots of problems. The only he promised himself to take proper steps as soon as he will be back in the office.

Robert spent on the farm a few days and as he thought it was just a waste of time. Once, late at night he heard very heavy track. It was very normal matter that all tracks are coming here late at night but this time it wasn't any track which could belong to the farm. He could easily hear that it is very heavy track and didn't stopped as other by the kitchen only went straight towards the workshop. Robert left the tent quickly but then the sound stopped and he couldn't find anything. In the morning he asked security on the gate but the guard didn't heard anything and didn't see any track.

'Why he is lies to me?' Robert asked himself. 'The track was here and he must open the gate because there is no other way. What's wrong?' He couldn't find any answer except that something isn't right. 'Well, Captain was right about this place.'

Robert had search the whole place but couldn't find any marks if a track. There were some marks next to the workshop but he had no idea where it went. He came to conclusion that it will be pointless to stay here so he decided so he decided to make a call to Captain Robertson.

'Hi Robert,' Captain greeted him and asked how he is to be on holiday.

'I think that I am wasting my time here only. Over the night a heave track passed the farm but I have no idea if it was a dream or a true because nowhere I can see the marks. I've been asking security but the guard said that he didn't see any track. It is possible that it was track from the base but I don't know abut it anything, perhaps you can check it, sir.'

'In other words, you are telling me that you didn't see any track.'

'Exactly, do you think sir that I have to be awake for twenty four hours? It was a night and I was sleeping.'

'You just surprise me Robert. I am sorry to say that but you have to stay there on the farm and find out all about the tracks. I have to tell you one more thing no phone calls unless it will be something really very serious. Bye.'

'Captain, it isn't about the tracks only because I have many reasons to come back here to the farm or send police. Things here are not right. Many people suffer with tuberculosis, old people are beaten . . .'

'I think that I told you clear what you have to do and this is the end of our conversation,' Captain finished dropped the phone and Robert stood with his phone and didn't know what to do with himself. He didn't like to be here any longer but it was not up to him to change the situation. On the same day he took some more photos and walk all over the farm. Finally he decided that if he has to be on vacation then he has to take things more easily.

He didn't wait for long to hear another track. It was a night as any other when the same sound woke him up. This time the track didn't drive through the farm but it stopped next to the kitchen. Robert was about to go out but at the same time the leader entered the tent and told him to go and help to offload the track. They walked together between the tents and after they came close to the kitchen the leader said to him.

'Climb on the track and help to offload, the other and waiting for you. You will offload the staff by the workshop.'

Robert went on the track where a few people set in darkness. It seemed that they have to wait for him only. The driver started the track and drove off. Surprisingly they didn't stop by the workshop but went further on into the direction of mounts. He quickly realized that he never seen those people before so he asked a man sitting next to him.

'Are you from the farm?'

'I came now only.'

'What about the others?'

'We came together.'

The night wasn't too dark but soon Robert lost his orientation as they went into completely darkness. Suddenly the track picked up the speed. They drove very fast.

'I like to see this idiot driver,' Robert thought.

He noticed that even of very high speed the road was very smooth. He fell that the engine has a sound similar to a jet. Robert fell that his ears are blocked in the same way as it might happen when water goes into them. From time to time he thought that they stay in one place. Robert fell a little pain into his ears.

Suddenly very bright light blinded him for a while and after he was able to see again, he looked surprisingly at the people on the track.

'Why I didn't see it before?' Robert asked himself looking at the men dressed in army uniforms with black swastikas on the sleeves and the same swastika on their caps.

'What the hell is going on?' He thought.

'Don't worry,' said the same man with whom Robert has spoken on the track.

'Have I told you that I am worried? Did I tell you anything?' Robert asked.

'You thought and I heard it but I am telling you once again, don't worry,' the man answered.

'Don't talk shit to me,' Robert answered with anger.

'Don't you think right now that a smoke could be very nice?' The man asked with a smile.

Robert looked at him with wide opened eyes as in fact he was thinking about a smoke. He sighted at the man but the track stopped and everybody jumped off. Robert looked around the place which seemed to be a big city at night with lots of lights over the streets. Soon all the men went into unknown direction and Robert was standing together with the man who spoke to him.

'The boss is waiting for you,' the man said.

'Funny,' Robert thought, 'somebody has kidnapped me and I don't know who and even where.'

'You right but you did look for trouble,' the man said and at the same time Robert was quite sure that he really can read his thoughts. It was beyond his imagination. They entered a big building and the man said.

'Now you can enjoy your cigarette while waiting till I will be back.' He gave him a cigarette and lit it then he left and Robert stood alone in a very long corridor. It happened for Robert first time to meet someone who could read his thoughts. It worried him a little.

Robert knew one for sure, he was underground and now he understood where the heavy track went on the other night. The only thing, he didn't know where and how.

'I will know it, oh yes, I will but firstly I have to go out from here as soon as possible,' he thought and at the same time he heard the same known him already voice of the man who brought him here.

'Do not worry about the way back.'

'Shit, I cannot think in this place even,' he thought and looked into the man's blue eyes and his strange smiling face.

'You have to pay more respect,' said the man and continued. 'If you will pay respect, you will avoid unnecessary problems. Now follow me because the boss is waiting. By the way, you can smoke while we walk.'

Robert walked slightly behind the man and tried to make use of his mobile-phone but the man turned back and warned him so it become very clear that his situation isn't too simple. Soon they entered an office where behind the desk was sitting a man wearing similar army uniform with swastika on the sleeves.

'Sir this is agent Robert who is known as Pete on the farm.'

'Thank you, have a sit Robert or you prefer your nick name. I see you don't.'

'Shit, another one who can read my thoughts,' Robert thought and the man replied immediately.

'Just imagine, it could be funny if you have to remember for all times that your boss for example can read your thoughts,' he laughed.

'It is impossible,' Robert replied.

'Only at the present stage of your development but it might be very useful to help you in this matter so this stinking world of yours wouldn't stink as much as it does at the moment.'

'Actually what do you mean? Don't we stay in the same world?'

'You really surprise me Robert, as a great agent you should know by now that you are in underground world. The most important advantage that we can read other people thoughts is that we are not putting labels on anybody forehead as you do in your world. It is one of your biggest problems that you are labelling people but you don't know them, and don't even try to know them.'

Robert reminded the girl from the farm's office which treated him so badly and the man quickly responded. 'You see, it wasn't nice at all to be named a junkie but it is only one of your illnesses up there in your stinking world.'

'Sir, would you mind to me where I am, please.'

'I told you and I am going to tell you once again that you are in the underground world and since now this world will be yours as well because you will stay here for the rest of your life.'

'What are you talking about? There must be something wrong up there inside your head.'

'You shall worry rather about your own head and once again, you have to know that there is no way back from here.'

'Actually, how do you know me?'

'You must be joking do you think that we will take here anyone? By the way, do not be afraid because our world is much, much better then yours.'

'Perhaps this is the reason that you are killing our people.'

'You are very wrong because we didn't kill anybody but our people have been killed over there and you don't have any clue who and how it did.'

'Wait a minute, you have told me that your world is very good and suddenly your people are gone to my world and have been killed. If here is as good as you telling to me then where is the point to go somewhere else? It has no sense.'

'This is not your business but I can tell you that this is for experimental reason only but let me ask you Robert. What is your profession? What are you doing for leaving?'

'Didn't you say that you know me? Why are you asking?'

'Just to remind you that if that world of yours could be without swindles, you will be working in completely different field,' the man said that proudly.

'Oh yes, perhaps if you wouldn't interfere in our world and the question is what for if you have your own world?'

'In general we do not interfere but our scientific work needs some experiments and what is more important this work is very important for your world. It looks that you will need our help more then you can dream even.'

'Is it?'

'Sure.'

'Did anybody ask you for any help? Who could ask you if for example I am hearing about another world for the first time and the other thing is that who could give you right for any intervention?'

'We don't need to ask anybody and nobody have to ask us, and I have never said that we will help you but perhaps there will be a need to heal your sick world.'

'Oh Jesus,' thought Robert, 'another one who likes to make happy other people.'

'What did you say? Doesn't matter, you didn't say but remember, do not use this name again in my presence.'

'Sorry, I didn't know that you are so much religious.'

'It isn't your business but I am telling you once again, do not use this name again if you don't like to see me cross. There in your world you are using His name as a slogan but I am telling you that if He could come to you again, you people will kill Him much quicker then before. I wonder what type of death you will prepare for Him this time.'

'You must really be a little sick up there,' Robert knocked his forehead. 'You have to know that everybody loves him. I mean all Christians.'

'The creator made the world in order but you putting everything into places according to your imagination and without any common sense and if you are so sure about that then show me those who can hear truth about themselves. The other thing is that you have to remember abut your situation so if you knock your forehead, watch out because you might be knock very badly.'

'All what you are telling to me is strictly big nonsense.'

'You are the one who tells nonsense. Your lives have nothing to do with any religion. Actually I am not too sure how to say that but first of all you seems to be not enough mature to have any religion and it seems to me that you created all religions to protect your dirty lives. To cover your every day dirty matters and to use them for own advantages only,' he slightly raised his voice.

'Not everybody,' Robert reminded the owner of the farm who's helping other people but the man said quickly.

'Those on the farm are exactly the same and don't be mistaken because they are millionaire's. They pray on Sunday and on Monday they carry on with their swindles and all what is on their mind is how to use poor people to be more rich.'

'Actually I don't understand you, sir.'

'You Robert surprise me more and more.'

'Do I?'

'Cannot you see yourself that your sickness is only to be rich? You try to tell me about religion but in fact you have your biggest problem is to be rich and thereafter how to possess power. With the power never enough but there is no way that there will be someone who could rule the word.'

'Do you think so?'

'Oh yes but very often creates serious problems and tell me if there are any other matters that could ruin your world. There is nothing else but you and only you who try to destroy your world.'

'Not only because there are many other serious matters like, like AIDS for example.'

'Robert, you have no right talk like that because you should know that I have told you about something else but if you about AIDS then you should know that that illness is giving big opportunity for many crooks to be more rich. You know that you cannot help in this matter but you do not try to help there where you can like tuberculosis for example.'

'Whatever you say, nothing allows you to interfere into other people lives.'

'Don't worry because soon you will face problem that without our help your stinking world will be destroyed and you are the one who is guilty.'

'Is it?'

'The way your world goes takes you nowhere but we will be able to replace your stinking world with healthy population.'

'I cannot get you.'

'You see, our genetic engineering is far advanced from yours, if you have any,' he laughed and continued. 'We still need some more experiments but somehow you destroyed our job.'

'Wait a minute, are you telling that you are busy with clones?'

'You can name that as you like it but remember that for centuries you have been dreaming about a perfect worker. Now you can get one which will be the best, better then slave and better then robot. I would say rather robot-human which can only work, isn't it amazing? Oh yes, you will need us for sure because not too many of you will enough money to plant their seeds and have children like Ricky Martin.'

'Firstly I have never heard that name and that what you are telling is just nonsense, seems to me that you are very ill.'

'The nonsense is there in your world,' he laughed and said. 'You are creating a new model of live and you told me that AIDS is your problem but I am telling you that another epidemic will kill your population and this is homosexuality and you are one of those who are guilty but believe me that it will make our world very rich.'

Chapter 11

It was very difficult time for Alice but she knew that John has serious reason to feel upset because practically the case has been taken away from him and suddenly he became a suspect in the whole case. She fell sorry for his family even before her arriving to his home but there was nothing she could do about that except just to be here.

It started new sunny day and soon after Alice got up, and before she went to take bath, she entered the kitchen where she met John's mother.

'How did you sleep my dear?' Mrs. Carol asked.

'Thank you, I slept like a baby. Firstly, I couldn't believe that there are so peaceful places in the world. I am only worried about John because he isn't in good mood and he is a little ashamed of the situation so he stayed in his dad office for the whole night.'

'I can see that he isn't alright my dear but you see, he was very close with his father and I think that for him it is a very big shock. Would you like a cup of coffee my dear? I have made it right now and you might have one for John as well. Mean time I will prepare a breakfast.'

'Oh it is very nice of you Mrs. Carol, thank you very much.'

Soon after Alice knocked on John's door then she went inside. John was still lying on the floor covered with blanket. 'Good morning John,' she said.

'Good morning,' he answered and asked. 'What actually are you doing here?'

'John,' she took a chair and set down. 'Do not start the day from talking nonsense. There is no need to show everybody that we are not together. Your mom asked me to bring you coffee so what I suppose had to tell her. Perhaps, sorry it isn't my business. You cannot make shit for her or you like to make one very big.'

'No, I won't, I am sorry.'

'Then drink your coffee and I'll go to have a bath.'

'Bath?' John nearly shouted.

'Yes a bath. Don't you bath or shower in the morning?'

'Of course I do but I just thought about something else,' John answered and his mind where all the death people he saw before. Suddenly he saw baths filled with strings and floating heads. He kept quite and didn't say a word when Alice left the office.

After the breakfast John and Alice left for town and as they have planned they went to the hospital, to see his father. Alice didn't learn too much from that visit and she thought that it has to be accepted that he passed away naturally. She wasn't too sure about it but from the other hand she didn't like to put John into much deeper depression as he already was. After they left hospital she asked.

'John, I hope that you wouldn't mind to show me your father's yacht>'

'Of course I do mind but what it can change if I have to follow your orders. Do I have another option? I don't see any.'

'I thought that you have stopped that nonsense.'

'Let's go to see the yacht,' he said ignoring her.

They entered the yacht club and after they parked the car, hey walked along the line of yachts. Suddenly John's sight went to the yacht standing next to his father's. He stood for a while and Alice asked him if he knows the yacht but he couldn't answer if he saw it before or not. They went on deck of his father's yacht and as soon as they entered the cabin Alice said.

'Something stinks here like hell.'

'For quite long time nobody was here so, what do you expect?'

'John,' she asked, 'do you know the other yacht?'

'I am sure that I saw it not long ago but I am not too sure where it could be. Anyway it looks very beautiful.'

'Well, by now I like to see that one.'

'What could you see here? A cabin like many another and deck as many other, most probably you can fond in this marina many much more nice boats then this one.'

Alice looked everywhere with interest and asked about many things as she never seen it in her life. She listen John's explanations for some time but soon Paul arrived to the yacht club and joined them on the yacht.

'Hi, how are you? I was quite sure that I will find you here. What can you say about the yacht Alice? I think is beautiful.'

'To be honest I didn't see too many yachts before but all I can say it is very impressed.'

'You must be joking, our father's yacht is just a middle class but if you look at this one,' John pointed the yacht which stood next to them, 'you know that it must be worth a fortune.'

'I don't know the owner but he must be very rich. For quite long time nobody is coming here and some time I am asking myself what for the man bought it if is not using. It seems that he has plenty money and is jus a snob.'

'I wouldn't notice that,' said Alice looking at very beautiful yacht especially that she saw it already on the photos and knew that it must have some connection with the investigation, they were busy with.

'Never mind the yacht, tell me Alice how do you like our small city?' Paul asked.

'To be honest, I didn't see too much yet, we went to hospital and thereafter here but I like it, is very quite.'

'All you can do is t go sleep,' said John.

'John, do not say that you don't like here because I know that you do.'

'You see, she likes here and there is no other option but stay longer, perhaps you can go for a day sailing even,' said Paul smiling.

'I never went sailing in my life,' said Alice.

'Paul, don't you see any difference between a funeral and a picnic?'

'Look John, it could be good for you because it will bring your memory of the time which you spent together with our father on the sea.'

'John said that he doesn't know how to sailing.'

'Alice, it isn't true because he spent many days on the sea and I would say that much more then I did. Even on that yacht he went sailing.'

'Alright, I went sailing but it was many years ago. Actually I don't understand why you are asking me to go on the sea. The air stinks here, could we go to the bar?' John didn't like the conversation at all.

'Let's go,' answered Paul and added. 'Leave everything open so the fresh air will come in.'

They left the yacht and as they have been passing the mentioned yacht, John stopped again but couldn't remember where he saw it then Paul said.

'It is beautiful but you see it isn't like that because even most expensive yacht is not like mine one. I truly love my yacht and no other one could be compared with it. I really mean it. I spent many days on the sea and I went through many difficult situations so it is like a member of my family. Let's go, she for sure isn't as much beautiful as my yacht.'

They laughed on Paul's explanation and went to the bar inside the yacht club and Alice found it very cosy. As they walk towards the bar she left them going to rest room. Both men set down and Paul said.

'John, you told me that she is not working for police but I can see that is not true. It makes no difference for me if you marry a doctor or somebody else. I t isn't my business at all.'

'Paul, I have told you that she has nothing to do with police and this is true, and I think that I am the only cop she knows.'

'John,' Paul didn't like to give up, 'you two look like a couple which spent together no less then ten or more years and you don't treat her as your fiancé at all. You invited her into our home but if I look at you and into my past where I had many girlfriends, I don't know what to say.'

'Paul, it isn't like you thinking and you have to understand that after I have received the information about our dad I am not myself. This is the only reason that I might be seen in bad mood. How could be?'

John finished as Alice came to them. She took a sit and said. 'Oh, I see that you have a drink for me as well, thank you.'

'We've been waiting for you,' answered John and added. 'I hope that Scotch and soda will be ok or it is still too early for you.'

'Oh no, is fine,' she answered and then she said. 'I think that Paul had very good idea with that sailing. I am very far to say that this is good time but from my side if it could be possible to see how it looks alike will be wonderful. Who knows when we will again come here,' she looked at John's face and asked him. 'What do you think John?'

'I don't know what he thinks,' said Paul, 'but I think that he shouldn't be alone because of the time when many strange thoughts come to us and personally I think that a day or two could be good to spend on the sea.'

'Paul, if you like to show Alice the art of sailing or the beauty of the sea then why cannot you take off a day and take your family and her for a short race so at least I might have peace at last. I haven't got a fixed leave which means that at any time I might be gone back to work. Do you think that my bosses will accept my holiday on the sea,' John suspended his voice looking at Alice.

'John, you have remember that I have my own business and it isn't possible to be off even I would like it. Believe me that if I could take off, I will.'

'Oh yes but you have time to sit in the bar,' John replied.

'It is only because I have to say hello to you.'

'I think that we have to drop the subject but personally I think John that one or two days on the sea might make good affect on your spiritual life.'

'What do you think is wrong with my spiritual life?'

'Alice is right, yes, she is right,' said Paul and John firstly sight at him then at Alice, and somehow he came to a conclusion that it might be really better to agreed and see what will come from this all story then he said.

'Ok, I will make a call to my bosses and ask them for a few days or so but I cannot be sure of anything so do not take it wrong if I couldn't be able to go on the sea. Anyway if it will be possible then the yacht cannot go on the sea as it is now so there will be need to do some job and prepare it for a race.'

'Now you talking sense,' said Paul smiling.

'Thanks Paul but now you owe me a drink,' laughed John.

'With a great pleasure but for two of you only because I have to go, some customers will come to me this afternoon but I will come to see you later.' Paul said and stood up. He left the bar and John with Alice set with silence for some time.

'It is quite good idea and it doesn't matter if we will go sailing or not but at least during the day we will be out of the house and in stand to face your mother, I will work on the yacht and doesn't matter what you will ask me to do. Thereafter at nights we can be in your father's office and chat.'

'You talk with sense but what do you mean about nights? How many of nights are you planning to spend here?'

'If it will depend on me then you have to be sure that we will be gone as soon as possible, even today.'

'I think you right, there is no need to stay in the house,' John finally agreed.

'John, I will do any job you will ask me,' she said.

'We have to back to the yacht because everything is open and in case of rain it will be one big mess,' said John

It was difficult day for both of them. The idea of working on the yacht allowed them off for some time from John's home. The atmosphere even was better between them. John still wasn't too friendly but at least he had to explain what Alice has to do on the yacht. By the end of the day they set again in his father's office and spoke or rather

Alice asked him about many different matters. Many times she repeated some of questions which made him more and more nervous.

'John, I know that I have asked that before but tell me please do you really think that your father took that photo?'

'What the hell is wrong with you? You are coming to the same matters every now and then. How should I spouse to know who took the fucking photo? Perhaps it was in the log-book perhaps not. Did you put it there?'

'I am asking only,' she answered and added. 'This is the only photo with UFO in this room but if he took it there has to be another one. It is practically impossible that a professional photographer will take one shot only if he is facing such possibility. What do you think?'

'It makes sense and I don't mind if you will search house, I mean the office,' he answered.

'It is on my mind that you will help me in this matter, John.'

'Well, I do believe that if it was me in such situation, for sure I will take more then one shot. At this stage I cannot help you because I don't have any idea what's going on. Anyway, if anything will come up, I will tell you immediately.'

'Would you like some more coffee?' Alice changed subject.

'Yes, please,' John answered shortly.

After Alice came back with coffee, she found him looking at the same log-book in which she found the photo with UFO. It gave her some hope that he is interested in the case so she said.

'I see that the matter started to be interesting for you.'

'I don't know, the photo looks to be genuine but how he could get it, no idea.

'John, I hope that you wouldn't mind if I will make a call to Captain Robertson.'

'Don't ask me stupid questions, it is obvious that I cannot tell you no. Do what you have to do.'

After Captain answered the call she said, 'Sir, I am calling to you in connection of the photo, the thing is that there is no other in the house. We still have films that have to be developed but it came to my mind another idea.'

'What is it?'

'Captain, it is possible that on the yacht of John's father we can find what we cannot find here in the house.'

'Why don't you look there?'

'You see Captain I thought that it might be possible that if we will go on the sea then it might happen that . . .' She couldn't finish as Captain shouted.

'Are you mad?'

'No, I am not but the photo was in the log-book and if John received a message then we have to follow it.'

'What message are you talking about?'

'I think that you told me about his journey, Captain. You know very well that he drove at the same time when his father has passed away. It must be somehow possible that he was about to put his attention on something that we do not know but it is possible that it has connection with UFO.'

'If I understood you correctly, you will go on the sea to look for UFO, well who will pay your wages, I do not know but for sure not me,' Captain said and added. 'It really sounds very funny to see big agent on endless vacation.'

'Then I don't know what the whole story is about. We have to carry on with the investigation or we have to drop the case but then right in the morning I will go home and the comedy will be over. By the way, it looks like we are on right track and how it is possible that we have to give up.'

'One you have to consider, we might be on track but I would rather say mysterious track.'

'Look Captain, we are busy with the case for long time and it cost money so why you sending me here if I have to stop at the time when we should go forward. There is nothing to search in the house and nothing on the yacht, and the only sea is the place where we have to look if we are still serious in the matter. If I have to stop now then I have to leave John's home and go back.'

'Alice, you have to follow my orders and not look after mysteries.'

'There are mysteries in our lives and one of them was John's journey. If we don't follow it then we waste time and money. Except that we are playing fool with ourselves.'

'Is anything else you have to tell me?'

'Yes, there is a yacht and it looks as the one on the photo.'

'I know and I think that we'll see each other before you will go sailing.'

'What do you mean? Do you agree for that race?'

'I did not say yes but I will see you soon, good night.'

'Good night.'

Alice finished the conversation and looked at John then she asked. 'Did you see the photos there in the house? You must see the yacht which is in the yacht club.'

'Perhaps I did see but I am not too sure about it but tells me please, who is the boss, you or Captain?'

'You present very bad attitude but it doesn't matter.'

'Nothing wrong with my attitude because if I have a question, I ask and I think that we have to search that yacht which is next to my father's one,' John came up with an idea.

'There might be some possibility of connection with the case but that we have to leave to Captain as he is very interested and by the way, he doesn't like the idea of sailing as you are.'

'Well, we can go sailing because I see that even Captain cannot change your ideas.'

'I don't know what is it but I have such feeling that it will push the all matter forward.'

'Do you really think so?' John asked and started laugh.

'There is nothing to laugh about we have a job to do.'

'This job belongs to you and I came to attend the funeral but anyway look here but look very carefully.'

John put a map on the desk and Alice came a little closer she asked why is putting the same map which they have already see before.

'Look, this is the only map which he could use during the race in which he might take the photo of UFO. I cannot see any other map corresponding with the log-book. Do not think that I really believe in that story.'

'Are you sure?'

'I am not but I hope that I am right and we go away as soon as possible. Firstly show me the farm where I was driving around.'

'It has to be somewhere here.'

'If there is any connection between that place and the photo then the photo has to be taken somewhere in this region.'

'Now you talk with sense.'

'I have to do whatever possible to go as quick as possible from my home. If you will check the log-book then you will see that it was the only place. He has been sailing around but funny that there is no other course on that map. One what can help is that there is a spot where he might be fishing and most probably he spot UFO over there. Anyway if we have to go sailing then we must repeat the same race. I wonder why there is no other map from this region.'

'What I can say is that slowly I start to believe that we are going somewhere and we are on right track.'

'We are but on a mysterious track.'

'The same told me Captain.'

'He is right.'

'John, do you mind to explain me how do you read all this lines?'

'This is the course and here is the place where he took his position. The same note you will find in the log-book. If you are on the sea, you have to know where you are at all times.'

'Very interesting and I hope to see it personally.'

'Look, I can go sailing with you but I do not remember too much and I am honest with you so you are going on your own risk.'

'Paul said that you know sailing very well.'

'It was very long time ago, of course I still remember many things but after such long time many things is gone from my memory.'

'What about satellite navigation system? What I know nowadays it is a common.'

'Well there is satellite navigation system and I am taking the risk but if something will go wrong then who will be responsible for your safety. Do you think that my father's death isn't enough for me?'

Alice listen him seriously and it came to her mind that perhaps it will be better to drop the case with sailing as it could be really dangerous but it wasn't in her nature to give up. 'It will be what it has to be,' she thought looking at the map on the desk.

Chapter 12

Robert found himself in such situation that he couldn't freely think about escaping from underground to his freedom. The conversation started to irritate him more and more. The man who clime to be in charge laughed a lot while expressing his opinion about the world.

'I am more then sure that you will need our help. Just look at your new model of family.'

'What about it?'

'You are breaking the law of creation.'

'I don't know what actually you are taking about.'

'I would say that you don't like to know but what about homosexuality.'

'I have nothing to do with it.'

'No, you don't but I am not too sure about it because your quite is equal to support. This is disrespect for order of existence of the world. Because two lesbians or two gays cannot and will never be able to multiply. Where they can have children from?'

'I don't see any reason to be worried about.'

'Me either but it sounds funny. Once homosexuals where people who most likely can be affected by AIDS, suddenly they can get married. They can get married in the church so in other words even Vatican is accepting homosexuality. On top of that they can adopt children and It seems that you don't care about morality at all.'

'Where could you see my fault?'

'I tell you where, you like them or even love them.'

'How could you talk shit like that?'

'Then who goes and clap hands while watching tennis game. Who loves the best tennis player ever that no other woman can beat. The biggest ever woman's tennis player but from other hand just a lesbian and do you know when she could be a hero in my eyes. Only if she will say to the whole world, "forgive me but all my achievements wasn't right, I am too strong for a woman but too weak for a man." Act like that I can name as heroism but no one will do it and slowly this world of yours is becoming a world of stinking fagats.'

'She might be a lesbian but still is a woman,' Robert answered then added. 'I have never said that I like it but what I can hear from you is just a crime in my eyes.'

'Look, I have learn your history and seems to me that if the matter will give a development then no crime will be involve but if we are talking about homosexuals then except that tennis player I can tell you that you people are making them heroes. Just simple incident in Benelux where a boss of British homosexuals jumped out of the crowd to attack a president of one of African's country, wait his name is Mugabe' the man looked at Robert very seriously and continued. 'Do you think that this is correct to create a hero in an interview on radio? Your media is making big damage but it's good for us.'

'I don't know what you are talking about.'

'No, because for you is nothing to see in a magazine a photo of big singer Elton with Sir Title married to another one and proudly posing while even can adopt children. Actually I did believe that to get a title like Sir a man must present high moral value and what actually means that for Queen, nothing, just a joke from all nations. I cannot understand how you people can look peacefully at a show of Mrs Oprah glorified another singer Ricky Martin who advertise modern family that he is alone with two children. Daddy, where is mammy? I am your mammy. How can you accept shit like that? I wouldn't even mention that but it is a prove that in nearly future we will be very rich.'

'I am not interested with things like that.'

'Of course not because you are not interested that your stinking world stinks more and more every day,' he became very serious but then he said softly. 'I can see that you like to have smoke so help yourself. Personally I am not smoking but I don't mind if you do or anybody else,' he started to laugh.

'How could you breathe underground if people smoke?' Robert asked.

'This is our difference you sit in your parliaments and create more and more prohibition using taxpayers money but no one even thinks that it might be completely another solution. I would say simple, just install similar to ours or better even extractors and there will be no problem. Here underground you can smoke as much as you like,' he laughed.

'It sounds interesting. There are many places that I use to go but because of smoking prohibition, I don't like to be there at all.'

'You see here in underground world we have to find a solution for any problem. Just imagine what could happen if all our vehicles will drive and there is no possibility to prevent smoke.'

'Ok, now I see where goes our fuel,' said Robert.

'Oh no,' the man laughed, 'we have some trade with you but your fuel is not for us. I can tell you that because you cannot take from us this information. You still have a lot to learn to achieve our level of technology. Just imagine what could happen if we will use your fuel, impossible. We are using silicon.'

'Impossible.'

'Well, I'm telling you that we are using silicon supported with electromagnetic field so there isn't any unnecessary smoke and what is most important, we can achieve very high speed. Our fuel is highly economical.'

'I guess that you know my next question but still let me ask you about another matter. 'What connection do you have with Bermuda Triangle?'

'Well, I have to tell you that personally I have nothing to do with Bermuda Triangle or any other similar places.'

'What do you mean—any other places?' Robert asked and after a moment forwarded next question. 'What means personally?'

'You see our world is situated in many places, same like yours and if there is some military training there is no need to inform anybody. Perhaps I know something in this matter, perhaps not. Of course our communication system is much faster then yours and is possible that from time to time an accident can take place. Enough to say that our ships can reach very high speed and in general are safe,' he said looking at Robert proudly.

Robert thought about the matter which he worked with and sight at the man on the other side of the desk. The man laughed only then he said.

'You see Robert the problem is that you went too far with this investigation of yours. Perhaps you don't know even but at this stage you could be very dangerous person for us and what can I say, there is no need to worry because even if you will go back, which is impossible there in your world nobody will take you seriously. In other words for the rest of your life everybody will treat you as a mad person. All we need from you is to take information which you have in your brain.'

'What for you need it and how it is possible?' Robert asked smiling.

'There are many reasons one of them is that you cannot find out who killed our people. Another matter is that somebody ahs to substitute you and work for us.'

'You really talk rubbish.'

'It isn't any rubbish. I told you that we are practically able to produce the same person if we can get genes from that person.'

'Oh really, and what afterward, are you telling that the substitution will fuck my wife. Is that so?'

'Sorry to say so but it is strongly possible and I don't see any other option.'

'Why don't you just kill me?'

'No, no there is no need to kill you because it might be a need to use you for other experiments. Most probably we will keep you on the farm.'

'Are you trying to tell me that the people on the farm are just rabbits?'

'Not all of them but mostly they are rabbits.'

'In other words I was right that this is a court case.'

'Nobody can help them on the farm and all we do is for development purpose.'

'Who's development, not our for sure.'

'I told you Robert that you will need our help and remember that you already have many our gifts and you don't even know about them.'

'No I don't.'

'Of course not because what could you know how did you get radar or laser. That you will never know.

The conversation has stopped because to the office came the same man who brought Robert here. Now Robert looked into his blue eyes and very calm face.

'Sir,' he said, 'I hope that you wouldn't mind to give him an injection right now.'

'Not at all just do your job,' the man answered and added. 'Just do your job. There is no need for him to stay here for nothing. I did spoil myself a little with the conversation, that's it but nothing serious.'

'I don't need any injection,' said Robert.

'I have no need to ask you and you are not the one to decide here. I can let you go free but where could you go and who will help you, nobody.'

'Perhaps I will be lucky to meet some good people.'

'Perhaps, for example those from the farm you idiot,' he answered and continued. 'I told you already that all what they have are from charity and never mind because the farm actually belongs to us. I did listen to your conversation with Captain Robertson and we know all about that plan of yours to close the farm but we cannot afford that.'

Robert looked at the man who wears by now a white overall and once again into his eyes. The man took Robert hand and placed on the desk then he pulled up the sleeve. From the box he took early prepared syringe and inserted the needle into Robert's muscles. Soon Robert fell as a liquid is filling his whole body. Suddenly he fell dizzy and there was some strange sweet taste into his mouth which stayed for a while. Robert concentrates his mind on the box with cigarettes so no other thoughts could come to his mind. The man behind the desk said to him.

'I told you that you can smoke and don't be ashamed because I know that you have big problem with your addiction.'

Robert lit a cigarette and then he fell that something isn't right with him. He didn't know what is happening but the man behind the desk knew very quickly what took place and pressed a button behind the desk. Somewhere from a speaker came a voice.

'Sir, what can I do for you?'

'Max, come here immediately with the doctor who was here in my office.'

'Sir, I never sent any doctor you.'

'What are you talking about if a few minutes ago came a doctor who injected Robert some shit and as a result he lost his memory.

'It is impossible, I will be there right now,' Max answered.

The man who was the boss in this place looked at Robert from behind his desk for awhile then he said. 'You don't remember anything from your life but you still remember how to smoke fucking cigarette. Don't worry, I can ensure you that your memory will come back, you bastard.'

Chapter 13

John came to the office with two drinks and put them on the desk. 'I made Scotch with soda for you,' he said then he continued.

'I cannot understand how it could be possible that you never went sailing. I am quite sure that you are earning quite good money. Every day you are wearing very nice clothes which I think are expensive so why cannot you spend a little for a vacation on the sea.'

'John, I am not looking inside your pocket and except that I have never thought about sailing before. Most probably I will never think about it if not that stupid situation.'

They spent some time on conversation then Alice sighted that John's glass is empty so she went to pour him another drink. In the lounge she met Mrs. Carol.

'I came to make a drink for John,' she said to her.

'My dear, you shouldn't ask even. I am very glad that you are with John and I have a little hope that you two will settle here sometime in the future.'

'It is very difficult to say because John doesn't like to be in small place and I am quite sure about that, never mind his work. He is involves into his job very deeply. Except that I have my job and I don't think that I might have a job here.'

'Anyway, let me have a hope my dear.' Both started to laugh.

'What is so funny?' John asked while he entered the room.

'Nothing my dear,' answered him mother, 'I just try to help you two to settle here for good.'

'What?'

'John, nothing wrong your mom will miss you after you'll be gone to work.'

'Ok, give me my drink, please. I need to clean up and make some order in dad's office.'

'Nobody is stopping you my dear.'

John left them and soon after Alice came into the office as well. He noticed smile on her face but didn't said anything.

On the next morning they left the house shortly after the breakfast and went to the yacht club. John opened the cabin and said to Alice.

'Ok, you can do some work here and I go shopping.'

'Firstly, I don't know what can I do here and secondly on the yacht we have to work together and if there will be a need to go shopping then we have to go together as well.'

'Why?'

'Because I have to be with you at all times.'

'Would you like to tell me that I have a secrets or I might be lost.'

'Let's say that I am your body guard and please don't make more difficult situation as it already is.'

John didn't answered he stood in the cockpit looking around and suddenly he spotted some people coming to them. Firstly he thought that it is his brother Paul but then he nearly shouted to Alice.

'Look, some people are coming here and I think this is your Captain. Shit, I think that Oscar is with him. What they are doing here?'

'I see they are coming with security guard.'

'I hope that they will stop you from going to the sea,' John laughed.

The security guard stopped in front of the yacht which stood next to his fathers' one. They have spoken for a while then he left. Alice couldn't wait so she took her mobile and made a call.

'Hi Alice, how are you?' Captain said.

'I am fine but what are you doing here, Captain?' She asked.

'I thought that I have small business here.'

'What business?'

'I found an advert in the paper and friend of mine is a sailor so we came together and perhaps I will buy a yacht. It looks very impress. My friend is an expert so I need his advice before I will decide anything.'

They have spoken for a while and thereafter Captain Robertson and Oscar came to John and Alice. Soon they set together in the cabin. There was light breeze and nice sunshine but no one of them was too happy.

'What abut my race Captain? We already cleaning the yacht,' Alice asked him.

'Well, I think that I have already agreed the matter is who will pay for this holiday. By the way, I hope that John knows about sailing.'

'Captain, never mind his sailing but you have to be a little serious about my money. If there will be really a problem then much better if we stop all the nonsense.'

'Wow, not so quick.'

'Captain,' John couldn't wait for the moment to say anything. 'I would like to know what you are doing to me.'

'Actually I don't understand you John.'

'I have been working with the investigation and now the case seems to me is against me. I cannot even go to shop on my own.'

'Didn't found you a photo with UFO?'

'She found it not me and except that I am not sure because she might to put it there as well.'

'Cool down John and stop talk shit. She is not here with you to play a game. Most probably there is mo to look for in this case. One thin you have to remember, this is serious matter and what we are asking for is to cooperate.'

'Do you really thing that we have to go sailing?'

'Perhaps not but why cannot you. I think that we have to sit in the bar for a while because the air here strictly stinks but before I like to see the photo.'

'Sorry but it is in John's home as I never expect to see you so soon.'

'Ok, we will make a plan but now let us go to the other yacht so see you in the bar.'

Captain left together with Oscar and Alice said to John that she cannot make coffee because the machine is not working. 'Could you fix it?'

'That what I know about coffee machine is how to switch it on but nothing else.'

'Then we have to be without coffee on the sea.'

'We will simply buy another one.'

'John.'

'What's now?'

'I just thought that you knew about the photo.'

'Is it? It seems that whatever I will tell you it will be impossible that you will believe me. I see that the coffee machine works.'

'Yes and coffee might be any time you wish.'

'Why you told me that it is broken?'

'It was but I fixed, simple so it will safe you some money.'

'Me? I am not the one who is organizing the race.'

'Why we haven't the log-book with us?'

'You didn't order but I think that we have to go to the club so let's go. The cabin must be open so some more fresh air will come in.'

They left the yacht and went to the club where Captain and Oscar set already by the bar. They took places next to them. It is quite interesting that whatever we might say abut sailors, they always will find themselves as very good friends. John ordered two drinks and said to Captain.

'I see that you have very beautiful yacht.'

'Oh no, she isn't mine yet but I hope to buy it very soon. There was an advert in the paper and I came together with friend of mine to see it.'

They have spoken for a while then they decided that John and Alice will go to town and come back with the photo as it was very important for Captain including undeveloped films. It took them less than half hour and they were back in the club. This time Captain with Oscar set by the table and they joined them.

'Where is the photo?' Captain asked.

'This is it,' Alice gave him the photo. He looked at it for a while then gave it to Oscar asking. 'What do you think?'

'Quite exciting, for the very first time I see UFO on a real photo; I can say that I saw some photos in the news papers but never took it too seriously.'

'John,' Captain asked him, 'did you know about the photo?'

'Sorry but I didn't and it seems that you don't believe me,' he answered smiling.

'Is that possible that your dad made a fake?'

'Captain that you can easily check and I do believe that you will but where is the point to do fakes,' John answered and added. 'The thing is that I don't have any idea how such photo was in his log book. It is really possible that it was just coincident.'

'Did you check the book properly?'

'Actually why you asking me such question if she works for you not me. You are the one who sent an angel here and this is her mission. I came here to attend my father's funeral and you not giving a damn about anything and anybody.'

'John, you have to understand our situation. We are busy with the case for long time and only now we have a few points so there is no way that you will turn around and say, fuck you people this is not my business.'

'It means nothing for me. I am a free man and do you know what? I am very close to get another job.'

'Do not complicate your life because you might face problems as well and we can send you for quite long time away so much better for all of us and for you especially to make your mind.'

'It does not mean that you have to play on my emotions. Anyway what do you expect from me?'

'Firstly cooperation and secondly you have to go sailing with Alice.'

'Oh boy, what more,' John nearly swallow his words.

'Inspector, you have never said that you know sailing,' Oscar came into the conversation.

'Well, you didn't ask but actually why I have to talk about my private life. I always enjoyed while listening about your sailing. Actually I don't understand that at all because you came here as an expert.'

'To search the yacht but you are sailing with a big S not like me, inland.'

'Don't talk shit Oscar because you can go sailing on the sea as well and I said the same to her,' he pointed Alice. 'Both of you getting enough money to go sailing on the sea,' John answered.

'Inspector, you are my manager at work but what I do in my private life can not be in your competency. People have right to live their lives independently like independent countries because if not then trouble is around the corner.'

'Sorry Oscar, it was a joke only. Captain he should go sailing,' said John smiling.

'John,' Captain said with angry voice, 'I hope that you know that the investigation is under my supervision. In other words you report to me which means that you have to obey my orders. Oscar works with me and we have other things to do.'

Oscar looked around and said softly, 'even I wish, there is no way as I don't know anything about sailing on the sea.'

'Whatever you will decide and whatever will take place, you are responsible and one you have to remember that on the sea anything can happen,' John said seriously and after a while he continued. 'Actually it looks very strange because not long ago I was busy with investigation and then took place a trip in which I drove nobody knows where so I became a suspect and now is possible that the yacht might even vanish on the sea. You taking big risk Captain and zero chances to find UFO.'

'Well, I have never said that you have to find UFO and I am against a black magic but in this case we have to follow some signs which are very logical. Anybody should be sure that I don't like to send anyone sailing and honestly for sure not you John.'

'My brother is asking every now and then if she works for police,' said John.

'Nothing wrong with that,' said Captain and added. 'You have to be ready go sailing as soon as the funeral will be over and I hope to meet you tomorrow on your yacht or here so we can speak about some matters before we will leave.'

'Ok Captain what else I can do,' said John with deep breath.

John and Alice left the yacht club and after they arrived home Mrs. Carol said to them that she is waiting with lunch. It was difficult to say that they are not hungry especially that Alice quickly said that she like her cooking very much. After they set together by the table Mrs. Carol was quite happy that they decided to go sailing. John didn't fell too well.

'You see mom,' he said, 'Alice never went sailing so it might be nice experience for her to see how it looks alike. The other thing is that who knows when we will be here again.'

'I do believe that you will come soon and I am very happy for you my dear and for sure that you will enjoy sailing together with John.'

'Have you been sailing a lot, Mrs. Carol?'

'Not really because of seasickness.'

'I hope not to catch one,' Alice laughed.

'I hope that you will be ok and you John have to look after her,' said Mrs. Carol.

'Mom, the weather is very nice and nothing can take place during a day sailing,' answered John.

They have eaten for very first time their lunch very quick and left for yacht club. Before they left John took some maps and the log-book in which the photo has been found. On their way they stopped to make more shopping. On the yacht they worked together and Alice found it very exciting.

'Whatever you'll say about sailing,' she said, 'I feel much better to be here then stay in your home.'

'You tell me about it. I am actually glad that we have to do something here but at the same time I have a hope that Robertson will change his mind.'

I don't think that it could be possible as we are working for quite long time on the case with UFO and our government put already too much ;money into this project.'

'Whatever is going to take place I do not know how to talk to my mother so it is really much better to be here or go to the sea or to hell even but not to look into her eyes.'

It was already late afternoon when they left yacht and entered the bar where Captain Robertson and Oscar waited for them.

'I thought that you have forgotten about us completely and never will see you here tonight,' said Captain.

'You should know that we are working on the yacht,' John answered.

'We thought so.'

'Why didn't you come to see us there?' John asked and added. 'I think that we should go there so we might have more free conversation.'

'Of course we can do it,' Captain answered and John went to the barman to explain that they invited their new friends to pay short visit on the yacht and soon after they left the bar. The cabin was quite comfortable for four people even it wasn't too big.

'Would you like a drink?' John asked, 'we bought a rum and whiskey.'

'I'll have a whiskey but show us the book as it is very interesting,' Captain answered.

Alice gave him the log-book, the same one in which the photo she found and Captain looked at it very carefully for some time then he passed it to Oscar telling. 'Look at it and perhaps we will come to some conclusion.'

'Well, I have to study firstly before I would say anything but let me see,' he answered and took the book.

John put a map on the table and said, 'I think that if my father took the photo the place has to be somewhere here. If he really took it because it is possible that the photo was here just incidentally.'

'It is possible but perhaps we'll never know it,' Captain answered.

'He was very lucky because to take a photo like this one it might happen once a life only,' said Oscar.

'I am thinking how many lives we'll need to see UFO and when you will decide to call us back from the sea,' John laughed while putting drinks on the table.

'I am far from asking you to see UFO but there is nothing too loose but actually I don't know why you have to go sailing if I have to be honest.' Captain said that a little sadly.

'Inspector,' Oscar's voice sounded with excitement, 'you can be sure that if I know how to sailing, I would go even now.'

'John,' said Captain and waited for a moment then he continued. 'You don't know but one of our agents is on the farm, the same about which you have told us and is searching for some information. He made a call to me and said that very heavy trucks passing the farm but it isn't all and you might be very surprised if I'll tell you that the owner of the yacht we are interested with most probably stays in India.'

'Does he selling the yacht?' Alice asked.

'Not at all, we put an advert in the paper so we have possibility to search it.'

'Isn't the same man who was killed?'

'We are not sure as there wasn't possible to identify the body.'

'Did you get any information from India? I've been asking Indian's police,' asked John.

'They sent something but nothing that we can learn from it. Most probably we have to check our self.'

'Why are you steering at me?' Alice asked. I have enough of travelling and after my present trip I will need a brake, for sure.'

'To be honest, I've been thinking to send you over there but if you are going sailing then we'll need to wait for a while,' Captain answered smiling.

They have had a long conversation as there were many matters to discus. Independently from UFO case they came to conclusion that the killing is connected with arms or drug trafficking.

Just before they had to leave Alice said to captain that she has a microfilm which he might need and it made John very angry so he didn't said a word on the way home. After his mother has greeted them John started talk again so she couldn't suspect the real visit of Alice.

Chapter 14

Robert watched the man sitting behind the desk who started to express the anger and didn't look the same as before.

'This is over! I will not accept this nonsense any longer,' he shouted for a while then he pressed a button on his desk. A moment later very noisy sound of sirens broke the air.

'Enough is enough!' He shouted when to the office came very tall man and asked.

'What is the alarm about?'

'Look what happened, he lost his memory. Now, now was here a man and I thought that you sent one of your doctors but mean time he injected him some shit and all is left from Robert's memory is to remember about fucking smoke.'

'I do not understand how it might be possible that anybody is able to do sabotage in our place.'

'Me eider but there is no time for conversation. You have the command and find the man. Independently of that you have to give Robert into somebody's hands so we might be able to know what shit he has inside. That's all Max and now go and start to do whatever you need to do, and Robert will wait here for attention one of your doctors but you have to inform me about it.'

'Ok sir,' said Max and left the office.

Suddenly the man changed his attitude towards Robert and asked him softly. 'Would you like a cigarette, Robert?'

'Yes, please,' he answered and took a box from the desk.

'Tell me please, do you know your name?'

'Yes sir, I am Robert.'

'Do you know where you are?'

'Of course that I know, I am in the office.'

'Tell me please, what are you doing here?'

'I do smoke my cigarette.'

'Robert, do you know where have you been yesterday?'

'No sir, I don't know. I do not remember.'

'I can't understand how it could be possible that you know that you need a smoke but you don't remember where you've been yesterday.'

'I don't know it sir but I like smoke very much.'

'Do you know how did you come here?'

'I don't know.'

'I really believe that that illness of yours will be for short while only and soon your memory will come back, and we will have possibility to have a chat again.'

Robert didn't give any answer as he didn't know anything else except smoking. For some unknown reason the other man gave him an injection in such way that except very strong hunger of nicotine he didn't fell any need.

'I think that you have to go so I could carry on with my work. Shortly to the office came a soldier and Robert left together with him.

'Remember that this is our very important visitor and has to be treated with high attention. Anything he will need has to be given to him, food coffee, cigarettes and whatever else.'

'Yes sir,' answered the soldier leaving the office. Soon they walked through the passage and stopped in front of one of many doors. The soldier opened the door to a room or could say that it was an apartment.

'Sir,' said the soldier, 'here you will find anything you'll need and I am giving you my cigarettes but I will come back just now with another box. If there will be anything you'll need just pick up the phone and I will answered immediately.'

'Thank you very much,' Robert answered and as soon as the soldier left the room, he lit a cigarette and stopped in front of a coffee machine. He watched it with interest until the soldier came back.

'Sir,' he said, 'here are the cigarettes for you. Sir Bernard said you are very important visitor so here is the best quality I can get.'

'Thank you. Could you tell me what is it?' Robert asked pointing coffee machine.

The soldier looked at him for a while then he shrug his arms and said. 'This is a coffee machine and it is very simple to use it.' He set up the machine and said to Robert. 'The coffee will be ready just now and if you will need a hot meal just pick up the phone, please but now I have to go.'

'Thank you,' Robert answered. The soldier left and he came close to the door. He tried to open it but it was locked. He held the handle for a while then on the wall appeared a big screen with Sir. Bernard and Robert turned into his direction.

'Where would you like to go? You lost your fucking memory but you still know that you have to go but where. Do you know where, you bastard?'

Chapter 15

Alice was glad that the funeral is over and finally come the time that she will leave the place and stop to play game with John's mother. On the day that they have to leave for the sea very early morning the whole family gather in the yacht club. Mrs. Carol stood quietly as she really loved Alice from the first moment and it was perhaps the reason of shining tears into her eyes.

Actually it was most difficult time for Alice as suddenly she understood what painful it might be for John's mother if she will know the truth. Suddenly she understood a purity of mother's love to her son and that worries her a lot.

The yacht was ready for the race but John still was checking if everything ok. Perhaps he rather tried to avoid any conversation. He knew the feeling of his mother and somehow he knew that his mom suspects that there isn't everything between him and Alice as suppose to be. Even Paul seemed to have questions and his body language shows that he does not believe that Alice came with normal visit. Most of the time John had feeling that he looks a comedian rather and not a serious man who came to attend his father funeral. Alice stood dressed with white crew-like jersey and white jeans nervously looking at John then she asked when he will start the motor as she liked to leave as soon as possible.

'Well, there is no motor on this yacht.' John answered with smile then added. 'I thought that after the time you spent already on the yacht you know about it. You should know by now that the yacht is prepared for solo sailing.'

'What shall I do?'

'I'll be working with sails and you have to be on the helm.'

'You must be joking.'

'No, I'm not. All you have to do is to follow commends and I hope that you understand me very well.'

'I am not too sure.' Alice's voice sounded very softly.

'One you have to remember, any commend has to be obey right after it was given to you. It is really important that all you have to do what you've been asking for and another thing is that there is nothing like, "oh, I thought that it might be better or I thought something else." It isn't a motor car and rules are n o t the same.'

'Why can't you be on the helm yourself?'

'It's simple you don't know what to do on the deck. If anything will go wrong then we will go back and nobody will force me go on the sea any more. By the way, I am not going to take passengers on race. The most important is that you have to follow my instructions and do not worry about anything else. It is highly important that you have to do exactly what I will tell you.'

'To be honest I am very sorry for that stupid idea and I am not too sure if I shall not to resign from the race right now and go home, even I might be fired from work.'

'Very good idea, so thereafter you might go to some sailing school and learn how to sail under professional supervision but now we are here and we have to leave harbour. All my family is watching us so better listen to me and stop worry. It isn't difficult but you have to follow commends and believe me that everything will be under control at all times. I will tell you when to turn the wheel and when to stop it.

'John, I am really worried.'

'Well, it was your idea, don't blame anybody. Are you ready?'

John once again he shook his brother hand, and gave warm hug his mother, and Paul's kids. Paul gave him the bowline and the yacht stared slowly to move backward. The wind helped a little as it blows from the front.

'Now turn the wheel slowly to the right. Not too fast, very gently. Ok, enough.'

They passed slowly the neighbour's one and at the same time John asked to turn the wheel to the other direction. For a short moment they stopped in standstill. Now they moved away from the other yacht. He worked very quickly on sails and suddenly all three sails of beautiful ketch caught the wind and they moved forward. John came to Alice and put his hand around her arm. She sighted at him surprisingly and he said.

'That's for them as they shouldn't be worried too much.'

They stood and waved to John's family. Alice looked at Mrs. Carol and tears came to her eyes. It wasn't too pleasant but who know what different people think in situations like this one.

'Your first manoeuvre was ok but soon we have to stop for departure and I hope that you have your passport on you.'

'Yes, I do have,' she answered softly and asked. 'Don't you think that it will be much better if you will take the wheel?'

'Don't you think that all what you did was to move the wheel a little from one side to the other? I told you that you have to follow instructions and the yacht will go to the right direction. If it will be possible I will explain to you how it works but now try to fell how the steer works and relax.'

'I will do whatever you will tell but I am stressing a lot.'

'There is no need to stress. If there will be more people on the yacht, I can promise you that I'll be sitting and doing just nothing.'

'Don't you understand that I am for the very first time on the sea?'

'Look, stop worried because whatever will go wrong it will be my fault only. Any mistake or any wrong manoeuvre, I'll be the only responsible and don't think that I will destroy my father's yacht or to risk your life.'

'I am not too sure if I will go sailing.'

'Too late,' said John and added. 'Turn the wheel to the left, ok. Now, do you see that point over there?'

'Yes, I do.'

'Ok, straight the wheel and try to keep the course on that point. There are no other yachts so you don't need worried. You will need to turn a little one or the other side but do it very, very slowly. There will be a need to turn to the right but only when I will tell you and again, not too fast.'

'We shall have an engine.'

'Turn a little to the right there is no time for conversation so I go to work with sails before it might be too late.' John ignored her and left her alone on the helm.

They sail through the canal which now turned slightly left. Not far from the turn on the right hand side there stood a coast guard soldier together with custom officer watching as they were coming to them closer and closer. John said to Alice.

'Just now but not yet and wait until I'll tell you when but this time you'll have to turn the wheel very fast. I mean really fast.'

'Ok,' she tried to say something but it was too difficult at the time.

'Now turn, turn. Ok, don't worry, you're ok.'

The yacht turned to the right and suddenly all the sails stopped their work. John looked at them for a moment and gave the rope to the coast guard without even throwing it.

'Good morning sir,' said the guard and added. 'We thought for a while that you will run away. As far as I remember the old man used to come here with one or two sails but you came with fully rigged yacht. It was beautiful and I have to tell you sir that all the yachts are coming here using engines.'

'To be honest I was a little afraid but I still believe that there is no need to have an engine.'

'Sir, nobody can do it better. I am very impressed.'

Alice was listening to the conversation and looked at John. She stood on the helm very worried at all the time and now only she understood what John was telling her for a few times. Now she knew that he was the one who sailed the yacht.

'How could I know when to turn the wheel?' She asked herself.

After they received stamps in their passports and John took the rope from the guard the yacht started to move slightly backward. 'Turn a little to the right but not too much,' he said to her. 'Ok, keep as it is now.'

John took the jib sail and shifted as far to the right as he could. The bow moved slowly to the left and he set quickly sails. Then he asked Alice to turn to the left. The yacht suddenly caught the wind and moved forward. Alice looked at the two men as they started to clap their hands. She experienced something which was beyond her imagination. John asked to move a little more to the left and the yacht moved faster on the water. Their bow moved slightly up and down as the pier was already behind them. After all the sails have been set properly he came to her and said.

'Now the race began. I have to tell you that you did very good job. I have never thought that you could be as good as you were. All sails in place and now we to check if our course is the same as the one on the log-book. One thing will be different for you by now there is no point on which you could to keep the course. Now you have only compass. Remember not to move the wheel too fast because you will go from side to side and sometime the sails might stop work. I'll be soon back so good luck'

'John.'

'Yes, I am listening.'

'You have told me that you don't know sailing but from the conversation I have had possibility to listen I think that you are the master. I feel like a fool.'

'Perhaps, I would say for sure you didn't see a good sailor. By now what you need is to know where the wind blows from.'

John left her alone on the helm. He made a note on the log-book then he checked again if their course is the same as his father was. There was another steering wheel and the compass in the cabin so he didn't worried too much about Alice on the helm. After his job was completed he came back to her and said.

'I see that you are doing very well but I can change you by now so you might be able to make coffee.'

'I have to tell you that all the things are very excited.'

'Do you know which side the wind blows from?'

'I think,' Alice stood surprisingly for a while then she ended. 'Actually, I don't know.'

'You will now do not worry but right now I am looking forward to have coffee, please.'

After Alice went to the cabin, he stood on the helm for a while then he set autopilot and went to the cabin as well.

'And now, what happened?'

'Nothing, I told you many times that the yacht is prepared for solo sailing so how do you think my father went on the sea alone. Do you think that he never went sleep?'

'Ok,' she answered and put two coffee mugs on the table then added. 'Please, here is the coffee.'

'I came down to show you that our course is the same as the one in the log-book.' John set down by the table and took a sip of coffee then he lit a cigarette. They set quietly for a while then he asked Alice to go to the chart table. He explained a little about the notes on the map and in the log-book.

'As you see for our race we have a new map so no lines will be mixed but as you can see the course is the same. In other words we are sailing according to your wishes, commander.'

'Don't be silly.'

'I'm not.'

'I've been listening to you about our route and even it seems to be quite simple I think that you spent many hours to know all this things.'

'At this time we are using satellite navigation system so it is not difficult at all.'

'How we will know when to change our course?'

'Please do not ask me stupid questions because I've been talking to you for half hour and it seems that you didn't listen to me at all. I don't know when because all depends on the wind and our speed. Perhaps it will take two or three hours. It might be more. It is possible that the wind will change direction so we have to go on another course as well.'

'I rather drive a motor car.'

'To be honest whenever I am driving motor car I have a dream to be on the sea.'

'You must be joking.'

No, I am not. The traffic is very similar but nobody is as much aggressive as you can see the people on our roads. I would say on the roads of the world.'

'I wouldn't be so sure.'

'Is it? How many times did you speak on the phone about just nothing and thereafter drove your vehicle using hooters because suddenly you realised that your time is limited and on top of that you don't know what to do first, change the gear, carry on with your make up or answer a call.'

'I've got automatic motorcar and the rest does not affect me at all.'

'John, you are trying to tell me about my driving or any other irresponsible drivers if at the same time as we talk, you are sitting here cicely and do not know what is going on around us. Perhaps another yacht or ship is near by? How do we know?'

'Look here you should know that this is a radar and I have to see what's going on at all times so don't think that we are going blindly forward.'

'Still I do believe that the road is safer and easy as well,' Alice wouldn't give up.

'It might be easy but not safe. Just think that if here I know that I have a right, before I will do anything, I have to take into consideration that the other yacht or ship is aware that I have the right. I have to consider that the other ship is not facing some problems with manoeuvres or perhaps the all crew is sick and there is nobody who can drive the ship. Finally I have the possibility to have a conversation on radio. On the road drivers think about themselves. They think that each and every one of them is a navel of the world.'

'What will happen after we will be gone sleep?'

'Practically there should be somebody on the helm at all times and it is the reason that we have to split into two watches so the yacht will be never left alone on the sea.'

'You still confuse me, once you are telling that your father went sailing alone then you are telling that we have to split into two watches. It was you who told me that your father slept as well.'

'Look, solo sailing is always risky but you have to remember that there are very big ships on the sea and sometime they cannot even see a small yacht during night time. By the way, didn't you tell me that you will see how the sailing looks alike?'

'Yes, I did.'

'Well, in other words you have the possibility to learn sailing and to look for the UFO of yours. Nobody will disturb you, just you and the ocean.'

'Wait a second. Are you trying to tell me that I have to be alone on the helm over the night?'

'Exactly,' John answered shortly.

'I don't think that it is possible. How should I know what to do?'

'You will know when the time will come. I have to go, sorry.'

John left the cabin and sat by the steering wheel. After a while Alice came to him and asked.

'John, do you think that I can take some photos?'

'Sure that you can, I thought that you made a use from this secret camera long ago.'

'John, I would like to take some photos of the sea.'

'I don't mind at all and you can take any photos you like to.'

'John, do you think that the yacht can be a little straight?'

'No, it has to be as it is,' John answered smiling.

'Look, I am sorry but I was doing my job.'

'I do understand that you have to do the work but if you are asking for cooperation then there is no need to take secretly photos. This isn't any partnership and I think that you should take some photos of our log-book just in case that something will go wrong.'

'To be honest, there is a need for proper documentation of the race but now I would like to take private photos which I might be able to show my family.'

'I told you already that you can do whatever you like to do. By the way, I have forgotten my coffee, would you mind to bring it, please.'

Alice left the cockpit and soon came back with coffee. She stood for a while and asked, 'John, what are we going to do here?'

'I thought that you know that awe are sailing.'

'I do know but except that because I do not know how we have to spend our time together.'

'I think that I have told you that there is a need to have two watches so how do you think will you stay on the helm if you do not sleep during the day. There is another matter you have to know, the person who is out of duty has to work in the galley. It is very important to have a proper food and on time. There are rules which even a solo sailor shall to obey. By the way I think that is coming time for breakfast and if I am on the helm you have make it. I know that we have had a snack before we left but I think that now is time for a proper one.'

'Of that I will do it but let me to take the photos firstly.'

Alice was busy taking photos and looking at John's town which was still visible behind their stern. The view awoke nostalgic thoughts. Suddenly she thought that still could see his mother standing with tears in her eyes.

'I enjoy the view,' she said.

'I'm glad to hear it.'

'Do you have any wish?'

'One only, the food has to be eatable.'

'Do you know what I'm thinking about?'

'How could I?'

'I think that the idea with the race wasn't too good because mostly I will listen to your taunts.'

'You can switch on the radio in stand listen to me and it will be very good because I will know all about the weather.'

'Ok, I am going to make breakfast.' Alice left the cockpit but she came back shortly and asked. 'John, shall I cook some eggs?'

'It doesn't matter, is up to you.'

'Ok, I will cook the eggs but would you like soft eggs?'

'I told you that it doesn't matter.'

Alice went back to the galley but not for long because after a while she came back with another question. 'John, I thought that perhaps you like an egg well cooked.'

'Excuse me but once again I'm telling you that it doesn't matter.'

'I really do not understand why you can't tell me what eggs do you like.'

'Because I do not know,' John answered with irritation.

'I have never seen someone who doesn't know what egg he likes.'

'Listen, the egg has to be tasty, that's all. Perhaps I don't like eggs at all.'

'Why did you buy eggs if you don't like them?'

'Would you like to make a breakfast or not and if not then I will do it,' John answered.

'Of course that I will make it,' Alice sounded confused.

'Then go and do it, and do not look for a company. If it will be an egg which I wouldn't like, I will tell you so you will know for the next time. By the way I like scramble egg,' he finished the conversation.

Alice left for the galley and did not come back before the breakfast was ready. Their first day on board wasn't worse but with the time it became much better even the atmosphere wasn't too good. She kept her watches and when it was possible learned about sailing. John started to look forward while thinking about the spot where his father caught his biggest marlin. Before they left eh bought bait with hope that at list he might have a fun with fishing during the race. They have been on the sea for three days already. The weather was still was very nice with moderate wind.

It was afternoon. John stood on the helm and looked at the ocean. They had very good sailing conditions as the wind was still the same but he looked around with some irritation. He left the cockpit and entered the cabin.

'Did you listen to the forecast?'

'Yes, I did and they said that they don't expect any weather changes during next twenty four hours. A long time forecast doesn't expect any changes as well,' Alice answered softly.

'Did you write it in the log-book?'

'Yes, I did.'

John left the cabin and set down by the wheel. He lit a cigarette and looked at the ocean. He started sailing in very early ages together with his father. Later on he joined a navy yacht club and there he became a skipper. During the time spent sailing he has learned that a respect has to be paid to the sea at all times. Now he reminded the time when he made his skipper's rank and went back to the cabin.

'It is possible that I have forgotten a lot about sailing but one which still is on my mind I will never forget.'

'What is it?'

'Sailing is the only school to learn delegation.'

'What do you mean?'

'A delegation is something which is needed to be a good manager and to become a skipper you have to keep control over the situation and how to use your crew members at all times. Oh yes, many people shall look at sailing a little differently and see that on the sea they can learn basic skill of management which is delegation.'

'Which means I can not be a manager yet,' Alice came up with a conclusion,

'Perhaps not yet but you are on good track. You have learned a lot but let me go up.'

John left and Alice started to think about his speech. The time they have spent together didn't put them closer at all. She kept her duty and tried to learn as much as she could. Though John wasn't too kind with her, he posses a gift which allowed him to teach other people sailing in such manner that they have to fall in love with sailing for ever and with Alice was the same. Very quickly she feels a need to know everything about the art of sailing and it was perhaps the reason that she accepted John's sadness.

He spent sometime on the helm and went back to the cabin saying. 'Listen, I need you on the wheel for sometime.'

'Don't you see that I am cooking?'

'I see but all you have to do is to switch off the stove and leave it for later. Make it quick because I'm waiting.'

Whatever Alice could say about John she knew that he is serious about their race but before he left the cabin she asked. 'I so not understand what's wrong, the weather is very nice.'

'I don't like the sea and I need you to be on the helm until I'll change the main sail.'

'What if you could be alone on board?'

'As far as I remember, I have told you something about rules on a ship so stop talk shit and do it.'

'Ok,' she answered and after she switched off the stove she left the cabin and took over the steer. Alice looked at John who worked by main sail. After he finished his job he came to her and said.

'I think that the jib should be changed as well.'

'You are telling such way that I shall to give you advice. I do not understand you at all. I think that you know very well that the weather is very beautiful and one what I can tell you is that my biggest wish is to be back home.'

John didn't wait to until she finished but went to change the jib sail. Alice looked at him surprisingly as he moved on the deck very quickly. Shortly the sail was changed and the yacht was ready for storm. He came back to her and said.

'Look at the sea.'

'I do look but at the same time I'm looking at you and do not understand anything.'

'Don't you?'

'No because there is no difference between yesterday and today. I see the same ocean as before and even more calm then before.'

'Aha you noticed it. The forecast didn't say anything about a storm but somehow I can feel that the ocean looks like lifted up. Strange,' he kept silence for a while and then continued. 'It's really strange I have never ever seen something before. I you could be a little longer on the helm I will make coffee for us.'

Alice didn't answer as he didn't offered coffee since they started the race. He stood for a while then he left. She looked at him totally confused and even more after he came back with two drinks and said.

'The coffee machine is sat up but before it will be ready I brought for us drinks. You can have some rest and I will change you on the helm.'

It didn't take long and few sips Alice asked, 'Shall I check if the coffee is ready?'

'Sure that you can, it is still my watch.'

'Do you think that I can finish cook?'

'I'm not too sure I think that it will be better if we'll wait for a while.'

'It seems that you might be right about the weather,' Alice said after she came back with coffee. 'I don't understand why is as much quite.'

'Didn't you heard that before a storm or even very strong wind there always is very quite?'

'I heard something but never have experienced that type silence. You prepared the yacht for a storm but waves are even smaller then before'

'I am not too sure that it will be a common storm because it seems that very heavy wind is on the way.'

'Shouldn't we hope that it will go away?'

'Sure that we can hope but it looks that firstly it will blow and I think that it will happen very soon.'

John wasn't mistaken because suddenly the wind became very strong and in every moment was stronger and stronger. He went sailing during heavy storms but it was his very first experience as he never seen a storm like this one. The ocean became really violent. Alice who never experienced any heavy wind on the sea firstly was fascination and she thought even to take some photos but suddenly she fell that she has difficulties to stay on her feet.

'We have to change our course a little but it still will be close to the original.'

He turned the wheel and after he set the new course said, 'you have to stay for a while because it is important to make a note in the log-book and mark the new course on the map.'

'Ok,' she answered shortly.

This time to be on the helm wasn't too easy. The ocean started to be more and more violent. Very high waves went through the deck so Alice had to hold strongly steering wheel but mostly to secure herself rather but not to keep the course. The yacht started to turn into different directions and even she tried to do her best it became impossible to stay on the course. Alice couldn't follow the compass and sails moved furiously from one side to the other. She was close to cry but luckily John came back.

'Why are you going around?' He asked and added, 'we facing a magnetic storm as well. Give me the wheel. Why the forecast didn't say anything about the storm?'

Alice kept silence and he added. 'It might be possible that the storm was created because of high temperature. The wind blows from different directions.'

'Perhaps we are not in the place where we suppose to be.' Alice said.

'Of course we are not in right place.'

'I mean that perhaps we are not in the place which is marked on the map.'

'I know what you have on your mind and I'm glad to hear that the whole navigation is just bull shit and we are going nowhere.' John replied sadly.

'Sorry but sometime I do not know where we are except that we are on the ocean.'

'Ok I need you to be more on the helm because I have to drop the main sail and try to keep the yacht in such way that the wind will blow as much as possible from the front.'

Alice looked at him worried as she looked at him while working on the main sail. The job was very difficult as the yacht jumped into different directions. The bow goes up very high then it was fallen down into a hollow between waves. John faced problem to drop the sail even it was already much smaller then the normal.

'What could happen if the wind will stay as strong as it is by now,' came to her mind. She couldn't control the course any longer as she had to grip the wheel to try to prevent from washing herself out off the deck. This situation made John's work even more difficult but finally the sail was down and he came to her.

'It will be much better if you will go down to check for life jackets. Actually do not come back but put the life jacket and stay inside. The storm is getting more violent with every second.'

She was glad to go to the cabin. Very high waves which went over the deck wetted her completely. Now, after she entered the cabin she looked surprisingly around as there was plenty of water. Firstly she thought that there must be a hole in the board but then wave went over the yacht and gallons of water came into the cabin and she understood that the water is coming from the cockpit. Alice started to look for the life jackets waking in deep water when a noisy sound came to her ears. It sounded like an explosion so she stood quietly for a while and listened.

After Alice left the helm John tried to straight the course somehow so the yacht will go into one direction. Never experienced something more difficult as for the first time perhaps he had to prevent himself from washing away by the water. The waves went over the deck covering everything with gallons of the water. It looked like the whole yacht will overturn at any time. It reminded a wild horse trying to free himself from the rider while its bow stood suspended high in the air. The yacht stood in this position for a while then suddenly fell into a deep hollow of the ocean.

John gripped the wheel strongly. Once noise came to him from the main mast and just after that the water took the yacht up. Another wave went over the deck. This time the power was too strong and coming from different direction. Most probably it was the reason that the mast fell down. He saw fallen mast to the side but then the yacht was turned into another direction and the mast went to the place where stood John. It was too late for him to avoid an accident. The mast hit him over the head and just after that he lost his conscious, and fell down next to the console with the wheel. The blood came out of his wounded head like from open tape.

Alice noticed that there is something wrong. She forgotten about the life jackets and tried to go out of the cabin forcing to go to the entrance into deep water. As soon as she went out she straight noticed what made such noise.

'No! John!' She shouted and kneeled next to him. Firstly she didn't know what to do then she checked his pulse. There was no pulse. A high wave nearly washed away both of them from the yacht. Alice spotted a rope and she tied him with it around his waste and around the console. John was bleeding so badly that even waves couldn't wash the blood of his face.

Alice knew that every second is very important. Once again she tried to check his pulse but there was not even sign of it. She pushed him into safer place in the cockpit which wasn't too easy as the ocean became more violent then before and high waves went over them every now and then.

'John! Wake up! Please wake up!' She shouted but couldn't even hear own words which were mixed with the noise of the ocean.

Some time ago she attended first aid courses but it took place in different scenario. Now it was even difficult to kneel next to her casual because of jumping yacht and the water covering the deck. She began CPR and from time to time checking his pulse but there was nothing. She couldn't stop herself from shouting. The hurricane pushed waves from different directions with wild power.

Slowly she became more and more weak. Suddenly she saw John's mother standing next to the yacht on the morning when they left the town. On both Alice's chicks slipped big tears. She couldn't see any longer properly but still worked very hard to bring his life back.

'John, I am so sorry. Please open your eyes,' she screamed without understanding that not long ago she couldn't stand the anger of John's eyes. 'I am so badly sorry,' she repeated and then she fell like something moved under her fingers. With new power she started to carry on with the rescue. After a while she was sure that his pulse works again. Two big tears of happiness went down on her chicks.

'John, wake up! Wake up!' she shouted again and again even couldn't hear herself.

Alice cleaned his face with her white skirt which wasn't white any more as she fell down many times since the hurricane began. She didn't know how long it took before John started to breath again. She still ahs to fight with devastating water to stay next to him. Her face was marked with blood as she blew the air into his mouth. Furious hurricane didn't and their situation was very dangerous.

Suddenly once again she saw face of John's mother who was standing in the same place in front of their yacht. 'I'm sorry,' she looked at John's chest and some hope came to her mind as she thought that she fell some movement under her hand. Now she knew that his conscious must come back. She knew that he has to be alive then came a moment that John started vomiting. She helped his to keep his head in the right position and soon he pulled the air on his own.

It was perhaps most happy moment in her life. With crying voice she started to repeat his name. It took quite long time before he opened his eyes and looked around surprisingly. Alice found that the rope which she used to tie John to the console is long enough so she took it and went to the cabin then tied it around the mast. The cabin was in one big mess but luckily she found some bandages and clothes. After that she went as quickly as it was possible back to the cockpit. She washed John's face and head then she tried to make a dressing on his wounds still worried that one of the waves might take her off the yacht. Finally the dressing was finished but it became quickly red from his blood.

She put a cloth on top of the bandage and looked at him proudly then she said, 'John, wake up. Wake up, please.'

She tried to put him into a sitting position but it was rather impossible as the ocean still was shaking the yacht and most of the time they have been covered with water. After John opened his eyes she asked him repeating her questions. 'John, how are you? John, say something. He reminded silence as he was till in shock and mostly he couldn't hear her voice mixed with angry ocean.

'Would you like anything to drink?' she asked and without any answer she went to the cabin where she found a container with water. He was very weak and only with her help could swallow few drops of the water. 'Sorry but coffee isn't ready yet,' she tried to joke.

John looked around and then asked. 'You did it?' He pointed on the rope.

'Yes, I was worried that you might be gone with the water.'

'Thank you. I must heavy strong hit over my head.'

'You are still bleeding. Would you like some more water? I don't know if there is anything better for you at this moment.'

'A shot of whiskey could be cool but the water is ok as well.'

'There is a big mess but I will try to get you something,' she answered with happiness in her voice and stood up from her knees. The time she was next to John she tied herself with the rope as well but now she loosened the knot. Alice moved toward the cabin and at the same time a big wave hit her from the back so badly that she lost her balance. She fell down still trying to hold anything possible on board but this time the ocean was much stronger, and with gallons of water she flew into the deep wild sea.

John didn't see for a while as he was covered with water but as soon as he could open his eyes again in a split of a second he realized that he is alone on board. It was a flesh when he could see Alice taken out of the yacht. He has forgotten about any pain and weakness. With difficulties he tried to lose the knot made by Alice.

'Shit, I must teach her proper knots,' he thought and then another thought came to his mind, 'if I will meet her in heaven.'

Chapter 16

'I don't know,' Robert answered softly.

'You have to remember that there is no way back for you, Robert. Do you enjoy your cigarette?'

'Yes Mr. Bernard.'

'How do you now my name?'

'The soldier was telling your name sir.'

'Sorry that I didn't introduce my self to you but I have simply forgotten. You have to enjoy our coffee and the time.'

The screen went off the wall and Robert stood in the room a little surprised. He poured himself coffee and set down by the table. At the same time in the office sir. Bernard watched the monitors and the soldiers running in different directions as the action goes on. Sir Bernard looked at the screens and thought about Robert who picture appeared on the wall screen as well. He watched as the room entered a soldier together with Albert who said.

'Hi, I am Albert and since now on I'll be your doctor and one you have to remember that except me nobody is allowed to give you any medicine or injection.'

'Why do I need a doctor?' Robert asked with surprise.

'You have lost the memory and this is quite serious matter. Firstly I will take your blood for test but soon after I have to take a piece of your muscle as well.'

'Why would you like to take my muscle?'

Suddenly on the screen appeared a screen with sir. Bernard and said, 'Listen Albert, before you will do anything I need to have a word with you and be so kind and come to my office.'

'Ok sir,' answered Albert.

After he entered the office sir Bernard told him to have a sit then he asked.

'I hope that you now why I have called you here.'

'To be honest not really,' answered Albert.

'Don't tell me that you lost your memory as well,' sir. Benedict.

'Seriously I don't have any idea.'

'Do not make me fool and try to tell me that you don't remember what happened in India.'

'Sir, you know very well that it was just an accident and incidentally I cut myself. It has nothing to do with Robert.' Albert was talking very quick.

'It is your point of view but I know and I do believe that I am correct that it was your ignorance that you cut your hand.'

'I cannot agree with you sir.'

'Don't say anything because this accident of yours created all the problems we are facing right now. Do you understand?'

'Sir, I cannot see any ignorance in this incident.'

'But I see do you understand? I, Bernard tell you that and there is no need for any further discussion. Firstly it wasn't too easy find proper people to create clones then after your incident the trouble began. Our clones have been killed, the people in India broke up and Lisa's husband started with his experiment how to use silicon as a fuel. Do you need more?'

'It cannot have any connection with my accident.'

'How could you explain that Albert works with silicon?'

'Well, it could be very difficult to explain but there is slight possibility that my accident has some connection with the matter.'

'Now you are telling me completely different thing but even without that I knew that somehow you did transfer your knowledge into Albert's system. By the way, you have started with a project about the same matter we are talking about right now. If I am not mistaken it began few months ago so what can you say about it?'

'Sir, we are working on the matter but you have to remember that every day thousands people have blood transfusion but never ever together with blood information has been transferred. Our research is all over the world and it seems to be a job without any end.'

'Perhaps you are right in this matter but still I am not too sure if in this case it was possible to transfer information as well. At this moment we don't know who injected shit into Robert's system and for sure they possess much higher development then us so we are facing big problem. We have no idea who is destroying our job and for this matter we need Robert.'

'Sir, one you have to remember that I am a doctor only and I have very little knowledge about other matters.'

'Well, many matters which have been impossible in the past are very simple by now, on the earth as well.'

'Sir, for me the matter is very simple, Albert looked at the sand and very strange idea came to his mind, why cannot use silicon as a fuel. Sooner or later people will find out how to do it.'

'Perhaps but personally I am not too sure that all the information did not came from your blood.'

'Perhaps but I am not too sure if incidentally Albert didn't received more information from you. Well, this is history and what right now important is how to find who every now and then is destroying our job. Something more is important, they can find out about things which they never should know.'

'Sir, every time I do work, I try my best and this time will be the same,' said Albert hoping for an end of the conversation. 'The fact that Robert lost his memory means that someone has a reason to destroy our job.'

'In other words I do understand that you will seriously and work responsible.'

'Sir, what are you going to do with Robert after we will recover his memory?'

'It isn't important but is possible we'll keep him on the farm if there will be some need to use him again for any other type of experiment. Go and do your job, please.'

Chapter 17

John realized that the situation. Somehow he shifted himself to the stern. There was an anchor on the stern which his father used mostly for fishing purpose. John took it out and cut the rope. He threw it into the cockpit and tied the rope around his waste. Down in the ocean he saw for a moment something which he thought is Alice and with a new power he jumped over the railing. He flew down into the ocean and thousand of thoughts came to his mind. First what came to him was the other side of the rope which was running fast from the winch. He saw the winch turning and suddenly he saw the end of the rope flying off the deck.

'It will be very quick finish for both of us,' he thought and then he reminded a similar situation in on of the harbours he visited many years ago. John saw himself throwing the rope which sank quickly in the canal.

'The other knot was worth a bottle of whiskey but if this one is lose then it will cost two lives,' he thought. 'Why I didn't check it?' he asked himself. 'The winch can be block it self,' another thought came to him. 'At list we'll die together.'

Suddenly he asked himself, 'where is she? Why I cannot see her? Well, it will be quick finish for two.'

At the same moment he hit the water luckily at the place where Alice was and both of them dive deep into the ocean. They stayed in the water for quite long under water and John started to swallow salty water. Alice was already unconscious and lost her breathing long ago.

The water of the ocean pushed them up of its darkness perhaps to teas them and to give them the last possibility to see the world. It is known that some respect is paid to those who strong and John has been given a chance to pull a fresh air into his lungs. At the same time the rope on the winch reached the end and John feel strong pain as he was pulled into another direction. The pull of the rope was so strong that he nearly lost Alice from his arms. He held her strongly and for some time he couldn't anything else as the yacht pulled them into different direction, and he couldn't have any control of their movement. John had difficulties with breathing.

'I can't lose you now I cannot because if I will lose you now it will be impossible to catch you again in this boiling water.' John gripped her and nothing else he could do.

'Why cannot she hold me a little?' he thought while he started to feel his injury as well. 'Well she isn't conscious I can forgive her but fuck she looks like a woman making love and avoiding touches her partner for unknown reason.'

Whenever they went out of the water he tried to tie a rope around Alice's waste but unfortunately the rope was a bit too short. The other thing was that he held her with his both hands and if he will to freed one hand then it was possible that she might be gone. John faced very difficult situation because it was clear that he has to tie her urgently and at the present moment it was for him the most important matter because it could be the only solution to safe her life.

It wasn't easy but finally both of them were tied with the rope and after short brake John could begin to start with her breathing.

'I cannot wait until we'll be back on the yacht,' he thought and after a while another thought came to him. 'If we'll be there sometime with Father's help.'

The hurricane didn't slow down and around them was still boiling water which covered them every now and then. John carried with rescue until Alice started to breathe again. Practically she was still swallowing the water and her breathing was irregular but he thought that it will be waste of time if they will be too long behind the yacht.

John started to pull the rope but it was really difficult as Alice was in front of him and his movement was limited to minimum as he had to pull the rope behind her back. It took him long time but finally the yacht became visible. Of course from time to time only but it enable him to see the distance and keep in hope. It gave him extra power. He understood that he might lose rapidly his power and it worried him a lot. He tried to be as quick on the board as quick as possible but he pulled the rope very slowly. Though that there was more and more rope behind him. It came to his mind that if he could have a loop on the rope it will give him possibility to have a little rest. It took him some time but finally there was a loop on the rope and he was really happy to insert his foot into and rest for a while.

Suddenly John reminded the day when he went fishing together with his father on the river at the time he was still very young, perhaps nine or ten. The river was wide and they took a boat to go to the other side. There was no puddle on the boat only two long poles which nearly could reach the bottom of the river. A few days before they went fishing there was heavy rain and the water very deep. They came to the place that the poles couldn't reach the bottom and it was the reason that the stream took them down the river and his dad lost control over the boat. They turned around into different directions and suddenly they were close to the bank with trees. John was pushed on the bottom of the boat by his father who told him, 'lie down and don't move.'

Now somewhere on the violent ocean John saw himself in a square boat and looking at his father's face. He could hear even noise of braking tree's branches growing by the river. 'What am I thinking about?' he asked himself then he sight at Alice then he was lucky to see their yacht which wasn't further than thirty foot. Sudden pull of the rope brought him back a little to the reality but then he saw again the story from many years ago.

Once again he saw himself again with the boat. 'John, keep going. We have to keep going, we cannot lose the boat.' He heard voice of his father.

'What's wrong with me?' He asked himself and gripped the rope much stronger. With hard moves he pulled the rope and soon they were not too far from the stern of their yacht.

'Don't worry,' he said to Alice but surely she couldn't hear him.

They were behind the stern but now it started to be more dangerous then before. High waves moved the yacht up and down so he had to pay attention that no one of them will be hit by the board. Suddenly he felt strong pain with any movement. Some invisible power tried to take the rope from his hands. It was clear for him that is losing his power. Now he knew that there is no time to be wasted especially that right now the Father gave the possibility to save their lives.

John understood the situation and after he saw right moment then with some acrobatic move he caught the railing of their yacht. Wild waves covered them every now and then but he tried to push her on the deck. John felt cramp in the arm which he held around the railing. During the battle he lost a lot of blood and now he was weaker and weaker. He sighted at Alice and said; 'don't worry,' but she couldn't hear him for sure. They've been suspended behind the yacht and suddenly Alice started vomit on his chest. He moved his face slightly to the side and said to her, 'no problem.'

At the same time another high wave went over the yacht covering everything. John's hand was already very weak and he wasn't strong enough to hold both of them. He opened widely his eyes trying while using all his power to hold to the railing and prevent to fall into the ocean but then another high wave threw them away from the yacht and then they flew together into deep water of the ocean. Once again they went deep under the water like two bags thrown without any mercy.

'A sailor belongs to the sea,' John thought and another thought came to his mind, 'At least I've two loops on the rope.' Suddenly they have been swollen by the ocean.

Chapter 18

Since John went to attend the funeral of his father Oscar mostly worked with Captain Robertson and he was rather a visitor in own office. This morning on the way to the office he thought about the time, which he spent together with John and about sailing as well.

'Isn't it unfair?' He asked himself, 'some people won't go sailing but they have to. I have promise my kids to take them to the lake but until now it is still impossible. The life never goes smoothly.'

Oscar entered the office and surprisingly stopped in the door as Captain Robertson set behind his desk.

'Good morning Oscar,' Captain greeted him while he was still standing in the door.

'I hope that you don't mind to take your place but I couldn't find myself too well this morning so I came here.' Robertson continued.

'Good morning Captain, even I will say that I mind I don't think it might change anything. To be honest, I'm not too often in this office lately anyway. Funny but I'm not feeling too good as well. The whole story changed all my private life completely.'

'What's the problem Oscar? I have never heard any complain from your side.'

'I promised to take my family to the lake but now can have time. When it will change, when the life will be normal?'

'Look, if this is urgent we can make a plan, I don't see any problem. The investigation doesn't go forward anyway. Actually this is the reason that I came here this morning.'

'I wouldn't say Captain that we didn't have progress, Captain.' Oscar answered.

'Well, don't understand me incorrectly, please. We did some progress but there are many questions without any answer. Until now we don't know how it was possible that the films went blank. Of course we know that there is some radiation but too much we know about it.'

'An open lens by the camera will destroy any film and that isn't big deal.'

'My bosses asking for a proper report but I know perhaps a little less then they know. I'm not able to give any report.'

'Many matters are already solved.'

'Not really Oscar. There is a problem with DNA of the victims. Benjamin still stays in the hospital and it has very close connection with the matter but what more, we don't know.'

'I wonder when he'll be realist because last time I was told that he has no blisters on his body any more.'

'There are no blisters on his body but mentally he isn't ok. It isn't too good because from him we could learn a lot about many things.'

'Captain, did you hear anything from John and Alice lately?

'Well this is another story which worries me a lot. Since they left the town I didn't received any call from Alice.' Captain Robertson answered.

'Luckily the weather is very good, I would say is prefect.'

'The weather is perfect but the race is another one because as far as I understand they cannot be friends.'

Captain stood up and went to the wall with a big map. He looked at the map for a while and said, 'according to the log-book they suppose to be somewhere here.' He pointed a place on the map.

'We have to hope that the weather will stay as it is for longer time.'

'The next matter is that there is something wrong with Robert. We lost a contact with him.'

'Perhaps he is facing some problems.'

'I have no idea what problems he might face but there is very urgent need to send somebody over there as soon as possible.'

'Do you think that there might be something wrong for him?'

'I have no idea what problems he might face but it seems to me that we have to send somebody so we will know what is going on over there.'

'I wander what could happen.'

'Well, it is difficult to say but I have such feeling because Robert is highly experienced agent and we cannot lose contact with him. By the way, I think that we have to go once again through all the files we have because there is something missing but I don't know what.'

'Captain, most or I would say that all the files are in your office so I don't understand what can we do here.'

'Well Oscar, perhaps you are right, in this case let go.'

They have been about to leave the office but at the same time came Oscar's boss Captain Paul and said. 'Good morning gentlemen. I thought Oscar that you are no longer working here and now so big surprise.'

'Captain,' answered Oscar, 'if you don't see me here, I am together with Captain Robertson.'

'If I good remember, I've been asking you to be here this morning but it seems to me that you are not interested to say hallo.'

'Captain, we are quite busy lately,' Oscar answered.

'I do believe that you are busy but our situation here isn't too good as well. Actually I have to ask you Captain Robertson, if you people took over the investigation I don't see any point to keep my people.'

'What can I do, Captain.' Robertson answered.

'We have a lot of work but practically one department doesn't exist.'

'Look Captain,' answered Robertson and added, 'you know very well that the case is important for all of us and no one can change that. My bosses are waiting for any result and all I can say they are giving orders and don't ask what we can.'

'I don't know what is the whole story about but what I know for sure is that John should be at work and not on the sea sailing like on holiday. What's going on?'

'Actually we don't know but as soon as we will know anything you are the first one who will be informed, I promise.' Captain Robertson said that with smile.

'What the fuck are you telling me? How it is possible that you are talking such nonsense? Do you think that I have tome for some stupid jokes?'

'Captain Paul,' Robertson started seriously, 'I am telling you the truth and as the truth you have to take it or not. It is up to you but nothing can change the present situation and most probably you have to look for new people.'

'Are you crazy or you trying to fool me?'

'No, I am not but it seems to me that Oscar will not come back to you and this is not a joke for sure.'

'What John is doing on the sea?'

Difficult question but perhaps there will be an answer in the future. By the way, I think that John will not come back to you as well.'

'Listen, this is too much. Right now I am going to take proper steps and then we will see what you will achieve.' Captain Paul was really angry.

'Well, what can I say, I am really sorry but nothing we can change in this case, no one of us. If I have to say anything about John, I am very, very worried. One I can tell you that the case which you handed over to us has some connections with another case which for long time we are busy with. Perhaps there is only a slight connection but there is no way to ignore it.'

'I do understand your position but how I have to do my job? What I shall do after you have told me that John and Oscar will never come back to work?'

'Well, I hope that you will find many good people who will be happy to work for you and will do same job as John and Oscar so I don't see any need to panic.'

'Do you mind to ask you what is happening with John? It isn't common case that right after his dad funeral you sent him on the sea.'

'Well, we have been spoken with Oscar before you came here and we are very concern that since John and Alice left the town they never contact us. It seems to me a little suspicious and I am worried a lot.'

'Captain,' said Oscar who was busy with a coffee machine. 'After Inspector John left whenever I am coming to the office, first what I do is to set up the coffee machine. Do you know Captain that Inspector John is highly skilled sailor? I hope that he will accept my invitation after he will be back so I might to learn from him a lot about sailing.' Oscar's voice sounded excited. He came to the wall and pointed the same place which has done Captain Robertson not long ago and said.

'We suspect that Inspector John and Alice should be somewhere here. The weather is ok and there is nothing to be worried about.'

'Actually,' said Captain Robertson, 'I think that we can make a call to John's home and ask his mother if perhaps she heard anything from him.'

'That's brilliant idea,' said Oscar.

'What? Why are you staring at me?' Captain Paul asked.

'Well, you are his boss,' answered Captain Robertson and added. 'You are the one who should make a call.'

'Oh no, this is too much. You are strictly trying to fool me. What shall I say?'

'Not much, just ask if John phone to her and whatever you like.' Robertson answered.

'Why cannot you make a call to your agent?'

'Sure that I can,' Robertson answered and dialled Alice's number. He held the phone for a while then he gave the phone to Captain Paul. It was clear that her phone is switched off.

'Well, now you have to make a call,' Robertson said and gave the receiver to Paul.

'Ok, let me try his mother but I have no number,' said Paul.

'Here is her number,' said Oscar and gave it to Captain Paul.

After a while he could hear voice of Mrs. Carol. 'Good morning, I am Captain Paul your son John's boss. Firstly I would like to say that I am very sorry about your husband. I do believe that it was painful lost in your life, please take my condolence.'

'I thank you very much,' she answered and asked. 'Is anything wrong with John that you are calling?'

'No, not at all I just like to know if he contacted with you since he left the town. You see Mrs. Carol I know that he is sailing right now but except that that he lost his father and he needs to have a rest but you see at this time of a year we have a lot of work and I thought that you perhaps know when he will be back.'

'Sir, he went sailing with her fiancé and I don't think that they are worried about anything. I have to tell you that she is lovely lady and I love her so much. I am very happy for John, really very happy sir.'

'I thank you very much and wish you nice day.'

Captain Paul took the phone off his ear and covered the microphone with his hand looking at Robertson and Oscar surprisingly but still could hear voice of Mrs. Carol so he said to her.

'Sorry Mrs. Carol but somebody was coming to the office.'

'Sir, tell me please, is there anything wrong with John?'

'I can ensure you Mrs. Carol that there is nothing wrong with John and I have to tell you that I am calling because he is our best investigator and it will be good to have him back here at work. This is the only reason of my phone call. The weather is nice so let them enjoy the race.'

'In other words you like to call him back to work, sir.'

'Not really but if you know anything let me know, please,' Captain Paul finished his call and dropped the receiver then he kept quite a while looking once at Oscar then at Captain Robertson. Suddenly he said.

'Now you have to tell me what a fuck mystification are you producing to me, do you think that I am fool? What fiancé is with him? What are they doing on the sea? Actually I don't need to know anything, you can do whatever you like but one you have to make sure that I must have people to run the department.'

'You don't understand Captain that they had to introduce somehow our agent Alice. What do you think they shall say, hey, this is my body guard and a woman looking if something is not right with me but this is not all because one of our agents is on the sea another one on the farm and suddenly we have to send there another one. Do you think Captain that we have no other jobs to do?'

'If you are sending people on the sea then seems to me that you shall be a little mo responsible. Right now I am facing a case with serial killing and nobody to do the job. I think that I need your help this time as well. Perhaps the case is connected with your case as well.'

'Captain, I cannot promise you anything but let me see if there will be anything I can do for you. I will contact you as soon as I'll be back in my office.'

'Now you are talking with sense Captain.'

Chapter 19

The hurricane still moved massed of the ocean and high waves covered the yacht which jumped up and down like a toy. Once again John held them to the railing waiting for a right moment to push them on the deck. Open wound on his head were bleeding and he felt very weak. This time they had more luck and with some acrobatic movement he pushed Alice on deck.

'You see, you are safe,' he said but situation wasn't too good because the waves tried to wash them away every now and then. With difficulties he went on board as well and very quickly tied Alice with the same rope which has saved their lives.

Suddenly she opened her eyes and looked at John. She couldn't understand what happened. Alice had difficulties with her breath and her sight showed that she isn't fully conscious. John started to fell a cramp in his arm but even that he did not stopped with bringing her to full consciousness. Suddenly his sight went to the ocean. He couldn't believe his yes. Somewhere very deep in the water he spotted a blue light. Firstly he wasn't sure if it is true but then he started to shout at Alice showing blue place in the ocean.

'Look there! Wake up and look! You have to take a photo, Wake up!'

Most probably Alice didn't even hear him. For a short moment he thought about her camera but after he looked at her weak body he resigned. John checked the knot around her waste worried that she might fly again back to the ocean. He thought about the camera once again but then he started to shout.

'Look! Can you see? Wake up!'

John looked at shining light and then he reminded the blue grass on the farm. 'How it could be possible?' He asked himself. 'The same light was in the screen there in the house of the last victim.'

Alice moved her hand and immediately John asked her to look at the ocean but in return he heard only, 'ok, ok John,' and suddenly he thought that she is going to fall asleep.

'No, you cannot do it to me now.' He said nearly shouting and went to the cabin. John found a container with the water and came back to the cockpit. 'Shit, I cannot give you drink that water but any way you might vomit some more but better that then . . .'

John tried to give her the water but she couldn't drink at all. It took some time before Alice opened her eyes and he knew that she is again conscious even she looked at him still like sleepy eyes.

'Did you see the light?' John asked her. 'It was down there but now is gone.'

'No, I didn't see anything but I do believe whatever you tell me. I just do believe.' She answered with soft vice.

'Sorry that you didn't see it, it was fantastic and beautiful.'

'I didn't see but how am I here? How did you bring me back?' Her soft voice was mixed with noise of the ocean as the hurricane was still furious.

'One you have to remember for the rest of your life, never ever give up. Never,' he added and kept quite a while.

'I'll help you to go to the cabin. It will be much safer as the hurricane didn't slow down. These vicious waves might wash us away and this time it could be forever.'

They entered the cabin, which was full with water. It was difficult to move as except the water there was no light. The yacht jumped like young horse covered with high waves.

'There must be a hole somewhere in the board,' said Alice.

'I hope that there is no hole because if there could be one, we will be long ago down on the bottom of the ocean. As soon as we will be in the motion the water will be gone. We have very simple but effective system and . . . but firstly the wind has to slow down and then the water for sure will be gone. Well, the wind has to slow down firstly.'

'What shall I do here, everything is floating,' she asked.

'Nothing, just wait until the hurricane will slow down.'

John left the cabin and Alice tried to do something by the stove. At the same time he tied himself at the helm and surprisingly looked around as the noise of the ocean became much lower. The weather started to change very rapidly. On the sky there were still clouds but waves became much smaller. John felt that the wind started to blow from one direction and wasn't as strong as before. John loosened the knot of the rope which he was tightened with and went to the cabin.

'What happened?' Alice asked.

'I think the storm is over.'

'It is very quite, I cannot believe it.'

'I cannot understand because if I have to be honest it happened too quickly. I have never experienced something like that and never heard about but I'm glad that it is over.'

'What we will do now?'

'I don't know but it seems to me that I have to make some order on the deck and then try to sailing again.'

'If it will be possible, all I like by now is to be back in my home.'

John shrugged his arms left the cabin and stopped on the helm and looked at the compass then at the main mast lying on the deck.

'Luckily the mast didn't damaged anything too serious,' he thought and started to make some order with all the ropes which suppose to hold the mast in vertical position but unfortunately they failed as the power of the ocean was much stronger. Soon he has forgotten about his injuries and with a new power worked on deck. He shifted the broken mast to the foredeck in such way that the top goes far in front of the yacht. He tightened the mast firmly to prevent it movement from side to side and went to the cabin. John looked at Alice surprisingly while she was pouring coffee into the mugs and asked.

'How did you manage to do it?'

'I don't know but I think that you should have a dressing on your head. It's look terrible. Actually you should have some stitches.'

'Not now and for sure not stitches. Thanks for the coffee. Look, we are not jumping any longer and I need your help on top.'

John finished his coffee and put the mug on the table. From the after cabin he took some ropes and went back on the deck. He prepared mast to be tight and after everything was ready he tightened one side of the rope around his waste and the other side to the railing then he said to Alice who came to him.

'Firstly I need you to secure me because I have to go down and I will tight the mast so it will work as a bowsprit and thereafter we might be able to fasten a sail on it.'

'I do not know what is bowsprit but tell me what I shall do.'

'I need to go down and tight the rope on a towing hook and all you have to do is to be here, just in case.'

'What? Are you crazy?'

'No, I am not but you have to be here in case I will need something.'

'I don't think that I need to be here and look like you will risk fall into the ocean.'

'You have no other option if you like go home.' John said shortly.

John went over the railing and slowly moved down. It wasn't too difficult as he made loops on the rope so he could stand while he worked. Soon the mast was tightened and they had a long bowsprit going far out in front of the yacht. After he was back on the deck he said, 'now I must go on the mast.'

'What?'

'I told you that I must go on the mast. It is clear that somehow I have to fasten a sail up there.'

Alice didn't say anything and stood quietly looking at John who in just few minutes was on the top of the mast. There he tightened one extra two blocks and put ropes around them then he came down. Soon after he brought biggest sail he could find and clipped it around the rope between the top of the mast and the top of the new bowsprit. Thereafter he pulled the rope and since then they couth fresh wind into the sail. The construction was a little funny but after he saw that the sail works he stood and looked proudly at hi work then he said.

'Perhaps it isn't highly professional but we still have some possibility for sailing. Never mind that but I have to drop the sail and go underwater once again.'

'What do you mean about that?'

'Could you see that we are not going straight? The steer is blocked and I have to see if it will be possible to fix it.'

'I do understand what you are talking about but it came to my mind what might happen if suddenly the wind will start to blow. What do you think I will do?'

'Look, I have to take a chance and check what could be done so the steer will work again.'

'You are still bleeding.'

'It doesn't matter because I have to go down and you must help me.'

'One I have to tell you that if you really have to go underwater then I'll be better being gone down to the cabin.'

John didn't listened any longer but started to drop the sail and thereafter he secured himself with the rope and jumped into the ocean. Alice didn't feel too good while looking on the mark on the water when he has jumped. He didn't go up for quite long time and she started to be worried. Finally he went up and held himself for quite long time to the board before he went on the deck.

'He steer doesn't work but it is straight. Perhaps I will be able to do something later but at the moment we have to make some substitution.'

'Whatever you say I still not understand what is on your mind.'

John went to the cabin and brought a bucket and said. 'It will be our steer,' then he tightened it with a rope.

'How it will work?' She asked.

'Very easy but you will learn about it after you will start to use it. Now let me pick up the sails.'

After John set up the sails he dropped the bucket into the water behind the stern in such manner that it started to keep the yacht in one direction. There was a silence for a while then John said. 'Now we will if the water will go out from the cabin. Personally I do believe that the pump will work correctly.'

'I don't know anything about it and what I can is to keep quite.'

'I hope that you see that we are going forward.'

'Perhaps we are but I am not too sure about our sailing any more.'

'Well, it wasn't me who asked to go sailing.'

'I know that it is y fault and I am very sorry. Can I say anything more?'

'Do not take it too seriously.'

'Well but how we will know how to go back?'

'Good question.'

'Nothing works on board.'

'I know but the situation is much better then we were there in the ocean,' he said and looked at the sky. The sun went down to the horizon. His sight went from the sky to Alice's face. She had many still bleeding scratches. Her white skirt was now dirty and torn showing scratches on her knees. John looked again at the sky and pointed the first shining star.

'Everything is broken on the yacht but could you see that star over there?'

'Yes, I do.'

'When I was still young boy I watched this star many times and it shined over the ocean which means that if now we will go opposite direction, we should go home.'

'Are you sure?'

'No, I am not,' he answered with smile which little surprised Alice because she didn't see him smiling since they left the town so she asked. 'Why are you smiling?'

'Because I do not know where we are going to and I do not like to know' John answered laughing which made her a little worried.

'Why are you laughing? I don't understand you.'

'Well, it is simple; I don't care where I am going to.'

'I don't know what is so funny and what I think is that we should do something so we will be back as soon as possible.'

John stood up, came closer to her and said. 'Alice, I am very sorry but I was very wrong and now I am asking you to forgive me. You are very brave and you have saved my life.'

'You safe my life and I am very sorry for this very stupid idea about sailing.'

'Look Alice, I need to tell you that you are very beautiful and I have never met somebody like you in my life. I am thankful to the God that he put you on my way and brought into my life. I am very happy that we went sailing.'

'John, I am really sorry,' Alice didn't know what to say.

'On the way to the funeral I treat you very badly but actually I don't mind to have a boss like you.'

'John, I promise that I will never do anything stupid in my life and soon after we will be back I'll be gone immediately home.'

'You didn't understand me Alice. I try to tell you that I am in love with you and this is very serious matter.'

They stood in silence for some time looking each other eyes then she suddenly said.

'John, I think that I am in love with you as well.'

'Wait a minute,' John said and went to the cabin. He came back and said, 'you have too many wounds on your face and they have to be clean.'

John washed gently her face and looked at the tears falling on her chicks. From the first aid box she took a piece of cotton and put on his head where he had open and still bleeding wound. After a while their eyes met again and their faces came closer. Finally their lips met and they stayed for long time in their first sweet kiss.

The sun went down the horizon and the sky became red and the two of them like two silhouette stood on the board connected with kiss of pure love.

'Alice,' said John, 'I would like to you to know that since now on my life belong to you and I hope that the God will help me to be with you for ever.'

'John, my life is for you and the God has to help me to go with you the same way you go.'

'Do you know what is most important in life?'

'What is it?'

'I think that the most important is that a man should never give up.'

'You shouldn't think about it because if not this motto, we wouldn't be here right now. Yes, a man shall never give up and it is very important.'

'Wait a minute,' he said and went to the cabin and came back with a bottle of champagne. 'I have forgotten glasses.' He said and went back. This time he came back not with glasses only but with a warm jersey as well.

'I think that you have to put on,' he said and then he poured two glasses.

John waited until she was dressed with the jersey then he gave her the glass telling.

'For us and our lives and for our love which has to be for ever,' John picked up his glass.

'John it came suddenly and I don't know how it happened but I really love you,' Alice answered and they empty their glasses.

'I like Russians tradition,' he said smiling and trough his glass over into the ocean. Alice did the same and then they hugged each other and kissed. They stood on board for long time then John asked. 'Would you like a warm drink?'

'I'll make coffee,' she answered.

'Do you think that you can do it?'

'Never give up,' Alice answered and they laughed.

After they entered the cabin Alice set up the coffee machine while John worked by the stove. He made sure that there is no leak of gas and was safe to light up.

'I think that there is nothing with the stove and it can be use again.'

'Thanks, since now on whatever you'll say I will believe you.'

'Now we can have warm meal. By the way, the water is nearly gone.'

'I have noticed that but just forgotten to tell about it,' she answered.

'Tell me Alice, are you still in hurry to be back home because I think I am not.'

'Actually I'm not,' she answered smiling.

'In this case we can put the yacht in drift for tonight and tomorrow we can see where we are going to. We can do it even tonight but it isn't too important.'

'We have to go somewhere.'

'I think that we are not too far from our previous course as the hurricane turned us mostly around but is possible that I am mistaken and we are very far.'

'In this case where do you think we are going to?'

'One what I do know for sure is that we need to be in a place where we can get married.'

'John, I told you that I love you and it is forever. Nothing will change it.'

'Perhaps only the God knows how much I am happy to be with you, Alice and I do know that you love me. Though the love I think we have to make it official and that's why I would like to ask you—Alice, will you marry me in the first harbour?'

'I will do it anywhere you wish, John.'

'I need to tell you that I am really sorry that I have threat you as I did. I shouldn't react as I did but you have to understand that I was full of stress.'

'I know John. The most what worried me was your mom. I didn't know how should talk to her and I am glad that since now on I'll be able talk to her and look into her eyes.

'If I look at the matter now I see that you came to very excellent idea with the race. Two things happened, firstly, we are together and secondly we found the spot.'

'What spot?'

'The spot where my father took the photo and I do believe that it was the same unknown reason for us to go on the sea, and for me to drive around the farm even I didn't know if I really drove there or it was a dream only. I'm sorry that you didn't see the light.'

'I'm sorry John but I didn't see any light. I do believe that you have seen but I cannot remember even how you brought me back on the yacht.'

'We were very lucky.'

'What I do remember is how I was taken out into the water. But no idea how it was possible that you could catch me in that boiling water,' Alice looked at his face.

'Sorry to say it again but do you remember, never give up. Would you like more champagne?'

'Why not, it looks like our wedding and it isn't any common wedding.'

'You right Alice, it is perhaps informal wedding but for me it is more important then anything else in my life.'

'John many things happened today but it is most important day in my life as well.'

'Actually as a Captain of this vessel I have to make a special note in the log-book because it is the first wedding on this vessel and I hope that it will be threaten as normal wedding.'

The sun shined already high over the horizon when Alice and John woke up. It could be perhaps too difficult to answer a question how many hours has a night but they could never expect such happiness after heavy hurricane which nearly took away their lives. The yacht was still drifting on the ocean while they still were busy with themselves. It seemed that they have completely forgotten about bad experiences from previous day.

Once the ocean tried to take them for ever into its deep abyss and then suddenly the same ocean gave them pure, beautiful and surely for ever strong love.

'I think,' said John, 'that is the time to start some job but from the other hand nobody can dream even how much I am happy to be here with you.'

'John, my dear, I am very, very happy.'

With difficulties John left the bed and set up coffee machine then he left the cabin and looked outside. He looked at the sun and at his watch. Something wasn't right but firstly he couldn't notice any difference about the time so he shrugged his arms and thought, 'this watch never was late.'

He lit a cigarette and at the same time Alice came to him and said. 'John there is nothing wrong if you will smoke inside.'

'Alice, if I didn't smoke inside before why should I now? You shouldn't be harm with my smoke.'

'I wonder how you managed to keep your cigarettes dry.'

'My father has to teach me some manners and I keep it in my mind.'

'Perhaps the coffee is ready let me go and check.'

'Don't you feel sleep a little longer?'

'Why do you think so?'

'I don't know but I just thought so. Look, I can make a breakfast as well.'

'Do you know what John? Why did you feel in love? I don't think that there was a reason that I am a doll staying in bed until midday and thereafter taking long time to dress up or to use microwave for quick meal while there is a lot of time to make a proper food. If you need a doll then you can buy one in sex shop but I am a normal person, let say a woman. Please don't threat me as a doll John.'

'I am sorry but I am still little ashamed of the past.'

'The past gave us our present and the future. Oh yes, our future started in the past.'

'I love you Alice. Let's go inside to have a breakfast,' said John and they entered the cabin then he said. 'Perhaps I shall check our position.'

'I don't think so,' she answered and added. 'Coffee is ready and we can have it outside so you might enjoy your smoke as well and what is most important we will be together. There is something that is very important and it is that we cannot work for twenty four hours a day.'

'I do agree and I like a lot to be together but there is a need to know where we are.'

'As far as I remember you told me that you can go anywhere and you don't care for how long. Did you change your mind?'

'Actually you right, especially that we could be dead by now but we have to understand that for many years my life was my work and my work was my life.'

'I do understand you very well but now there will be a need to separate work from our private life. Nothing will change the situation if we will know our position even one hour later. It seems to me that time for yacht is work time and if we are off then is private life.'

'I heard something abut this but how to implement it is another matter.'

'I know John that you are the Captain of this vessel and you are the one who has to make sure that we'll be safe home, never mind our wedding but you have to make sure that we have a private life. We have to remember that after the race there will be a need to decide what we'll be doing with our life. Whatever we will be doing there will be a need not to disturb our happiness.'

'As you said I am the Captain of this vessel and I do agree with you to have our coffee outside. I have to tell you that it was most beautiful wedding ever I've seen in my life and you are most beautiful bride.'

'Remember that I still wait for my rings,' she answered smiling.

'Why rings and not one ring only?' John asked.

'I think that I shall an engagement ring and wedding ring.'

'Luckily two only,' he laughed.

'Two because I believe there never will be the third one.'

'What do you mean the third ring?'

'Didn't you hear? The third ring a suffering.' Alice laughed.

'Actually it isn't any joke because after the race we have to decide something about our lives.'

'Firstly will be wedding and then . . .'

'And then?'

'I think we will be officially married and you will be Mrs. Carol.'

'We have to stay somewhere.'

'It will be up to you because you know my house and you know yours so even now you can decide where would like to stay.'

'Well, your house is much bigger but that we can decide later but what is on my mind is what could make any difference if we know our position by now.'

'Not much but if I know where we are I could be more involve into our future. At the moment we are drifting and going nowhere.'

'If I can say anything about the future, I would say that the future is today, right now and not tomorrow. Perhaps we don't know in which place we will find ourselves by the end of this race, perhaps we don't know where we will stay but what I know is that the future is now and we cannot and will never feel a happiness of tomorrow if we cannot feel it at present time.'

'One you have to understand that we don't know anything about the weather and our situation is more then difficult. I cannot be in peace with myself until I will know that you are in safe place.'

Alice stood up and kissed him then she said, 'John, I love you and I do agree that the position is very important especially that nothing works on the yacht but I do believe that if the Father safe us until now He will make sure that we will be back home.'

'I think that you are right. I will check the radio later and perhaps I might do something.'

'What about our position?'

'I think that I like my present position very much and I don't feel to change it.' John answered smiling and kissed her.

'I don't get you.'

'I mean, I like my position next to you.'

'Sometime we will finish breakfast and what we'll do?'

'I'll be still next to you but seriously I have a feeling that we are not too far from our course but a proper position we might be able to find tonight only because at the moment I am not even too sure if my watch goes properly.'

'John, one what I know is that you will take us home.'

'Why are you telling that?' he asked.

'I think that you are the best sailor in the world,' she answered.

'Actually you are the only one so you have to be the best. Oh no sorry, I know another few, one of them is your brother then your son.'

'You have forgotten about Robertson and Oscar,' he laughed then he said. 'I think that if I will set the sails we will go somewhere. Never mind our destination but if we will consider that we are not far from the course then we can carry on into same direction.'

'I thought that we are going into some direction.'

'Since last night we are in drift and of course we are moving slowly but it isn't any sailing. Alice, I would like to show you something,' he said and soon they have been checking the map.

'My point is that we cannot be too far from the curse because the storm stopped shortly after I saw the light and the light wasn't different from the one I've seen on the farm.'

'John, please do not say anything about work.'

'Look, not long ago you tried to push me to say abut the case and now you try to stop me but I'm telling you that the light was beautiful. I cannot believe that something like that can exist in this world. At least I'm sure that our two cases are strongly connected.'

'Do you think so?'

'If we found the place you've been looking for, where do you think we have to go?'

'Home, I think,' she answered.

'Apparently our home is here on board this yacht and I think that it became our yacht.'

'Which means we should have special breakfast,' said Alice.

'If you said so, we will have a special breakfast. Our yacht is our home and I don't think that we can give it away as I thought before. Paul was right saying that his yacht is most beautiful in the world because I do believe that there is no other as beautiful yacht in the world as our one.'

'You are right John, our yacht is not only most beautiful but very special.'

It passed some time and thereafter John set up the sails, and they caught the wind, and they started to continue their journey. Somehow it happened that the course they started to sail with was to the East.

'Our first course was actually set up itself,' said John.

'Where shall we go?' she asked.

'If I could know where we are then it might be possible to say but to be honestly, I don't know.'

They set in the cockpit while Alice asked, 'John, I need to ask you something.'

'Ask me, please.'

'You see, I like to call you as nice as possible but I don't like to sound funny.'

'You are calling me John and actually I like it.'

'John, do you think that I can make a call to Captain Robertson?'

'Why not, I think that we should call him long ago.'

Soon they tried both their mobile telephones but no one of them worked even the batteries where not flat. 'It is strange, perhaps here is no signal. I'm sure that Captain will call us or perhaps somebody else.' John said and he asked. 'It is our special day would you like a glass of champagne?'

'Sure it is really special day.'

Chapter 20

John and Alice enjoyed the time and they seemed to be most happy people in the world and as soon as he estimated their position he asked. 'Do you know what?'

'I don't.'

I think that we are very close from the place which I marked on the map and if it is true we close to nice island.'

'It looks that you like to go there.'

'Why not, it is obvious that we have to go somewhere and wherever it will be, no one shall say a word against because it will be an emergency.'

'It's up to you. You know that with you I can go anywhere you'll ask me to go.'

'All I can tell you is that it is beautiful place and you will love it very much.'

'It seems that you went there before.'

'Yes, I went there long ago with my father.'

'Well, our mission is over and as you said we have to go somewhere.'

After a lovely night they spent another beautiful day. Slowly came an evening and they enjoyed superb food which they prepared together. The yacht was clean and only missing mast and funny sail could say that they went through heavy storm. After the supper John took Alice into the art of navigation. She learned quickly and n the same night she was able to find position on her own and it made her very happy.

'John,' she said, 'now I can see that we are really not far from the place which you've been telling about.'

'If we will be lucky, I mean if the wind will be still the same then some time tomorrow we should be on the island.'

It was about midday of the next day when John heard a plane and asked Alice if she did hear as well. 'John, you are professional sailor so you can spot and hear anything on the sea but not me, sorry.'

After a while they could see a few planes and John said, 'I hope that they are not looking for us so we will still enjoy our honey moon and the nice holiday.'

'I don't think that anyone can look for us, John.'

'Alice, according to my calculation soon we should see the land and then one more hour and we'll see the harbour.' John said and he was right because about one hour later they could see the island . . .

'Soon we will be entering the canal but I reminded something.'

'What is it?'

'We have to know to listen. Listen even small matters because the people have a need to share what they have inside their hearts. Sometime we are looking for an answer and many times it might be many years and we might have the answer. Perhaps if we can understand better the universe we will know that we might have the right answer. Perhaps we are in condition to safe many problems.'

'To be honest I don't understand what you are talking about.'

'No problem, I don't understand myself as well but what I know is that we have to avoid a situation that others asking us to do their washing as it might be possible.' John kept quiet for a while then he said. 'Alice, soon we will be in the canal and it is very important that everything will go smoothly.'

'I am really worried.'

'You shouldn't but anything might happen. This time of a year there are many people on the island. Listen please, the canal turns to the left so the wind will blow from the back. After we will find a place we have to turn around then we will be against the wind. I hope that the bucket will do the job. Just remind cool and believe that everything will be ok.' John kissed her and went to the foredeck. Alice stood on the stern a little worried as she never ever could imagine that she will operate with a bucket in stand of a steering wheel. She didn't know if she has to be happy that she will be on the island or cry and have a hope that everything will be all right as John said. Suddenly John came back to her with a paddle and said.

'Alice, here is a paddle, if you will see that the bucket does not work, you will need to use the paddle.'

'How shall I do it?' She asked.

'The paddle is long enough and all you have to do is to put it into the water on the side in which direction you have to turn and work against the water.'

'Now I am really worried.' Alice answered.

'You will be ok, dear,' he answered and went back on deck.

Chapter 21

Mrs. Carol sat in the launch watching TV when the bell rang. 'It must be Paul she thought and went to open the gate and soon he stopped his car in front of the door, and came inside together with his family.

'Have a sit and I will make coffee, please.' She said.

'Mom,' Paul asked while looking at the TV. 'What is the good news, you have to tell us?'

'You cannot imagine,' Mrs. Carol answered from the kitchen. 'I have had a call from John's manager.'

'Did he ask to come back John to work?' Paul laughed.

'No, not at all, he knew that John went sailing.'

'Then what type of good news did you get? As far as I know bosses rather don't like to say anything good if they are making calls to someone who is on leave.'

'The most important is that he told me that John is the best investigator.'

'Oh yes but John wasn't home so he couldn't call him back to work.'

'Why are you trying to be silly?' his wife asked.

Paul changed the TV canal and looked for a while at the news then he shouted.

'Mom, come here, quickly! What the hell is it? There is John and Alice on board. I know this island.'

What they say?' Mrs. Carol came to the launch.

'I don't know but look, it is our yacht. Why they have broken mast? I don't understand what they did.'

Mrs. Carol stopped close to the TV set and listened to Paul's comments.

'Look, John is on the deck but what happened to their steering?'

'How do you know that it is broken?'

'Mom, don't you see that they have a rope on the side of the yacht with a bucket.'

Suddenly the picture went off and Mrs Carol asked, 'what did they say?'

'I didn't hear.' Paul answered and added. 'How could I hear anything if you've been talking at all times.'

'Who was talking if not you? I was you who talk all the time and this is your big problem because you don't know how to listen and on top of this you don't let other people listen even to serious matters.'

'Are you sure? I don't think so.'

'Oh yes and I would say that it is your biggest problem even at work.'

'Leave my work, please.'

'I am not talking about your work at all but in general. You don't know how to listen when other people speak and what they have to say, and it makes your life very difficult.'

Paul looked at his wife ready to say something but at the same time Mrs. Carol said that she must make a call to John but Paul replied.

'Mom, you cannot call him now.'

'Why not, he is my son.'

'Mom it was life on TV and he has no time to have any conversation. I don't know what could happened to them but I am not too sure if can manage to go into the small canal without steering and with some funny tackle.'

'He is a good sailor.'

'He was but many years ago and she doesn't know anything. Actually I don't understand why John is taking chance and asked her to operate with the bucket. I think that he has no other option.' Paul answered his own question.

'John's telephone is off,' said Mrs. Carol.

'Mom, give me the phone, please.' Paul said then he took the hone and after a while he said. 'You are right, his phone is off. It isn't any joke.'

'You see,' his wife said to him, 'you cannot believe your mom that John's phone is off.'

'This time of a year there is many yachts on the island and he can easily damage somebody's boat. Perhaps he did already and now they are showing how it was happened.'

'What could we do?'

'Mom, nothing you can do and nobody can help him right now but I can not understand why they have broken mast if the weather is so excellent.'

On TV screen came back the picture with John and Alice, and Paul said.

'Look, look they are showing them again but now we have to be quite and see what is happening with them.'

'Then shut your mouth.' His wife said shortly and everybody watched how John's yacht is coming to the small harbour with a big sail suspended between the mizzen sail and the broken the top of broken mast working as a bowsprit. The yacht was passing the canal quite fast as the two sails were taking as much wind as they could.

Alice moved the bucket to the left and the yacht turned to the left as well, and they moved even faster between many yachts. On the side there were plenty people, who stood and watched unusual yacht. Perhaps the time of a year and many prominent made that the TV operators were there as well. John started to drop the main sail from the mizzen mast.

'We are too fast,' John thought and went to drop the mizzen sail then he ran quickly to the fore-deck. He took the boat hook and watched one of the buoys. Very soon he was able to pick it up and he didn't missed the right moment. As soon as he caught the buoy, he inserted the rope into the eye of it and fastened the yacht. He felt like a hero after a big battle.

'Alice, you can leave the bucket,' he said and went to her. 'You are beautiful and perfect.' John gave her warm hug and she returned then their lips met in a kiss.

'I will pick up the mizzen sail once again then you have to lose the rope but slowly. Do not hurry, please.'

Alice started to lose the rope and John shifted the sail to the side. The yacht turned slowly to the side and soon they were able to move into one empty space between two other yachts. John dropped the sail and soon they have been moored to the wooden pontoon but for them it was a real land. He went to Alice and gave her a hug. They stood together for some time expressing their happiness with warm kiss. Suddenly very loud shout of the people woke them up and they looked at them surprisingly.

'Let us finish the job,' John said and he fastened the ropes properly so they could easily walk on the land but before they did it Alice asked him.

'Tell me John, how did you managed to be very cool making all the manoeuvres and even every time you've been telling, please.'

'It is simple and I love you, and I knew that we have to do it. The other thing is that the wind was our friend let's go as we are finally on land.'

Soon as they left the yacht they had to answer many questions as everybody was interested what happened to them in such nice weather. One of questions given by a journalist from TV station was if they came here to spend a holiday and John answered.

'Not really, to be honest we came here mostly to get married.'

Very loud applause went into the air. One gentleman came to them and introduced himself as a Captain of the yacht club. His name was Daniel.

'When would you like to make your wedding?' He asked.

'I think that you misunderstood me, sir because we will get married. You see, our wedding already took place on the sea and now we have to make it legal. The best if we might be able to do it today.'

'I think that this is possible but at what time would like to do it?'

'If now is two o'clock,' John looked at his watch, 'then I don't know at what time your offices are stopping to work.'

'Your time isn't correct because right now is three o'clock but doesn't matter. Tell me, where would you like to make the ceremony, in town?'

'If you ask me such question, I have to tell you that the best place is our yacht but I don't know if it could be possible.'

'Of course it will be possible, John but let me introduce to you people my wife Nancy, if you don't mind, I hope you don't. Nancy will take Alice for shopping so she will look a little different for your wedding. I wouldn't say that you look bad but your dress reminds some big battle. To be honest I still cannot understand how you could experience heavy storm if the weather is so beautiful. Anyway, I think that the time when Alice will be gone with Nancy, you will go with me so you will change yourself a little as well. I think that we can meet in my office, lets' say in two hours time.'

'It sounds very nice but could I make a call?' Alice asked.

'Of course you can, no problem, lets' go to my office.' Daniel answered.

They entered the building of the yacht club and as soon as they were in Daniel's office he said. 'Let me leave you with your call and I will be back very soon.'

Alice dialled Captain's Robertson number and after he answered she said. 'Hi Captain, Alice is speaking.'

'Where are you? Why didn't you contact me? Why your phone is off and why your phone is off? I've been trying to call you for long time?'

'Captain, everything is ok. There was a little storm but the most important is that we found the spot.'

'What spot? How could you get a storm if the weather is excellent?'

'Look Captain, I told you that there was a little storm and there was a storm but to be honest it was a terrible hurricane. You should know that anything might happen on the sea. What I like to say is that we found the place and most probably John's father took the photo.'

'How could you say such thing? Did you go on the sea and there was a sign?'

'I don't know if you like to have a talk with me or you are joking, Captain.' Alice answered sadly.

'Ok, ok when you will be back?'

'I don't know because our yacht is very badly damaged. We have broken mast and broken steering. Well, nothing is working on board. No navigation system, no radio . . . just nothing. We came to the island which was closest from the place where we were after the storm.'

'In this case you have to come with a plane.'

'We have to buy a new mast and fix many things but there is something else I have to talk to you about, Captain.'

'What is it?'

'I hope that you remember that I still have my leave and now I need to be off for a few days, say two or three weeks.'

'What? Two weeks? Don't you know that you are working on the case?'

'I do know but to be realistic I might be dead by now and the other thing is that I can't be there anyway as we have to fix our yacht.'

'I can't imagine how it might be possible for you stay there and quarrel with John for two weeks more.'

'I think that you should have a word with him,' she said and gave the phone to John.

'Halo Sir, John speaking.'

'How are you John?'

'To be honest fantastic, I have never have had such beautiful time in my life.'

'What are you talking about? Alice told me right now that you went through very heavy storm and the yacht is badly damaged.'

'Oh yes, the yacht looks bad but it doesn't matter. The thing is that we are getting married.'

'What?' He couldn't be more surprise.

'I said, we are getting married,' John answered smiling.

'John, I think that you have to make another call to me because I don't think that we can carry on with stupid conversation. If you talk to me, try to be a little serious. If you need to see a doctor then ask Alice to help you,' Captain was totally confused.

'Why did you drop the phone?' Alice asked. 'What he said?'

'He said that I should make another call but more serious. He said that you have to take me to a doctor.' John answered laughing and at the same time to the office came Daniel with his wife Nancy.

'I see that you are very happy,' Daniel said.

'Alice,' Nancy said coming to her closer, 'there aren't too much time and many things to do so it will be much better if we will leave right now. Let's go Alice.'

'I think that we have to go as well,' Daniel said after the women left the office. 'You dress isn't too presentable for wedding,' he added laughing.

They left the office and just before they had to leave the building the phone rang. Daniel went back and after a while he came to John and said, 'there was a gentleman on the phone who like to talk with you but I have told him that you've got no time because of the wedding. He asked who's wedding but after I told him that yours, he just dropped the phone. Strange,' he added. 'Let's go said Daniel,' and they left the club.

Chapter 22

Jack was the second intelligence agent who went to the farm. Captain Robertson couldn't find any other option as to send someone to check what's happening to Robert. Jack came late at night to the farm and in the morning the leader wrote his details into the register book. He saw Roberts name in the register book but he learned that his college left the farm and it surprised him or even made him a little worried what happened to his friend.

'What can you do?' the leader asked him.

'I am a motor mechanic but I can do whatever you ask me to do, no problem.'

'Can you work on diesel engines?'

'I told you that I am a motor mechanic and this is my trade so of course I can work on diesel motors.'

'Then you'll go with me because I've got a job for you, Jack.'

Jack walked together with the leader towards the workshop and listened some of the stories about the farm. He was very interested with everything especially now after he knew that Robert isn't here any longer. The only question which was coming to his mind was why Robert didn't contact the head quarter. They walked between igloos made from polyester when his sight went to a high construction.

'What is it?' he asked pointing the construction.

'Up there we have to make flats for single women but the construction has to be lowered firstly as it is too high.'

'Why did you build it so high?'

'It was much higher and we lowered it but it is still too high.'

'Why didn't you finish?'

'I told you that it is too high but we will finish soon.'

They stopped in front of the workshop and Jack looked at the vehicles standing around. Jack knew the place as he saw it while flew with a helicopter but still it looked a little differently from the ground.

'This is our workshop,' said the leader and at the same time came out a man who was in his middle sixties, short and with white hair. The leader said to him, 'Dennis, I've got somebody to help you with the truck. His name is Jack and he will help you because he knows diesel engines.'

'How many of them came here but they couldn't even change oil.' Denis answered with ignorance.

'Listen to me man,' Jack didn't like to owe anything to other people, 'you just put a label onto my forehead but you don't know me at all. I said that I am a motor mechanic, that's it. Do you think that you are the only one in the whole country?'

'I know what I am talking about.' Denis repeated shortly.

Jack looked at him for a while then he said, 'what do you know? Do you know me? I don't remember you. Where is the fucking van?' He said to the leader and they went to the vehicle standing right to the door of the workshop.

Jack looked for a while then asked, 'why can't you give me another job?'

'Because you have to help him,' he answered.

'He can do it himself. What I will do? Hold a spanner and listen to his shit?'

'Jack, we have some rules to obey and everybody has to work.'

'Then give me another job.'

'I have no other job for you and this van has to be finished today. If you don't like the job then you can go to the owner of the farm and have a word with him. You can leave if you like and I've got no problem with it at all.'

'Ok, I can go to the owner.'

'Can you work together?'

'Sure that I can but then he has to stop talking shit because I know already how good he is.'

'Ok, I am leaving you guys and I hope that the van will go to town tonight.'

The leader left and very quickly Jack ensured Denis that he knows his profession and there is no more than three hours to finish job by the van. It came up that Denis was worried that he might lose his position on the farm where since quite long time he was the only motor mechanic. That gave him quite big advantage but quickly became very friendly with Jack and it helped him to learn about the farm a lot and about Robert as well.

As soon as Jack learned that Robert went sleep and in the morning was gone and nobody knew what happened to him he thought to make a call to Captain Robertson but something stopped him and he decided to leave the place as soon as possible. Jack helped Denis to fix the van and the engine could be started at any time. During the lunch he went to the leader and said.

'Listen, I am leaving.'

'What about the van?'

'It isn't my business.'

'I see that you are like the others, like to be here and have a big plate of food without any work.'

'I think that I worked for my food but you can have it together with the other one which they brought to your place.'

'It seems to me that you are looking for trouble.'

'I don't care what you think or see.'

'It will be good if you'll finish your plate and just fuck of.'

'Watch your mouth because I am not one of them who you can punch in the morning as you like and it looks that soon you might say one word too much.'

'You better fuck off, you lazy ass.'

Jack didn't answer anything but left the farm. He caught a lift and soon he was again in the base GP-2 and made a call to Captain Robertson. 'Hi Captain, Jack is speaking.'

'I can hear that you are speaking but what have you to say.'

'I am in the base.'

'What?'

'I said that I am in the base. Did you hear anything from Robert?'

'No, I didn't.'

'Then I don't know what's going on because one man told me that one night they have call him to help by offloading a truck and he never came back. He is not on the farm, Captain.'

'Jack, nobody asked you to leave the farm.'

'Captain, it isn't about me but about Robert. I suspect that they keep him somewhere and if there anything goes incorrectly then after me you will send somebody else. I do understand that I should be still there but I think that we have to take proper steps.'

'What steps are you talking about and what you people do I don't know at all. One is vanished another doesn't listen then she is getting married.'

'Who is getting married?'

'What a day, I don't know what to do with you people. Who? Alice of course, who else could get married'

'Sorry Captain, what did you say?'

'I said that Alice is getting married. Don't leave the base as I'll be there soon.'

Chapter 23

'I knew that we will be the first,' said Daniel while passing the gate of the yacht club. He stopped the car and just before they left it John asked him. 'Do you think that our wedding on the yacht will be accepted?'

'Of course John, I told you that many times and stop worried about that. Look better at yourself and how you look alike for your big day.'

'What's wrong with me?' John asked while standing next to the motor car.

'Did I say that there is anything wrong with you? Man, you look perfect.'

They walked to the office and suddenly Daniel started nearly to run as he heard that his phone is ringing. He picked it up and answered with deep breath, 'Daniel speaking.'

He listened for a moment as somebody like to speak with Alice then he answered, 'no, she isn't here but she should be here soon, soon because she has to be on time for her wedding.'

Daniel listened for a while the voice on the other side of the line then he answered.

'Yes that you can, John it is for you,' Daniel gave him the phone.

'John speaking,' he answered and at the same time se sighted at a photo on the wall which shows Lisa standing together with her neighbour in front of the same yacht which was standing next to his one in the yacht club. He suspended his sight on the photo for a while with a big surprise then a voice in the receiver woke him up.

'John, what's happening?'

'Oh, not much except that we are getting married. Actually we are married but it has to be legalized.'

'Is that only what you have to say?'

'Yes, thank you a lot for a call and I will remember to send you a nice photo.'

'John, isn't anything wrong with you?'

'Look, Alice and myself we love each other so we get married and I think that you should wish us all the best as we planned to be together for the rest of time.'

'When can I talk to her and when I will see both of you?'

'It is difficult to predict because our yacht is badly damaged. One mast has to be replaced and except that we have to look for a problem with all our electronic system, never mind the steering.'

'What's wrong with your telephones?'

'The cell-phones are broken as well.'

'John, you have to make a call to your mother. They saw the news on TV and they are worried a lot.' Captain Robertson said that very softly.

'News on TV you said, what news?'

'Don't you know? They showed your yacht on TV as you were coming to the harbour on the island, the same were you are now. Your family is really worried about you.'

'Ok, I will do it and thank you very much.'

Daniel showed himself as very good organizer. Together with his wife of course who came right now into the office. He came closer to Alice and continued. 'Wow, I am totally astounded. Alice, you look fantastic and John is most lucky man in the world.'

He came to his wife and said, 'Nancy, I knew that I can always rely on you, my sweet heart. Thank you a lot,' Daniel kissed her chick.

'Well, she is stunning lady,' she replied and added, 'all I had to do was to find a right shop and any dress we looked at was perfect on her.'

Alice came closer to John who wore dark navy jacket and white trousers and said to him, 'John, I love you.'

'I love you too Alice.'

They kissed each other and incidentally they stood in such way that she could see the same photo which saw John not long ago. Alice couldn't believe her eyes and she whispered to his ear about it but he answered softly, 'we can talk about it later honey.'

'I think that it's time to go down,' said Daniel and added, 'by the way, you are not the first people getting married in our yacht club. Look there on this photo. Those people are our members and their wedding took place in the yacht club as well but let's go,' he finished and they left the office.

'There is something, I have to tell you, John,' Daniel said as they waked and continued, 'don't be surprised to see many people on your wedding party.'

'Why wedding party? What do you mean?'

'Look, your wedding is very important for us and you have to know that everything goes on our account so you don't need to worry about it.'

'Actually I don't know what's the story is about.'

'We own some number of hotels on the island and we need to give as many attractions for our guests as possible and this is the reason that your wedding is very important for us. By the way, I will see tomorrow what we can do with your yacht.'

'I don't think that here on the island you can do anything.'

'You might be very surprise. By the way, I think that I saw your yacht somewhere before.'

'It is possible because my father visited the island many times, I suppose.'

As they came closer to the place where stood John's yacht more and more people stood on their way. They watched especially John who walked as a movie star, dressed as a real navy Captain. For many quests it was a real attraction because it isn't a common to witness a marriage ceremony in the yacht club especially during a summer holiday. John looked at the people and asked.

'Daniel, would you like to say that all these people came to attend the party?'

'Not all but most of them, it is your big day John, isn't it?' Daniel asked with a smile.

Chapter 24

Robert enjoyed a cigarette while sitting in the same empty and locked room. Dr. Albert and two his assistants left very quickly. Robert didn't feel any pain and only a dressing tape on his grain reminded him that not long ago a piece of a muscle has been taken from that place and as Dr. Albert informed him it has to be send for a test. During that time Robert's brain has been tested as well. He never experienced something like that before or it could be possible that he couldn't remember because his memory went back to the moment when he received the injection in Sir Bernard's office from the strange man, who vanished right after that incident.

Now Robert looked sadly at locked door and asked himself what actually happened and suddenly he thought, 'I must have my memory back, I must,' he said that loudly and at the same time he heard a voice, 'not now, it's not right time.'

Robert looked around to see where the voice came from and then on the wall appeared big screen with Sir. Bernard on it who said, 'Robert, I am very glad to hear that you like to have your memory back and believe me that I will help you with it as much as I can.'

'Thank you sir,' answered Robert but then the screen went of as quick as it came on the wall. A few minutes later to the room came the same soldier who brought him here and said flatly.

'Sir Bernard is waiting for you.'

'Would you mind if I will take my cigarettes?'

'Not at all, sir,' the soldier answered.

Soon after they entered Sir Bernard's office and Robert looked around surprisingly because there on the wall was a big screen with plenty small monitors on it showing pictures from different places at the same time. He could see a lot of soldiers running in different directions and many vehicles which he thought didn't have wheels.

'Yes Robert, these vehicles don't have normal wheels but balls with special suspension. The wheels are used but the vehicles covered with electromagnetic fields they can stay at the right distance from the ground and move into different directions with very high speed. I have to say that they are perfectly safe.'

'I wouldn't say that, sir', said Max who entered the office.

'First of all you shall knock on the door before coming into the office.'

'Sir, I did knock for a few times but you couldn't hear it in this noise so I just came in.'

'Never mind,' answered Sir Bernard and he continued. 'Why are you saying that our vehicles are not safe?'

'Sir, just have a look at him and you will have the answer,' Max pointed at Robert.

'I don't understand you, Max, not at all.'

'It is simple, they have driven with high speed and as the result he lost his memory.'

'Do you really believe that it might be possible?'

'Sir, don't you remember what we have experienced in the past?'

'Well, the farm is far and what do you think, shall they travel two weeks?'

'Sir, you know very well that I'm talking about the speed they have been travelling so as the result he lost his memory because isn't prepared for such speed.'

'You can say anything you like about the speed but the truth is that the only reason for his illness is the injection which he received. Have you forgotten what the whole action is about,' asked him Sir Bernard.

'Sir, I didn't and I am responsible for the action but I do know as well that we are chasing for someone who could be anybody or who is gone by now.'

'Max,' Sir Bernard suddenly raise his voice, 'you are responsible for the action but on top of it our safety is in your hands and this shit should never take place. The other thing what I know is that this is unacceptable.'

'Sir, you know very well where they are coming from and you know as well that they are far more advanced then we are and except that there is another side of the matter.'

'What is it?'

'The matter is that we know our weak points but in stand to do something to reduce them we are busy with some nonsense which nobody ever will need.'

'What do you mean?

'Firstly Sir, let me tell you that this action cannot bring any positive result.'

'Max, you are the one who has to make sure that the action will be successful,' Sir Bernard became very angry.

'Sir, can't you see that the soldiers are running up and down and one knows who has to be caught.'

'Honestly Max, you strictly disappoint me.'

'Sir, as far as I remember you are the one who used to tell us many times about coexistence and where is the point to waste the time with clones? By the way, shouldn't he to be on a test by now,' Max pointed at Robert.

'Don't try to put me of the track but never mind, he has a small brake and I brought him here because I do believe that a little click is needed to get his memory back. It cannot be anything serious and on top of that we need him very urgently.'

'Sir, I'm quite sure that there on the farm they already looking for him so why cannot we bring someone else?'

'Max, don't you understand that Robert is highly marked special intelligence agent and he has been working on our case?'

'I suppose the matter is over and I don't see any point to carry on with something what cannot bring any positive result. The next thing is that if they will find out that the dead people are clones only then there could be much bigger problem especially after we will send another one over there.'

'It is impossible Max that they will find out it.'

'Sir, the intelligence agents are still busy with the case and another matter is that somehow they can meet the real people. It might be possible because Lisa left her husband in India and if she will go home, which is strongly possible then what you think will take place.'

'Max, right after the action will be finished, I have another mission for you.'

'What is it?'

'You should know by now Max that the mission is very important because as you said right now they might meet the real people and we cannot afford it so in other words you have to bring them here.'

'It must be some joke.'

'No Max, it isn't a joke and I don't care how will you do it but strictly I must have them here.'

'I cannot understand why you are thinking about more victims? Don't you think that there are enough problems?'

'The only problem is that we are not finish with our experiment and another thing is that we are in war. By the way, sometime I think that you are like one of those clones.'

'I wish, I really do,' Max answered.

'So I do because it might enable me to have a full control over your stupid brain.'

'Sir, I don't know why are you so upset?'

'Max, I see that you don't understand our situation.'

'If we didn't organize it then there will be no problem and we could have a piece of mind.'

'Listen Max I think that you should see a doctor together with Robert because there is something very wrong inside your head.'

'It's possible but let me remind you sir that nobody else but you has been telling that there shouldn't be any war in the world.'

'That's right and I can repeat it at any time because it became clear very long ago and everybody shall understand that the world is not to be destroy but it has nothing to do with our experiment.'

'Sir, as far as I remember since Hitler failed our politics should change but all what we do is more and more mess. It seems that it is our policy to find out where it's possible to make mess,' Max said that ironically.

'Max, we are helping for the whole world but you must see a doctor,' Sir Bernard was very angry.

'Sir, do you think that it is possible to force anyone to be happy or try to turn other people according to our thoughts?' Max sounded sarcastic but he couldn't predict what will take place vey shortly.

'Once again Max I am telling you that it has nothing to do with anybody's happiness but there are other matters which we have to consider because perhaps—well, many of that things like for example homosexuality will never affect us but we cannot ignore them and as I said we have to look into this matter right now because now we are building our future.'

'I would say rather that we are creating more and more problems and sooner or later nothing and nobody will save us from our own catastrophe. Those cops are busy with the case and I don't wish to see their visit here.'

'Max, I am quite sure that I have to suspend you with immediate effect.'

'Whatever you'll decide, sir will take place and I can go on pension as well. I think is the right time for me to retired, isn't it?'

'Max, I don't see any reason for you to complain as you live like a millionaire, actually you are a millionaire.'

'Yes sir, I am a millionaire without any freedom. Firstly I thought that I am a soldier but now I know for sure that mostly I am a common terrorist, especially that all my money always connected with dirty jobs.'

'Watch your mouth Max!'

'Is that our democracy? All what I am allowed to do is to keep my mouth shut and I will but sir, don't ask me to carry on with this shit of yours any longer.'

'I am sorry Max but I don't see any other option except to put you on the farm. Most probably in very nearly future Robert will be your friend and what you'll be thinking about a plate of food but I'm telling you that you will work and suffer. The food will be the only pleasure of yours' and no other matters will disturb your thoughts. In other words you will be finish as a human been.'

'At least I'll be free and unable to look and trying to understand this shit of yours as all the things is just a crap, stinking crap.'

'You are right because before you'll go your brain will be stripped to small pieces and carefully analyse so we might know what went wrong inside your head.'

'Sir, you can destroy me and my brain but you have to remember that you can not destroy or rule the world as you think.'

'You won't see what I can do, you won't Max.'

Shortly Max has been taken away from the office and there was a silence for quite long time.

Chapter 25

The news which John's family watched on TV has extended Pauls' and his family the visit by his mother. The children played out in the pool and they didn't even think about going home as they have good time especially that there was no pool in their place. Their parents were sitting in the lounge, trying to find out what could happen to John and Alice during such beautiful weather. Another matter was that the information which John gave to the journalists about the marriage didn't come to them as a fact and they have agreed that it was a joke only. They understood that that time of a year there are many prominent on the island and it is quite obvious that journalists are looking for any possibility to give as much exciting news as possible.

'What they are talking about?' Paul asked himself and then he shouted to his mother and his wife. 'Come quickly or you will missed John's wedding.'

Soon after they stood in front of TV set and Paul said with excitement, 'look, they are really getting married.'

Suddenly the telephone started to ring and Mrs. Carol went to pick up the call. Surprisingly she listened to man's voice. 'Captain Robertson speaking and I'm sorry but I have to ask if your TV is on.'

'Yes sir.'

'Mrs. Carol, did you know that John is getting married?'

'No sir, if you are surprised then I have to tell you that I am very surprised and do not know what to say.'

'I see,' Captain Robertson answered and dropped his receiver. Mrs. Carol stood standstill for a while and didn't know what to say.

'Who was on the phone?' Paul asked.

'It was Captain Robertson if I heard properly. I think that he is from John's work.'

'Why he phone here?'

'He asked if my TV is on,' she answered.

'I don't know,' Paul said and continued, 'what John is doing but it seeps to me very strange. Actually he shouldn't marry her.'

Paul, why are you telling that?' His mother asked.

'I don't think that she might be good wife for him. I think that she is too beautiful.'

'Wow, it sounds very niece, seems to me that I am ugly.' Betty said with irritation.

'Honey, I never said that, you are a normal woman but look there.' Paul finished and at the same time the picture on the screen went of and then he added. 'Look, I am quite sure that she looks like a movie star but why thy organized secret wedding on the Island. No, I do not like it.'

'Paul, I think that you shall wish all the best to his brother,' Betty asked.

'Look there, look. What do you think about a wedding like that? How much it can cost? A fortune and something isn't right. How it is possible that we are not there?'

'Daddy, why don't you like Alice?' Asked Allen who came from outside.

'I have never said that Allen,' Paul answered.

'Dad, I am glad that I have asked ankle John to do it.'

'What did you asked him?'

'To marry her of course,' Allen answered proudly.

Chapter 26

John's family wasn't the only who watched the wedding on TV because soon after Captain Robertson finished conversation with Mrs. Carol the phone rang again

'Captain Robertson, could you kindly give me an answer what the hell is going on?'

'I am very sorry but I cannot,' he answered.

'What do you mean, you can't?'

'Exactly what I said but actually what answer re you looking for? I don't know what are you asking for?'

'Don't make me fool. After the news broke up about John's wedding on TV nobody works in the whole building.'

'To be honest only now I know whom I am talking to and you have to believe me that I am as much surprised as you are. Shortly before you called me I have spoken with John's mother but she doesn't know anything as well which means something strange came up during the race.'

'It is your fault Captain, bye.'

The office entered Oscar and said, 'Captain, on the way here I've been asked a thousand questions about Inspector John's wedding but I don't know anything. It looks like nobody works in the whole building.'

'Don't worry, your boss told me exactly the same and I don't have any answer as well.'

'Do you think that this is serious?'

'You asking funny question, did you have had wedding serious or it was a joke only.'

'I think that I am the only one who did not see the wedding.' Oscar answered silently.

'Don't worry just now we'll be flying over there to see what's happening.'

Soon they left the building and went to a chopper which was ready to take them t the base GP-2. The flight didn't take long and after they landed and entered the building they met Jack who waited for them in the office.

'Oscar, this is our second office so feel free make coffee, please.' Captain sat down and asked Jack. 'Now you have to tell me what exactly happened on the farm and why did you left.'

'Captain, I know for sure that Robert was there until one night he was asked to help of-load a truck. Captain in the register book he is written off and it looks like he left the farm on his own but I know for sure that it isn't true.'

'How could you know that?'

'Captain, the farm looks like a country in the country and monks who are walking with blindness. The people over there seem mentally sick and it looks a Parkinson's disease alike. This is very serious matter.'

'Why it has to be serious in first place and I think that one of your tasks was to find out about the trucks.'

'Most of the people are coming to the farm healthy and then they are going somewhere and after they are aback then they are strictly sick. They are heavily bitten and for sure they will never be healthy again.'

'Wait, are you suggesting that Robert might be taken for such treatment?'

'Captain, everything is possible, well I know him for long time and I know about him a lot but it could be possible that after he made a call they found out who is he and then . . .' Jack suspended his voice.

'Shit, tell me how it could be possible that in such short time you know as much matters. How could you be so sure that Robert left the farm with the truck?'

'Captain, there is a mechanic who started to worried that I might find out something about his qualifications and his position on the farm could be in danger so he was telling me some stories until the lunch when I left. Firstly I thought to make a call but then I decided to leave because most probably Robert needs our help.'

'Well, perhaps it was a good solution in this case, who knows,' Captain came up with the conclusion and there was a silence for a while.

'What do you think we shall do?' Captain asked.

'Captain, I think that we have to close the farm and keep the owner and other until we will learn something about Robert.'

'Do you think that it will work?'

'I don't know but we have to do something. Farm is the last place which we know he was and we have to go there in any case.'

'I know that we have to find him.'

'Captain, even those people on the farm we will help as they are living in such conditions that can be compared to a concentration camp.'

'What we can do with them?'

'Captain, I don't now but perhaps we can leave over there our people for some time then we can see.'

'I am really worried about Robert but firstly we have to see what's going on over the on the Island while Alice and John are giving me no les headache.'

'I saw them on TV Captain and I can say that he didn't look as a cop at all. I would say he was like a movie star,' Jack laughed.

'There is nothing to laugh,' Captain Robertson took the receiver and dialled Alice's parents' number. After a while he said, 'Robertson speaking.'

There was a silence on another side of the line then her father said. 'I shouldn't talk to you but one you have to know, right now I am busy to clean my revolver and believe me that I'll get you.'

'At least the gun will be clean so I won't catch any infection.'

'All the years, we've been working together I thought that you are my friend and you might help my daughter but now I can easily see that you just using her for some nonsense. What means this shit?'

'Cool down, I have no idea what's happening over there and I will go and find out what is it about. This is the reason that I am calling to you.'

'Is it?'

'Yes Tom, I need to go over there but the most important thing is that I need to introduce myself as her father.'

'Look, whatever you'll do, I will get you and doesn't matter where you will go.'

'Ok, but I need to go over there and I have to make sure that you don't come there as well, it might some shit.'

'Ok, go for it.'

'Thanks', bye.' He finished the conversation as it was quite irritating. Captain lit a cigarette and set in silence then he said to Jack. 'Today is too late so you can take our chopper and go home. We will call you as soon as things come up, Jack.'

'Thanks' Captain.'

* . . . . . . * . . . . . *

The Sun was down over the horizon when Captain Robertson and Oscar arrive to the Yacht Club. The security guard send them to the main restaurant where another man came to the car and opened the door.

'Thank you,' said Captain and added. 'I am the bright father so could you announce me, please.'

For Alice and John to see Captain and Oscar was quite big surprise. Suddenly she became whiter than her wedding dress. 'What are you doing her?' she asked.

'Don't be surprised but tell me what you two up to. You cannot be serious with that wedding.'

'What do you mean, we cannot be serious. Did you see a wedding for fun? I have told you that we are getting married and where is the reason for you to come here on the Island?'

'Firstly, I came here as your father and there is nothing wrong for us to be here to see your wedding or to say more correctly to see what a show you are busy with.'

'If you are her father then I am your son-in-law and we are not making any show. As far as I know people are falling in love then they getting married. I thought that as a married man you know how it works unless you were born already married.' John laughed then he added. 'Dad, this wedding is very or even more then serious.'

'Well but as a cop how could you afford such party.'

'I thought that you know that my father-in-law is very reach businessman but don't worry because nobody will pay for anything.'

'What? Are you trying to tell me that all this things has fallen from the sky? I would say that here are no less than two hundred people.'

'Don't worry pa,' John answered and added. 'It isn't on your account. We are guests in the club and except that the owner is simply advertising himself on TV.

'Thanks God, for a moment I thought that it is a real wedding.'

'What are you talking about? It is real and wake up, please,' Alice was getting slightly nervous.

'Ok, we'll talk later but really I would like to know something about the wedding and I do believe that I deserve some proper explanation.'

'I told you pa already, I love your daughter and she loves me. Is anything wrong with it?' John answered with smile and Alice added.

'Yes dad, John is right and let join the party and be happy for us.' She laughed.

'Do you know what is happening?' Captain asked and then he answered his question. 'There is nobody working but just sitting and watching the wedding, and your families as well. You shouldn't be too happy John because her father is cleaning his gun to shoot both of us.'

'Well, what we can do about it? Let's go inside.'

'Alice, you told me about a spot.' Captain wouldn't give up.

'Not now, please,' answered Alice but still before they enter Captain said, 'Look Alice, I have to know everything because Robert vanished from the farm and we have to take very quick steps. It isn't any joke.'

They stopped the conversation as Daniel came to them and introduced himself.

'Hi, I'm Daniel and I am very glad to see you in our Yacht Club sir. I see that you care a lot about your daughter that you came here so quickly. Not long ago we have spoken on the phone, I suppose.'

'I'm please to see you too and in did I do care about Alice but tell me please why are you making big show on TV.'

'I'm really sorry for the show but as soon as I spotted the yacht coming to our canal which looked like one which left a big battle I immediately phone our TV station as it was really big attraction for our guests, especially after John said that they came here to get married.'

'To be honest I have never expected their wedding so soon and in a scenario as such.'

'Sir, there is nothing wrong with our Island and I have to tell you that any people are coming here to get married, and I really hope that after this wedding will be many more of weddings here.'

'Well, I cannot say anything wrong about the Island but personally I didn't expect that and I do not believe that TV is the best way to inform parents that their children are getting married. Don't you thing that some preparation should take place before any wedding.'

Sir, together with my wife we took care about everything and I hope that you will enjoy the party as well. For that occasion our chefs prepared really delicious and superb food. Of course Alice and John look fantastic.'

'Do you think that they will look the same after they will see an account after the party,' Captain wasn't too sure about John's information.

'Sir, Alice and John are our guests and the party is on our account. You have no reason to worry about it at all. I would like to tell you that the Club organized everything as a wedding present.'

'You must be very reach, sir.'

'Actually yes but except that we have very reach sponsors. One of them is Albert who was very happy after I told him about the wedding of your children. He asked me to make sure that the party and the wedding itself will be as much beautiful as possible.'

'Who is Albert?'

'Albert gets married in our Yacht Club sometime ago as well and nowadays is coming to us very seldom because of his business in India.'

'In India, it sounds very interesting.'

'He is our member and I will show you the photos but firstly let me introduce you to my wife so we could make toast for our special guests. Actually, why didn't you come together with your wife?'

'You see, we are on business trip and our visit here was unexpected. Our plane is waiting and we cannot stay here for long.'

'I see,' said Daniel and added. 'Let go inside.'

* . . . . . * . . . . . *

Later on Captain Robertson went together with Daniel to his office. Daniel took a photo album from a drawer and put it on the desk. He found the place where was a photo of Albert and his wife Lisa. Captain looked at the photo surprised as he never expected to see Lisa's photo together with the last victim especially in that place.

'Look her sir,' Daniel said with some excitement. 'Here are the same people I have told you about. Lisa and Daniel have had their wedding party in our Yacht Club.'

'Is that the same man you have spoken on the phone today?'

'Oh yes. Sir, I have to tell you that he is very interesting man. Together with his wife they have a big petroleum company in India and Albert works on a new fuel system.'

'Is that so? It sounds very interesting.'

For a moment Captain thought about the spot that Alice did mention to him on the phone and all the matters he already learned in the Yacht Club connected with the investigation. Even more carefully he listened to Daniel.

'Sir, I have to tell you that Albert is working on very serious project as he will use silicon as a fuel.'

'It cannot be possible.'

'Apparently it is difficult to believe in such things but when I am listening to Albert it seems to be very simple. He explained to me many times about structure of silicon and many interesting matters about chemistry so it is difficult not to believe in his story. Actually many things are made from silicon so why not fuel.'

'Well, I could imagine a situation that the people drive with a spade in side their boots.'

Captain turned a few pages of the album and surprisingly looked at the photos. He stood very confused but then Daniel continued. 'Your daughter is the next one whose photos will be in that album. I am really happy for them.'

'Never mind that I am confused, I am happy as well. Tell me please, did you show the photos to Alice and John?'

'I am not too sure about Alice but John saw the photo which is on the wall. Look here please.'

Captain looked at the photo and listened to Daniel who talked with excitement. 'You see, as soon as I have learned that this isn't a joke and they really would like to get married I did everything that all the things will go smooth. Oh yes, definitely I have to put their photo on the wall. I am really excited and happy as well.'

They have spoken for some time in the office then they went to join the party. Captain's thoughts every now and then went to the case and he was very glad when finally he could be together with Alice and John on their yacht. Captain and Oscar looked around and they couldn't believe that it might be possible that in such good weather the yacht is totally damaged.

'I hope that you don't mind to tell us now what really happened to you guys.' Captain said.

'What would you like to know? Everything is simple, we fell in love and now Alice is my wife and I am her husband.'

'I am talking about the yacht and what you have done to it in such nice weather.'

They stood in silence for a while and soon after they entered the cabin put a map on the table and said. 'Here is the place that the hurricane caught us. Exactly here the storm began,' John pointed on the map and Alice said.

'The forecast never said anything about the storm and I have never ever imagined that something like that could happen to me.'

'I think that you will remember it for long time,' said Oscar.

'You are right Oscar,' Alice answered and continued. 'John sent me to bring life jackets and suddenly I heard very heavy knock on the deck. It was broken mast which while falling down hit John over his head.'

'I have to say that your forehead doesn't look to presentable.' Captain said with smile.

'It wasn't any joke,' said Alice with excitement. 'All I can say is that I have experienced most difficult moments in my life. John was unconscious and very high waves went over the deck every now and then. I didn't know what to do.'

John took her hand and said. 'Alice brought me back to life but then one of the waves took her of the deck and she just flew over the railing into the ocean.'

'What?' Captain nearly shouted.

'Yes Captain, I don't remember how it happened because the water covered me very quickly.'

'Wait a minute, are you trying to tell me that you came back on the yacht even of a heavy storm. How it could be possible that you are still alive?' Captain asked.

'Ys Captain, John safe my life and I don't know how he did it or how he did jump into boiling water and brought me back on board.'

'John,' Captain asked. 'How could you do it?'

John looked for a while at Alice then he said. 'Could you see another option? Could I give up?'

'Well, a man shall never give up but what you are telling now seems to me impossible.'

'Captain, perhaps I didn't know at that time that I love her but the other thing is that at that time I didn't even think that I cannot bring her back on board. If I look at the all story now, I can say that it came very naturally and nothing special is in this matter. The most important is that if you really believe then you can do anything but you have to understand that word, believe fully but firstly we have to understand what really means, believe. The universe is big and we could look like pones on a chess board but we are not created for nothing. Never mind responsibility of a skipper or a fact that if incidentally I will come back alone I'll be for sure prosecuted. Well, I hope that by now you understand that we are together for real and for ever.'

John finished and there was a silence in the cabin for sometime then Captain Robertson said. 'Congratulations and to be honest, I can say that you two have been in my mind as a couple for quite long time. Perhaps not for too long but I felt something strange before you went on the sea. It's funny but I think that I have seen you John with Alice before I have met you even.'

'Perhaps now you understand everything Captain.' Alice said softly.

'Well, now I fully understand your decision but still you have to remember that Alice's father by now has clean revolver.' Captain laughed.

'Shit, both of you people could be death by now.' Oscar said.

'Oh yes,' said Captain and continued. 'Now I think is time to go back to the case. I like to know something about the spot that you have mention to me Alice.'

'The spot is here,' John stopped Alice from an answer and he pointed the same place on the map as he has showed where the storm began.'

'How do you know that there is the spot and actually what spot we you are talking about.'

'Captain, we've been lucky to find the same place where John's dad took the photo.' Alice said proudly.

'How do you know? The ocean is big.' Captain replied.

'I saw a blue light in the ocean,' John answered.

Captain looked at him for a while then he asked. 'Alice did you see the light as well?'

'I told you that I don't even remember how John brought me back so how could you expect me to see a light.'

'Alice was still unconscious at that time,' John added.

'Have you taken any photo?'

'Captain, you must be joking.'

'No, I'm not joking John.'

'Captain, do you understand our situation? Unconscious person on board and who I cannot leave alone so when do you think I could be able to take any photo. Of course that

I thought about it and I did ask Alice to look at it but she couldn't even understand what I was talking about.'

'Story with light is good for children but we are dealing with proper evidences.'

'Children story,' John repeated sadly and continued. 'Once again Captain, firstly you should experience a hurricane like this one and have somebody who's live is in danger then you might be able to say if this is a children story. Of course I like to take a photo like that because it was amazing but what can I say, it wasn't possible. By the way nothing worked on board and, well what I can say more, just nothing.'

'Captain,' said Alice. 'One you have to know and it is that even I didn't see the light, I know that there was a light in the ocean and there is no need to prove it. John has told me that there was a light and this is true. You don't need to have any suspicion because I know that John saw the light.'

'Captain,' John started slowly. 'In a marriage the most important is honesty and you know very well that only that can secure strong and for ever lasting connection. I have no need to talk nonsense but funny thing is that the colour of the light was very similar to that one on the farm and the same which I saw in Lisa's neighbour's house on the monitor.'

'You might be cross with me people but in any investigation there is a need for facts.' Captain replied.

'I think that everything is becoming more and more clear,' Oscar said.

'Firstly I would like to point the fact that a light is coming up not for the first time which is very interesting matter. Secondly somehow we are still on track. Oscar finished.

'Perhaps we are on track but I see that it is only a track of mysteries.' Captain said.

'Captain, I don't know how but I've got a feeling somehow our lives are connected with the whole case.' John replied.

'I wouldn't say that,' Captain smiled, 'but where is the end of the whole story?'

'Daniel told you about his conversation with Albert and according to the photos which are there in his office he has spoken with our victim. The man from the photos is death but according to Daniel he isn't death.'

'John,' Captain tried to answer his question. 'Everything is possible and I wouldn't be surprise that there are in the case involve big money.'

'There is another thing we have to look for,' Oscar said. 'I didn't see any report about a storm but this yacht looks terrible.'

'It's true,' Captain answered and after a moment of silence he said. 'John, there is another possibility but do not jump on me too quick.'

'What is it?'

'What Oscar has pointed by now is that you might have had an accident during the race and the yacht is destroyed.'

'You are going too far Captain,' John answered with anger.

'I didn't try to point any accident and we have to check again the weather reports as it is possible that I missed something.' Oscar tried to cool the situation.

'I think that all that matters are very far from me,' said Alice. All what I have on my mind is my future and right now I like to be happy,' Alice said and took John's hand.

'Well,' Captain said, 'if I knew that things will go this way, I will never let you go for the race. You are two irresponsible people,' He finished smiling.

'Would you like some champagne?' John asked and before any answer brought on the table glasses and a bottle of champagne. He poured glasses and said, 'we bought the glasses before the race and I actually didn't know what for but the life gave the answer.'

'Alice,' Captain said, 'I think that I have another job for you and you might love it.'

'It sounds interesting because I am thinking about another job as well, Alice laughed.

'I am serious because it could be very good to check on the people over there in India. Police from Delhi told us that those people living good and peaceful life but I think that it might be good if you go over there. It will be quite natural as Albert knows about your wedding here in the Yacht Club. What do you think about it?'

Alice looked at Captain Robertson for a while and she said, 'Captain,' she suspended her voice for awhile; 'As my father you know I suppose that I am an architect and this is the job I am thinking about.'

'What are you talking about? The case isn't finished yet.'

'For me the case is over,' Alice answered and she continued. 'You have to remember Captain what already said Oscar, if there will be another situation we could be death by now and I don't see myself any longer working as an idiot. My experiences with John's family did teach me a lot and on top of that I am a married woman. Please do not forget that, dad.' She added sarcastically.

'Well, you might have your right but let me to remind you that Lisa became married woman on this Island and in the same Yacht Club,' Captain said.

'If that are your wishes, thank you very much Captain, it's very sweet,' Alice answered.

'I know that it isn't too good time talk about such matters but you didn't go to John's family home for fun but to work. That is one thing and the other is that I do hope that after short brake you will be back at work. By the way, you have to know that Robert vanished from the farm and this is most important matter at the moment.' Captain was very serious.

'Why don't you say anything about me, Captain?' John asked.

'What shall I say? It seems that for sometime you will work with us and it will give you possibility to work together with your wife. Perhaps you might join her on a trip to India.'

'Daniel promised us to fix the yacht.' John changed suddenly subject.

'It might be possible that now we will have an engine,' Alice said looking at John.

'Say again.' Captain asked.

'I said that an engine could be very useful on board, simple.' Alice answered.

'John is it possible that there is no engine on your yacht?' Captain asked.

'Captain, our yacht has sails and it is enough if such good sailors are on board like my wife Alice,' John answered with smile and kissed her chick.

'I cannot believe it, Oscar said softly.

'Look guys, Alice made all the manoeuvres without a steering so I don't see any reason to have one on board.' John said proudly.

'John,' Captain said, 'we are going out of proper subject but I like to know if you seen any UFO together with the light.'

'Sorry Captain but I didn't see. I wish and it could me good to see it.'

'It could be possible because there is something in records in the base.' Oscar said.

'Cannot we talk about something else? Our wedding party goes on and why we have to seat here?' Alice complained.

'Perhaps but the most important matter is by now is that Robert vanished and Jack couldn't find anything to find out what happened to him. Robert is nowhere.'

'Sounds bad even I didn't know him,' John said.

They have been on board for some time and talked and actually they like to leave the yacht while Oscar said. 'Captain, I think that the time that the storm began which is noted in the log-book and the time when UFO has been registered in the base is the same.'

'We will check once again all the information we have so far but take some photos of the log-book Oscar.' Captain said to him.

'Oh, I see that you have changed your profession, Oscar.' John said smiling and added. 'Before you'll take any photo Oscar, take a note that there is a space so perhaps you and Captain will put your signatures.' He laughed.

'Well, Oscar might write his surname but I can sign only.' Captain Robertson said looking into open log-book and added. 'It might be not possible later as Alice's father might shoot both of us,' he laughed and Alice asked.

'What did he said after you told him that you are coming here, Captain?'

'I told you already that he was busy to clean his revolver. I think it is clean by now so we won't have any infection from dirty bullets.'

They have spoken for a while then they left the yacht and joined the party. Captain Robertson and Oscar left the Island early in the morning. The wedding party was over and Alice with John enjoyed their time on Island. They spent the time with Daniel and Nancy. Very often they used one of their motor cars.

Once, on their way back to the yacht club Alice said raising her voice. 'John, John please stop the car.'

'What's happening?'

'Actually nothing but for a moment I thought that I've seen Lisa sitting on the terrace in the café.' She answered.

'You must be joking.'

'Perhaps I am mistaken but we I think that we can have a walk and look over there.'

'Why not, lets' go.'

They left the motor car and walked slowly until they reached the cafe. The woman who was sitting by one of the tables looked in did exactly same as the one who they saw on the photo and exactly same as the other one who has been killed.

'I cannot believe my eyes,' said John surprisingly. 'I can swear that she is the one who I saw in the bath.'

They entered cafe and as soon as they took a table next to the strange woman, she stood up and said. 'Congratulations, I've seen your wedding on TV and to be honest it was something that took my breath away as some time ago my wedding took place in the same Yacht Club as well. As I know from TV you must be Alice, I wish you all the best. By the way my name is Lisa.'

After that introduction Alice and John were totally confused. It was amazing because not only the same woman they met but with the same name.

'Please to meat you Lisa, my name is John and Alice my wife you already know. By the way, I saw your photo in the Yacht Club. Why you didn't join the party?'

'I am sure there must be some photos in the Club because I think that our wedding was the first one in the Yacht Club. I couldn't attend the party because I had some other very important matters. The other thing is that I came here to have my own time and privacy.'

'To be honest,' said Alice, 'I don't understand because Nancy and Daniel are very nice people.' Alice said and John supported her.

'That's the point,' he said, 'I fully agree with Alice.'

'You are right and yes, they are nice people but it doesn't means that it secure my privacy. I don't fee talk about my life right now as it isn't too pleasant.'

John sighted at her and reminded the same face in the bath. He started to think about similarity of these two women and it came to his mind that Lisa most probably has a twin sister and there was something mixed up with names so he thought that here in the bath wasn't Lisa but someone else.

'You look at me in such way that I have a feeling that you look right inside me.' Lisa said.

'I'm sorry but you are looking exactly as on the photo which I saw in Daniel's office. Seriously, you look the same.' John answered quickly and added. 'I hope that you wouldn't mind to leave you for a while as I need to check something by our yacht. Alice, I'll be back soon, soon.' He knew that has to leave Alice alone so it could be possible for her to have some more information abut strange woman they have met.

'Oh John, there is no need for you to come back because I can drop Alice in the Yacht Club with a great pleasure.' Lisa said quickly.

'It was really very kind from John to leave two of us alone. He is real gentleman and you must love him a lot. Isn't it?'

'You right, I do love him very much.'

'I heard about that trouble of yours and I do believe that it was horrible.'

'Luckily it came to good end,' Alice laughed. 'What about you? Why are you so sad?'

'To be honest, not long ago I didn't like talk to anybody but I have say that it was a luck that you came here. I have to leave the Island tonight and I see that I have to talk to someone like you. I don't know why but I feel very comfortable with you, Alice.'

They have been spoken for quite long time and Alice with her diplomatic way of conversation which allowed her to learn about Lisa and her family. The most shocking for Alice was to hear about Lisa's maid Shivana, who still is very healthy in her house in India. Alice became completely confused because all the people who should be death by now are still alive so she started to think about very serious and well organized syndicate. She thought that the investigation connected with UFO has nothing to do with killing. Finally Alice couldn't understand who is who.

'Do you know what is most difficult for me?' Lisa asked.

'Tell me.' Alice answered.

'The most difficult is to be without my daughter who stays together with Albert.'

'Didn't she like to be with you?'

'I really don't know, really I don't know. All what I know is that it is my and only my fault.'

'Why are you blaming yourself at all times? Everything mast have some reason.'

'You see, I think that perhaps I have had too much money and too much time which I didn't know how to use.'

'Many people would like to have such situation.'

'Perhaps you are right but after I attended meditation course of Master Osho there in India, I changed my view on many matters. I still remember when I've been listening about sexuality.'

'I think that I saw a book of Master Osho but I cannot say that it impressed me as I didn't agree with it in many matters.' Alice replied.

'I have to say that you are right but at that time I did believe in any story I was told. I remember once I've been listening about sexuality as well and it came out that a man who is interested with female's breasts has a psychological problem because most probably his breast feeding was stopped too early.'

'Do you think that this is true?'

'I wouldn't talk about it if I believe. I've been watching your wedding and looking at two of you, sorry to say that but with jealousy,' Lisa was saying that with tears in her eyes. 'They showed some clips and it remind my own past. I thought about Albert and suddenly I felt that my breasts are taking more air. I did put my hands on them and I thought that Albert is holding them and I felt as they are getting harder and harder and bigger even. I felt Albert's sight on them and it was really strange. I can say that I made very big mistake in my life and I will never forgive myself.'

'We are making mistakes in life but we can fix them as well.' Alice told softly.

'You see, after all that lessons I have seen Albert as a monster. I saw faults everywhere but meantime I was the one who was faulty. I know by now that it has to be as it is because a male has to be interested with our body and nothing is wrong with that as we are created in such way. We are not those who shall correct the Creator.'

'In other words you didn't even phone to Nancy and Daniel.'

'No, not at all and luckily here are other hotels on the Island.'

'Tell me please but really honestly, is there any other reason that you broke with Albert?'

'I am the only reason, I think. You see, Albert is working on a project which is taking most of his time and it separated us as well. Slowly we stopped talk one to another and started to live different lives.'

'What project is Albert working on?'

'His project is another story because for me it is just nonsense. He believes that can use silicon as fuel.'

'Do you think that he can do it?'

'No, I don't but he doesn't know that it is impossible and since he came up with that stupid project our relationship turned upside down.'

'Why cannot you try to change it? It is normal that a man must have something to do if is not going fishing then must have them in a fish tank. If not that then has to do something else and anything will be better then sit in a pub or screwing around wherever is possible.'

'You are right but I know that it is too late.'

'Don't say that because there is never too late. Why don't you call him?'

'Then I will look even more stupid.'

'It isn't true. Anybody can make a mistake but only the wise one point himself as a guilty. An ignorant will stay in blindness for the rest of time. Most probably you know life better than me but you have to forgive me to say that most important in any relationship is compromise. There are many very simple matters which could be fixing with just a little effort. I do strongly believe that you should call your husband right now.'

'Do you?'

'Of course I do unless you have somebody else.'

'No Alice, not at all, the thing is that at the time I started to hate all the men.'

'Then you shouldn't wait,' Alice said and put her new mobile-phone in front of Lisa. She looked quickly at the phone and a few moments later Alice witnessed her conversation with Albert

'What is the whole story about?' Alice thought. 'Who is death and who is alive?'

Meantime Lisa finished her conversation and became completely different person. She started to talk with excitement. 'It was created by the God that I met you because in a short time I've got back my family.'

They agreed to together to the Yacht Club so Lisa could say halo to Nancy and Daniel before leaving the Island. Before they left the cafe Alice asked about Lisa's house.

'I thought to go there tonight even of all the memories but it doesn't matter right now as I have to go to see those who I love the most, my daughter and Albert.'

The time run quickly and soon Lisa had to leave for airport. After they came back to the hotel, Alice told about her conversation with Lisa. John couldn't believe how it was possible that his wife managed that Lisa went back to her family.

'For me the most interesting is that Lisa has no twin sister. For short time I thought that her sister was killed but now I have no idea who was the death woman.'

'Now everything became even more mixed up then before.'

'Do you think that we have to call Captain Robertson?' Alice asked.

'Well, I don't know but soon we will leave the Island and then we have to meet him anyway.'

'I think that you are right and actually we are on holiday, and somehow we are involved in our job again.'

'Yes but for a while only but tell me Alice, do you remember Captain's question about UFO?'

'I do but why are you asking?'

'Because I am thinking about something very similar,' John answered.

'What is it?'

'Sometime ago my father told me about a flying object. It was shortly before Second World War. He said that many people watched that funny object which looked like a big cigar.'

'Do you think that UFO might exist?'

'I am not too sure but if then they might even a base on earth.'

'Perhaps it is possible but do you remember?' Alice asked smiling.

'What I have to remember?'

Lech Lebek

'We promised ourselves not to talk about our work and suddenly the matte came up itself.'

'Yes you are right but isn't it exciting?'

'You are right, it is exciting,' Alice agreed.

'I have to ask you something Alice, because we have to leave the Island and it you like then you can take a plane. Actually both of us can take a flight because I don't think that there could be a problem with yacht. Somehow Daniel will make a plan to deliver it to us.'

'John, I am fine with sailing and I don't think that anything could happen this time.'

'Perhaps not but who knows?'

'In this case we have to go sailing once again,' Alice answered smiling and kissed John's chick.

Chapter 27

Captain Robertson and Oscar tried to sleep during their flight from wedding party and only when the plane was about to land Captain made a phone call to Jack.

'Jack, sorry for early call but it is necessary to start the action as soon as possible in other words you have fly to the base immediately.'

'No problem Captain. How was the party? Did they really get married?'

'No, they did it for fun and stop talk shit to me. Take all the material you have and I'll see you in the base.' Captain wasn't in good mood.

'Captain,' Jack was still on the line. 'As soon as you'll be in the base, you have to check all the reports especially from the labour. This is very serious matter.'

'What is so serious, what are you talking about, Jack?' Captain was a little irritated.

'You will see, bye Captain.'

The call was over and Captain looked silently at his phone then at Oscar who asked.

'What was that about?'

'I don't know some serious matter but why nobody informed me about it.'

They came to the base and in the reception Captain received a sealed envelope. In the office he opened it and read the letter. After he finished he put it in front of Oscar.

'What is it about?' He asked.

'Just check it,' Captain answered. 'It is difficult to believe in but I had strange suspicion for long time.'

'I am not too sure if it is possible,' Oscar said after he finished read the letter.

'Oscar, the report tells that all the victims except Mrs. Brown are clones and I do believe in it as how could be possible that Daniel has spoken with Albert if he was death.'

'Don't you think that somebody has been killed or Daniel has spoken with somebody else Captain.'

'As soon as the labour will be open we have to contact with them.'

'Captain, I think that our genetic engineering isn't developed as much that somebody can make clones. It seems to me impossible.'

'Who knows, perhaps somebody can do it, we'll see.'

Before Jack arrived to the farm, Captain and Oscar studied all the information they had together with the photos of the farm. Then Jack has arrived and the action began. The trucks entered the farm from different direction and stopped in most important places. In very short time the farm was taken over. In one of the trucks the office has been organized and into that truck the leader has been locked. Then Jack pointed the workshop and they went over there. In front of the workshop stood Denis whom Jack knew already from the short time he spent on the farm.

'Halo Denis,' Jack greeted the man and asked. 'Do you know why I am here?'

Denis looked at him and two other men with confusion as he never expected to see Jack again. 'No, I don't know why you are here and I do not know who are you at all, sir.' Denis answered.

They have spoken for a while and Denis said, 'Sir, I do remember you very well but I have no idea why you are here. When I saw you for the first time I thought that you must have a reason to be here o the farm but till now I have no idea what it could be especially now when I see all the army.' He looked around little worried.

'Look Denis, there is no need for you to be worried because we are going to take over the farm together with all the people which are here. The most important matter is that we need to know where Robert is. Well, you know him as Pete.'

'Sir, I don't know where he could be but I liked him very much. He used to stay in my tent and on one night they came and called him to offload a truck. Thereafter I have never seen him again.'

'Have you seen the truck?'

'I have never seen the truck or trucks as they are coming here from time to time. I mean very heavy trucks. It looks like they are passing the farm and going somewhere towards the mountains.'

At the time that they have spoken with Denis the soldiers were searching the farm but no one of them reported about Robert. Except the register book there was no sign of him on the farm. Denis looked around nervously in fear. He knew that there isn't a joke with the army on the farm but then he said.

'I don't know what Theresa will say if she will find out that I have spoken to you. I did like Pete a lot but now I am worried that I can have some problems before my pension will come and I will no place to go.'

'Don't worry and just tell us what you know.'

'Pete was here for very short time. Mostly he was alone in different places on the farm making drawings. He could draw, he really could and after I realized that he is not coming back I took all his drawings and I keep them in my locker. I thought that sometime I might frame them.'

"Could you show us the pictures?'

'Sure that I can but I am still worried that I will face problems.'

'I told you Denis there will be no problem. Your leader is arrested and I don't think that you will see that Theresa of yours. If you don't show them to us then we will still take them ourselves.'

'I have to go to my tent.'

'Sit in the truck.' Jack said and Denis went into it.

They stopped next to the tent showed by Denis as own then they went inside. He took from the locker a packet and opened it. Inside there were few drawings.

'Woo, they good,' Captain said. 'I didn't know that Robert has such talent.'

'Are you going to take them away from me, sir?' Denis asked.

'We have to make copies of the pictures then I will give you the originals back. Actually why don't you call me Jack?'

'Sir, I cannot, I knew that there is something about you, I knew that you are not the person who you told to be.'

'Denis, tell me please, all the places on the pictures are on the farm?'

'Yes sir, Pete went to different places on the field and set drawing. Firstly the leader told him shit but thereafter he saw the pictures he left him alone.'

'How it could be possible that people are working with me and I didn't know anything about them, Robert is really good.' Captain was surprised.

'The are very good drawings and we have to send them to the base to make copies and analyze so perhaps it could be possible to learn something from them except that I think that we need to fly over that place once again.' Captain's face was very serious.

After a while Captain together with Oscar and Jack flew over the farm, mostly over the mountain. Captain decided that they must have more pictures taken from the air and many places on the farm as well. Oscar and Jack kept quite for most of the time. After they landed all the people stood in one place worried what will happen to them. All three officers left the helicopter and stopped in silence in front of the people. It wasn't too pleasant as most of the people were old and dressed in dirty clothes.

'I don't know how we will do it but I think that must go the hospitals immediately.'

'Captain, do you think that it will be easy to find places for all of them.'

'I don't know and I don't care where they will go but they must be in hospitals.' Captain Robertson answered and added. 'Oscar, you have to start with that matter right now so fell free and go to do your job.'

'Captain,' said Jack, 'everything has been check and there is no sign of Robert. What are we going to do?'

'I don't know, really I don't know and I am very sorry. One what I know is that we have to do something the thing is that I don't know what.'

Chapter 28

For Alice and John time of the Island came to an end as the yacht was restored and ready for sailing again. Nance and Daniel helped them to prepare everything they will need during their race back home. In the day before they had to leave the Island many people came to the Yacht Club and many of them became already friends with John and his wife.

'Alice,' Nancy asked her, 'if you like to fly then there is no problem and we will find somebody to deliver the yacht to your home.'

'Thanks' Nancy,' she answered, 'we have spoken with John on the other day about it. I am fine with sailing and actually it will be very cool to be on the sea again.' Alice laughed.

'John, remember that you have to come back as soon as you can.' Daniel said.

'We will Daniel, believe me that whenever we will have a chance to come we always come here as the most beautiful memories we are leaving behind.'

'It is our Island by now as well,' Alice laughed.

'I think that this is one of last times that we have chance to be on our yacht,' John said and took from the fridge a bottle of champagne. 'I don't know how to thank you for all the trouble and to be honest I have never believed that it will be possible to fix our yacht so quick and with such good quality.' John said and poured glasses.

'John, it was a great pleasure,' Daniel answered smiling.

'What now?' John asked looking at him.

'Well, not much, I am just laughing because I have really surprised you with the yacht.' Daniel laughed and after a while he added. 'It isn't the only surprise.'

'I'm sure that there is something in this smile of yours.'

'Well, if you have to leave tomorrow then there is right time to say good bye so lets' go to the club.'

It was a real surprise as there in the restaurant of the Yacht Club Nancy and Daniel prepared big party for them and suddenly they thought that another wedding is taking place over there.

They left the Island early in the morning. They stood on the deck looking at the Island which finally became invisible The ocean was calm and they enjoyed sailing with fresh breeze. The time passed quicker then they thought and soon on the horizon they could see the land.

'Our race is coming to the end.' John said.

'I am little nervous but it was a good time.'

'A time never dies,' John said looking somewhere on the ocean's water.

Soon the city could be seen and Alice became more and more excited. Shortly they enter canal their Yacht Club. The atmosphere started to be nervous. On the pier there were a lot of people and right in front there was their family members. John fastened the yacht and came to Alice who stood on the helm and said. 'I love you, Alice,' then he kissed her chick.

Soon as they stepped on the land John mother came to Alice and hugged her warmly. There have been tears falling down on her chicks.

'Alice, my dear I am so glad that you are back and that you two decided to be together. I am very, very happy.'

'I am happy as well,' she answered trying to stop her tears.

Suddenly from nowhere came to them Allen and said seriously. 'I am glad that you took my advice uncle.'

'What do you mean?' Alice asked.

'Oh you don't know but said to uncle that he shall marry you as soon as possible.'

'Why?'

'Because I like you,' he answered proudly.

It wasn't the only surprise because Alice's father had something to say as well.

'You know, firstly I thought that I have to shoot Robertson and you as well that he sent you sailing but further on I have had possibility to learn that you are worthy to marry my daughter, John.'

'Thank you and I do believe that the God will help me to fulfil your words.'

In the restaurant there was another surprise waiting for them as another party has been organized for them. As they entered the Yacht Club they met Captain Robertson who came to greet them and said. 'I didn't come to greet you by the canal as I still don't trust this man,' he pointed Alice's father and laughed.

'Well,' John joked, 'Alice has got two fathers and I have two fathers in law.'

It came the time when Captain Robertson had had possibility have a talk with Alice and John. She asked about

Robert and it was sad to hear that he vanished without any trace.

'Now you have to listen to another story,' Captain Robertson said and continued. 'The victims except Mrs. Brown are clones.'

'It cannot be possible,' John said.

'Well, according to the reports they are clones. Except that we have contacted the labour and sorry but they are not humans been.'

'Captain, in this case those people are still alive and Lisa which we met on the Island was the real one. Her husband is in India and Shivana is in India as well.'

'Captain, isn't it possible that the doctors are made mistake?' Alice asked.

'Oscar and myself did thought the same but without any question, the victims are clones,' Captain answered and then added. 'To be honest as I have mentioned before I like to ask you to go to India and see your friends.'

'We met Lisa but how they might be our friends, that I don't understand,' Alice answered.

'Well, firstly they sponsored your wedding then you already met Lisa,' said Captain.

'Captain, we met Lisa but I have told you already that I'm not going to play fool as it took place not long ago by John home. I am married woman and I have my profession.' Alice reminded.

'I am very interested with Albert project,' said Oscar. 'It sounds fantastic.

'That's another crap,' Captain ignored. 'Silicon never can be used as a fuel. This is just good story for children. I just can see myself driving with a spade and in case I'll need then I will put sand into my tank. It's just crazy idea.'

'Well, it could be nice, free fuel,' John laughed. 'Personally I wish him luck.'

'Alice,' Captain said, 'I hope that after few days you will decided about the trip to India.'

'Well, I will think about it but I am not too sure as we have to organize our life,' Alice answered.

On the next morning John set together with Paul on the terrace and Paul asked. 'John, why did you say that Alice doesn't work with you?'

'Because she did not,' John answered.'

'John, you are not honest with me but let me to ask you something. Where is the photo from our father's log-book?'

John kept quiet and Paul asked again. 'Do you know anything about UFO?'

'Not much.'

'Did you see UFO on the sea?'

'No, I didn't what about you?'

'John, why didn't you ask me before the race?'

'Well, I'm asking you now.'

'Now I can say that it is very interesting matter.'

'Perhaps we can talk about it.'

Paul answered smiling, 'who knows, perhaps we will. I don't think that you might give up.'

THE END L L Lebek

I was born in Poland in 1946 and educated in textile. Firstly I started to write in very young ages and all I do remember is that gave me trouble only. Seriously I wrote in middle eighties while to power was coming "Solidarnosc" in the country. My articles have been published in national newspaper "Sztandar Mlodych" and as a result of it I was victimize and finally I have left Poland, and asked for asylum in Austria.

In South Africa I am since 1990 and most of the time working in textile industry. At present since two years I am on pension and looking forward to write full time.

I was married with four children and actually do not know what more to say, perhaps that I love skiing and sailing. From time to time I do go ice skating here in Pretoria.

Lech Lebek